T0247127

KUMA KUMA
KUMA BEAR
→ Vol.13

CONTENTS

KUMA KUMA KUMA BEAR

NOVEL
13

WRITTEN BY
Kumanano

ILLUSTRATED BY
029

Airship

Seven Seas Entertainment

KUMA KUMA KUMA BEAR Vol. 13
© KUMANANO 2019

Illustrated by 029

Originally published in Japan in 2019 by
SHUFU TO SEIKATSU SHA CO., LTD., Tokyo.
English translation rights arranged with
SHUFU TO SEIKATSU SHA CO., LTD., Tokyo,
through TOHAN CORPORATION, Tokyo.

No portion of this book may be reproduced or transmitted
in any form without written permission from the copyright
holders. This is a work of fiction. Names, characters, places,
and incidents are the products of the author's imagination
or are used fictitiously. Any resemblance to actual events,
locales, or persons, living or dead, is entirely coincidental.
Any information or opinions expressed by the creators of this
book belong to those individual creators and do not necessarily
reflect the views of Seven Seas Entertainment or its employees.

Seven Seas press and purchase enquiries can be sent to
Marketing Manager Lianne Sentar at press@gomanga.com.
Information regarding the distribution and purchase of
digital editions is available from Digital Manager CK Russell
at digital@gomanga.com.

Seven Seas and the Seven Seas logo are trademarks of
Seven Seas Entertainment. All rights reserved.

Follow Seven Seas Entertainment online at
sevenseasentertainment.com.

TRANSLATION: Jan Cash & Vincent Castaneda
ADAPTATION: M.B. Hare
COVER DESIGN: Kris Aubin
INTERIOR LAYOUT & DESIGN: Clay Gardner
COPY EDITOR: Dayna Abel
PROOFREADER: Jade Gardner
LIGHT NOVEL EDITOR: T. Burke
PREPRESS TECHNICIAN: Melanie Ujimori, Jules Valera
PRODUCTION MANAGER: Lissa Pattillo
EDITOR-IN-CHIEF: Julie Davis
ASSOCIATE PUBLISHER: Adam Arnold
PUBLISHER: Jason DeAngelis

ISBN: 978-1-63858-819-1
Printed in Canada
First Printing: February 2023
10 9 8 7 6 5 4 3 2 1

Name: Yuna
Age: 15
Gender: Female

▶ **BEAR HOOD (NONTRANSFERABLE)**
Can see the effects of weapons and tools through the beary good eyes of the hood.

▶ **BLACK BEAR GLOVE (NONTRANSFERABLE)**
Attack glove, increases power based on the user's level. Can summon the black bear Kumayuru.

▶ **WHITE BEAR GLOVE (NONTRANSFERABLE)**
Defense glove, increases defense based on the user's level. Can summon the white bear Kumakyu.

▶ **BLACK AND WHITE BEAR CLOTHES (NONTRANSFERABLE)**
Appears to be a onesie. Reversible.
Front: Black Bear Clothes
  Increases physical and magic resistance based on the user's level.
  Gives heat and cold resistance.
Reverse: White Bear Clothes
  Automatically restores health and mana while worn.
  Restoration amount and speed is based on the user's level.
  Gives heat and cold resistance.

▶ **BLACK BEAR SHOE (NONTRANSFERABLE)**
▶ **WHITE BEAR SHOE (NONTRANSFERABLE)**
Increases speed based on the user's level.
Prevents fatigue walking long distances based on the user's level.
Gives heat and cold resistance.

◀ **KUMAYURU (CUB FORM)**

▼ **KUMAKYU**

▶ **BEAR UNDERWEAR (NONTRANSFERABLE)**
Won't get dirty no matter how much they're used.
An excellent item that won't retain sweat or smells.
Will grow with the user.

▶ **BEAR SUMMONS**
Can be summoned from the bear gloves.
Can be changed into cub forms.

Skills

▶ FANTASY WORLD LANGUAGE
The fantasy world's language will sound like Japanese.
Spoken words are conveyed to the other party in the
fantasy world language.

▶ FANTASY WORLD LITERACY
The ability to read the fantasy world writing.
Written words become the fantasy world's words.

▶ BEAR EXTRADIMENSIONAL STORAGE
The white bear's mouth opens into infinite space. It can
hold (eat) anything.
However, it cannot hold (eat) living things.
Time will stop for objects that are inside of it.
Anything that is put into the extradimensional storage
can be pulled out at any time.

▶ BEAR IDENTIFICATION
By looking through the bear eyes on the Bear Clothes'
hood, one can see the effects of a weapon or tool.
Doesn't work without wearing the hood.

▶ BEAR DETECTION
Using the wild abilities of bears, can detect monsters
or people.

▶ BEAR MAP 2.0
Any area looked at by the bear eyes can be made into a map.

▶ BEAR SUMMONING
Bears can be summoned from the bear gloves.
A black bear can be summoned from the black glove.
A white bear can be summoned from the white glove.
Summons, Beast Cubification: The bear summons can be
transformed into bear cubs.

▶ BEAR TRANSPORTER GATE
By setting up a gate, can move between gates.
When more than three gates are in place, can travel
to a location by picturing it.
This gate can only be opened with the bear hand.

▶ BEAR PHONE
Can have long-distance conversations with others.
Phone persists until caster dispels it. Physically
indestructible.
Can call people that a bear phone is given to by picturing
the person.
Incoming call is announced by the sound of a bear's cry.
By using mana to turn the phone on or off, user can
make calls.

▶ BEAR WATER WALKING
Gain the ability to traverse water.
Summons gain the ability to travel on water.

▶ BEAR TELEPATHIC COMMUNICATION
You can call your summoned beasts from a distance.

Magic

▶ BEAR LIGHT
Mana collected in the bear glove creates a light in the
shape of a bear.

▶ BEAR PHYSICAL ENHANCEMENT
Routing mana through the bear gear allows for physical
enhancement.

▶ BEAR FIRE MAGIC
Gathering mana in the bear glove gives one the ability to
use fire elemental magic.
Power is proportional to mana and the mental image.
When imagining a bear, power increases even more.

▶ BEAR WATER MAGIC
Gathering mana in the bear glove gives one the ability to
use water elemental magic.
Power is proportional to mana and the mental image.
When imagining a bear, power increases even more.

▶ BEAR WIND MAGIC
Gathering mana in the bear glove gives one the ability to
use wind elemental magic.
Power is proportional to mana and the mental image.
When imagining a bear, power increases even more.

▶ BEAR EARTH MAGIC
Gathering mana in the bear glove gives one the ability to
use earth elemental magic.
Power is proportional to mana and the mental image.
When imagining a bear, power increases even more.

▶ BEAR ELECTRICITY MAGIC
Gathering mana in the bear glove gives one the ability to
use electricity elemental magic.
Power is proportional to mana and the mental image.
When imagining a bear, power increases even more.

▶ BEAR HEALING MAGIC
Can give treatment by means of the bear's kind heart.

DEZELT

KARINA
Daughter of Lord Barlimer. Ten years old. A resilient, polite girl with a strong sense of responsibility, but now very worried due to a mistake she made.

BARLIMER ISHLEET
Feudal lord of the neutral town of Dezelt. A kind lord who cares for his children. Requests a water mana gem from Elfanica, which leads to Yuna visiting the desert.

LISTIEL
Barlimer's cool and collected wife. Expecting her third child.

NORRIS
Karina's still small younger brother who's a bit shy.

LASA
Barlimer's maid. Cooks something that Yuna is craving...

JADE'S PARTY

JADE
The leader of the four-person party that teams up with Yuna during the golem extermination. Keeps meeting her by some twist of fate. Ends up working with Yuna in the desert.

MEL
A cheerful mage who is always smiling. Met up with Yuna again during the academy's festival, along with Jade.

TOUYA
A tongue-in-cheek, mischievous swordsman. Often the butt of jokes, he sets the mood for the party.

SENIA
A cool, knife-wielding woman. Always teases Touya.

319
The Bear Heads Out to Dezelt

As I was heading to the desert town of Dezelt at the king's request, I met Rosa and her party in the town of Kars—weird to think I'd met them all the way back in Mileela. After she told me the way to Dezelt, I left.

I didn't have any plans to revisit Kars any time soon, but I still decided to set up a transport gate so I'd have a place to stop over. You can never have too many gates, especially when there isn't a limit to how many you can make in the first place.

As I rode on Kumayuru, I glanced around. There were still a lot of big rocks lying around, so setting it up somewhere near a pile of them seemed like a good idea. The best hiding place for a tree is in the middle of the forest, after all. Hiding a pile of rocks? Same deal.

I used earth magic to make a rock face that looked the same as all the other ones nearby, then I set up a bear gate in a cavity in the rock. Once I'd covered the opening, it looked the same as everything around it.

After I finished setting up the gate, I rode Kumayuru in the direction of Dezelt. We traveled for a while until we caught sight of something tall and thin in the distance— probably one of those markers Rosa had mentioned.

From here, though, it just looked like a thin stick. Then again, if I *could* see it from this distance, it was probably way bigger than it seemed.

I had Kumayuru run toward the pillar. Sure enough, it steadily grew larger and thicker as we approached, until I could see it really was the pillar I was looking for. The closer I got, the more rock formations gave way to sand.

Kumayuru ran along until we finally made it to the pillar. Yeah, it looked like it'd be all desert from here.

As for the pillar, it was about the size of a gigantic tree. Four or five people could probably have linked hands and made a full ring around its base. It was pretty tall too. Even craning my head to look up at it hurt my neck.

I tried touching it. Hmm...it seemed like someone might've used earth magic to form it from the sand itself, but it was still hard as rock. It'd be kinda interesting to make one myself, now that I thought about it, but that might cause a little too much trouble. Nah, not worth it.

Out in the distance stood the second pillar, which really *would* make this whole journey easy. My bear mapping skill couldn't keep me from getting lost if I haven't been somewhere before, so it was nice to have something to keep me from losing my way.

I leapt onto Kumayuru's back. "Okay, Kumayuru, let's head to that pillar."

Kumayuru crooned in response and broke out into a run.

"Kumayuru, are you doing all right? It's not hard to run, is it? Or too hot?"

"Cwoon."

"Glad to hear it, Kumayuru."

Kumayuru sped up then, as if to reply. I looked down at Kumayuru's feet and realized that their paws weren't even sinking into the sand. It was almost as though Kumayuru were walking on regular ground.

Good job, big guy! Kumayuru could run for days and didn't bat an eye at long distances. Better yet, the whole running-on-water thing apparently applied with sand too. Add in some perfect fluffiness, and you really couldn't ask for a better bear buddy.

This all applied equally to Kumakyu too, obviously. I looked at my white bear puppet and gave it a comforting smile.

We passed by the second pillar, no sweat. This was my first time seeing the desert, and it was a lot prettier than I'd expected. Admittedly, the only reason I could appreciate it like this was because of my bears and my heat-resistant bear gear. Without all that, this would've felt less like a vacation and more like a death march. I probably would've been going as fast as I could instead of taking it all in.

That was just how barren this desert was. Sand everywhere, as far as you could see... Sand, sand everywhere. Oh, and there were dunes too! But dunes are *also* sand, so maybe that doesn't count.

It was beautiful but terrifying.

When I looked up, the only thing above was the blinding sun bearing down on me. If I took off my onesie, I probably wouldn't have been able to stand the heat. I sure was grateful for it right then.

"Kumayuru, just let me know if it's hot, all right?"

"Cwoon," Kumayuru answered, then ran even faster. Apparently, they really wanted me to know that nothing was wrong.

We must've been a real sight, this girl on a black bear galloping across a vast desert. Just imagining it felt odd. This probably would've been a first in this world—and maybe in my old world too. If only I had a camera, I would've taken a picture. A bear in the desert...that would've made a nice scene, right? An interesting combination! And as I thought all of that, Kumayuru kept running along, doing just fine in this desert.

After a while, we got to the third pillar and took a break. I could see the fourth pillar from where we were. It looked like I really wouldn't end up getting lost at this rate, as long as I kept following the pillars.

Which led me to another problem: I'd heard from Blitz that traveling across the desert could get real boring, real quick. In other places, there would've been nearby villages to gawk at as we passed by or maybe some pretty hills in the distance to watch as we traveled. This place just had sand—coarse and rough and everywhere. The most sightseeing I could do was checking out the little differences between the sand dunes. Other than that, it looked like the same scene continuing into the distance. Maybe I could leave navigating to my bears and take a nap?

Before I headed off to the next pillar, I traded Kumayuru out for Kumakyu.

"Thanks, Kumayuru." I gave my bear a grateful pat on the head, recalled them, and summoned Kumakyu.

Seeing a black bear in a desert was an odd enough sight, but a white bear in the desert? That seemed even more bizarre. I'd always imagined black bears living in the mountains and white bears living on little chunks of ice.

"Kumakyu, are you doing all right?" I asked, just in case Kumakyu didn't share Kumayuru's heat resistance. But my bear crooned in response and nuzzled me. Seemed like they were fine too.

I'd thought for a moment that they might have polar opposite resistances and that Kumakyu would fare better in the cold, but that didn't seem to be the case at all. I mean, Kumayuru *had* run up a snow-covered mountain once already, and there weren't many differences between my bears.

Hm. Maybe it wasn't that hot after all? As a test, I tugged down my bear hood slightly...and got practically blasted off my bear feet by the heat.

"H-hot!" I pulled my hood back on right away. "What the—? How can *anything* be this hot? Who could live in a place like this? Kumakyu, are you *sure* you're okay?"

I looked at Kumakyu, worried, but Kumakyu looked just peachy. They were as adorable as ever—Kumakyu might as well have been lounging in a bear resort.

Kumakyu gave me a quizzical look, as if to ask, "What is it?" I guess my bears really were just doing fine out here. Made me really impressed by anybody who'd made a journey like this without all my gear.

God, thank you for this bear gear, I almost said internally... but, uh, nah. If I did that, I'd probably be doing exactly what the god wanted, so I decided to just be *half* grateful about the bear gear and *all* thankful for Kumayuru and Kumakyu.

"Okay then, Kumakyu, I'm counting on you, even though I know it's hot."

I scritched Kumakyu's chin and got onto the bear's back. Kumakyu faced the next pillar and dashed into the vast desert.

As we made progress, I started to get bored of the sandy scene. I got a cold drink out for myself from my bear storage. I offered some to Kumakyu too, of course. But I could feel the drink heating up in my hands, so I had to put it back into storage as soon as I was done.

One more reason to be thankful for the bear storage. I could fit a gigantic bear house in it, the storage had no weight limit, and it could even keep things cold. It sure was useful.

As we ran along through the desert, Kumakyu suddenly let out a croon and slowed down.

15

I looked forward, thinking it was a monster or something, but I actually saw people riding on a lizard. They were called...laggaroutes, I think?

Since I didn't want them to freak out if they saw Kumakyu, I kind of wanted to just pass them without them seeing us. We used the dunes to sneak by.

Hmm...we were getting a little away from the regular route now, so we came across something that looked a lot like a wolf ahead on one of the dunes. Maybe that was one of the sand wolves that Rosa and her party had told me about?

I activated my detection skill. Looked like I was right. There were actually about ten of them scattered around the dunes. As I observed them using my skill, the wolves steadily started to gather, almost like they were hunting us. I could've just hightailed it out of there...but it might be nice to get Fina some kind of souvenir, right?

Normal wolves were gray and snow wolves were white, but these things had reddish-brown fur.

I dismounted Kumakyu so I'd be ready to fight any time. As I stood in the desert, looking defenseless, the sand wolves slowly started to surround us. They apparently thought they could take me and Kumakyu down if all ten of them banded together.

Cute.

One of them howled, and then all of them attacked at once.

I dodged one and gave it a wallop in the side with one of my bear punches. Kumakyu countered one of the wolves with a punch of their own. Then—*wham!*—we both let loose a double bear punch.

I shot an ice arrow at another wolf that came at us, piercing it right through the head. Kumakyu got another wolf with their sharp claws.

Moments after the battle had started, it was over. All the wolves lay dead on the sand.

Survival of the fittest was the law of the land. If they hadn't attacked me, I would've left them alone. Mess around and find out.

Anyway, I had a gift for Fina now.

KUMA
KUMA
KUMA
BEAR

320
The Bear Meets Friends in the Desert

AFTER DEFEATING the sand wolves, I headed for the next pillar. Because there was nothing out here in the desert, there was nothing interrupting my view that could make me lose sight of it, even when we were far away. We came across a few more sand wolves, but none of them tried to attack. Things went smoothly.

The sun began to set, dyeing the desert red. It was a gorgeous view...though I guess I could only appreciate it because I was so comfortable. Sure, a desert could look pretty on screen in an adventure movie, but from the viewpoint of one of the characters in the desert, it was probably the same as staring into your own despair. I didn't have that feeling of hopelessness, though, so I was free to enjoy the view that spread out ahead of me.

"Kumakyu, isn't it pretty?" I said.

"Cwoon." Kumakyu stopped and watched the sunset with me. Once the sun had fully disappeared, everything around us went dark. I decided we'd stop here for the night.

Since I knew there might be some merchants and adventurers who traveled at night while it was cool, I set up my bear house a distance away from the pillar...but there was nothing to stop them from seeing the bear house because there was nothing to block it. In fact, they probably would have spotted it just from the lights, so I set up earth walls all around me.

That would also keep monsters out *and* guarantee that I wouldn't find myself sanded in later. I sure wouldn't think it was funny if I woke up buried in sand.

Once I was done and headed into my house, Kumakyu followed me in.

"Wait! Kumakyu! Stop, stop!"

Kumakyu did exactly what I asked and looked quizzically at me. There were bits of sand between their toes. At this rate, I'd end up with a sandy floor too.

I recalled Kumakyu, then resummoned them. That was kind of a cheat move on my part to get my bears cleaned up. Next, I summoned Kumayuru, who was just as clean now—not a speck of sand on them. With this, they could head into the house without a problem.

(I also miniaturized my bears, just FYI.)

"Thank you, guys, for everything today," I told them, giving them head pats.

Then, I ate dinner and headed off to the bath with the two of them. A hot bath in the middle of the desert...it seemed kind of wrong, but I *did* need to wash off after spending all day out, and I hadn't taken one yesterday.

Plus, even though they'd been acting like everything was fine, I knew my bears had been working hard in the heat. I wanted to thank them by giving them a relaxing bath.

"Kumakyu, you're first today," I said. I felt bad always picking Kumayuru first, so this time I gave Kumakyu priority.

Kumakyu trotted over to be in front of me and plopped right down. I lathered my bear up and started to scrub them clean. Since I'd recalled them, they were already technically clean, but I was doing this for the experience.

Kumakyu narrowed their eyes, looking blissful. I scrubbed them head to toe—even their poofy little tail! Finally, I poured hot water over their head, and we were done.

"All finished," I said.

Kumakyu crooned in response and headed to the tub. My little bear clambered up and into the bath. They placed their head on the edge of the tub, looking like they were in heaven.

Kumayuru took Kumakyu's place in front of me and turned around, ready for me to start scrubbing them down. Okay, okay. Message received.

First, I poured the water over Kumayuru, and then I got to work scrubbing my bear. My bear's fur was black, but that didn't mean it was dirty. Even if it was hard to tell, they were clean. Once we were done, Kumayuru clambered over to the bath as well and got in next to Kumakyu.

They set their heads over the edge of the bath, both looking like they were on cloud nine. Even their faces looked relaxed. I guess the bath was just that nice.

I watched my bears, washing off myself, and slipped into the water too. Ahhh... That's the stuff. I stretched and relaxed.

It really didn't feel like we were out in the middle of the desert. The outside world was sand, sand, and more sand. There wasn't a single shrub to be seen—maybe just some monsters, at most. And here I was, right in the middle of that, taking a bath. Weird.

I sank even deeper into the water and let it wash away all the day's exhaustion.

Once I was out of the bath, I brushed my hair, then started to blow-dry my bears as well. After that, I brushed them—I wasn't planning to recall them tonight.

The day's work was done. Once I got back to my room, I burrowed into the covers of my bed. I asked my bears to warn me if anything happened while I was asleep, as always. Being snuggled under the covers was so nice, I almost forgot we were in the desert as I dozed off into a dream.

The next morning, my bears woke me up like usual, right as the sun rose. As it turned out, the sand hadn't buried my house, so we managed to make it outside with no problems. Even though I'd seen the sunrise plenty of times in this world, it was special seeing the sun rise over the desert.

Soon enough, I was riding out once again, trading my bears off as we made our way across the sand. We'd gotten pretty far, but how much longer did we have left? I'd even lost count of the pillars...or to be more accurate, I'd been taking naps and letting my bears handle navigation. I hadn't been counting the pillars at all...

We didn't even run into any hostile monsters—things were going along smoothly. But as I dozed away, relaxing atop Kumayuru, my bear came to a halt. Kumayuru jostled me to wake me up.

"What's wrong, Kumayuru? Are we there?" I rubbed my eyes and stared out ahead.

Up way ahead, I saw some people who looked like adventurers waving their swords around.

Wait, was that a tiny wyrm? No, not just one—it looked like there were several, leaping out of the sand itself. They were about as big as wolves, and the things were fighting the adventurers.

Behind the fighters stood what looked like a few merchants. Still, I couldn't be sure if they were merchants or adventurers or what—all of them wore mantles with their hoods pulled up.

Hmm... Did they need my help? I didn't really want to draw attention if they didn't need me, and I *really* didn't want to have to explain Kumayuru or get involved with a fight if I could manage not to. I couldn't tell from here, so I decided to get a little closer to use my detection skill.

The monster's name was "sand wyrm."

So, the adventurers were battling sand wyrms... They were smaller than the wyrm I fought before, but there were a lot more of them. I could see some slain wyrms on the sand, and it looked like the odds were in the adventurers' favor. Nah, they didn't need my help.

As I watched them, I realized I recognized their fighting style. There was the one wielding knives in both hands and deftly fighting, a swordsman wielding his blade as he gave exacting directions to the rest of the group, another swordsman who made a commotion while attacking the monsters, and a mage casting spells from behind and covering for them.

"Senia, you're too far forward. Mel, you need to stay closer to the clients. Touya, cover my right. Mel, strike as soon as you get the chance."

It was Jade's party. They'd helped me out when I'd headed to the golem mines in order to make a mithril knife. They were all pummeling the sand wyrms at Jade's expert command.

Not that I could've expected anything less from them. I'd planned to lend a hand if they needed it, but they were steadily offing the wyrms one by one.

"There's a ton of them!"

Jeez, they really were crawling out of the sand nonstop. I used my detection skill to check them out...and, uh, at a glance, it looked like there were about twenty of them, wriggling all over the place. Jade and the others were picking off the ones that rose to the surface, but there were just so many of them.

They'd be fine, probably, but maybe I really *should* help? I urged Kumayuru to run over.

"Jade, there's a bear coming behind you!" one of the merchants shouted after noticing me. The merchants all tried to run from me and Kumayuru.

Jade whipped around when he heard the shout, which was when our eyes met.

"Yuna?"

The merchants paused. Since I didn't want to have to explain myself, I just ignored them.

Senia and the rest of the party looked to me, giving me a quick greeting while fighting.

"Yuna?"

"Miss?"

"Is that Yuna?"

"Want a hand?" I asked. I couldn't just leave after seeing this scene.

"That'd help a ton," said Jade at once. "The dunes are crawling with 'em."

"Got it."

Since he already knew about me, that made things quicker. I used my skill to figure out where the wyrms were in the sand.

"Jade, I'm going to drive all the wyrms to the surface at once. Could you take care of them after?"

That seemed like the fastest route.

"Okay, but you sure you can do something like that?" he asked, and I nodded. "Mel, you guard the merchants behind you. Touya, Senia, Yuna's gonna get the wyrms to come up so all of us are fighting them together!"

I got off of Kumayuru and told my bear to stick with Mel. Kumayuru crooned in reply and headed over.

"Okay, guys, I'm going to start." I began running. Then I aimed at the wyrms registering on my detection skill and fired air shots at them into the ground. As they dodged, they leapt out of the sand like fish from the ocean.

"Touya—!"

"I see 'em."

I fired air shot after air shot into the sand. As the wyrms leapt into the air, they fell to the ground and writhed.

Hrk...nasty.

The wyrms tried to wriggle back into the sand, but Touya and Jade stabbed them before they could.

"Senia!"

"..."

Meanwhile, Senia minced the wyrms that were flying in midair before they even reached the ground.

"Hey, miss, you're going too fast for us."

"Touya, if you've got time to talk, you've got time to swing your blade faster."

I dug the sand wyrms up one after another.

"Yuna! There's too much sand in the air now."

Uh...okay, I didn't know how to deal with *that*. I hadn't thought that far ahead. But just then, the sand in the air was swept away by a breeze—Mel had cleared it with a spell. Now that they could see again, Jade and the other two went back to fighting off the wyrms.

"Okay, here's the last one!" I fired one last air shot into the sand. The final sand wyrm leapt out.

Touya started running toward it. "Looks like I get to finish the last one off..."

Right as Touya brandished his sword, several knives flew over him from behind and landed right at the center of the wyrm.

"Last one's mine." Senia held a knife in her hands with an empty expression. Apparently, she had other weapons besides the mithril knives. Touya looked irked by the whole thing as he stared at the sand wyrm's body.

"I was closer," Touya said.

"I was faster," Senia countered.

"I'm not slow."

"Sorry. I mean your legs are shorter," Senia quipped as she pulled her knife out of the wyrm.

"I'm not short or slow. That knife was just fast."

"Learn to be faster."

Uh, that didn't sound physically possible. But I guess Senia and Touya were just the same as always.

321

The Bear Reunites with Jade

I CHECKED FOR ANY remaining monsters using my detection before returning to Kumayuru. My bear was with the cowering merchants along with Mel, who was patting Kumayuru.

"It's been so long, Yuna. This is the bear I've heard so much about, eh?"

Come to think of it, I hadn't summoned my bears in front of Jade's party before—not even once. Still, Mel didn't seem spooked by Kumayuru at all. She was even petting my bear.

"So the rumors were true," said Senia, joining Mel in petting Kumayuru.

Though the merchants were scared, the two adventurers weren't at all. I guess that courage is the big difference between those two jobs.

Kumayuru seemed unsure of what to do, but as I was heading over to save them, Jade made his way over to me, his hands raised up.

"Yuna, thank you. You're a lifesaver."

Ehh, they would've gotten through without losing anybody. I just helped speed things up.

"What are you doing here, Yuna?" Jade asked.

I actually wanted to ask *them* that. Jade's party normally used the capital as their home base when they took jobs. Whether they were on the golem quest, out at the academy's practical training as guards, or at the academy festival, they got their jobs from the capital.

I suppose they did mention taking jobs in other places too, though. I ran into Blitz's party just a few days ago, so maybe work in the desert was really popular.

"I'm here for a job," I explained. "I have something I need to take to Dezelt, a town up ahead. That's where I'm heading."

"Same direction as us, actually. We're just on our way."

Come to think of it, even if you wanted to get to a neighboring nation, you had to pass through Dezelt. I suppose anyone using the pillars to travel *had* to be heading there.

"Um, Jade, who is this girl dressed as a bear and the bear accompanying her?" one of the merchants asked nervously.

Whoa, hold the bear phone! Who could be scared of Kumayuru?

"As you likely gleaned from that fight," Jade explained, "she's a full-fledged adventurer, no matter how she dresses. As long as you don't hurt her bear, it won't hurt you," I kind of felt odd about him mentioning how I dressed in his explanation, but I guess it was relevant.

The merchants gave me a dubious look even after Jade vouched for me, but they calmed down once they realized that Kumayuru wasn't a danger.

"But, Jade, isn't this your first time seeing Kumayuru?" I asked.

"I heard about the black bear from my adventurer buddies. You do know we hear bits and pieces about you when we visit Crimonia, don't you?"

"Yep. Lots of people talk about how you head out of town riding a bear."

Come to think of it, they knew about me defeating a goblin king and black viper too... They even seemed to know about the kraken, so it wasn't weird they'd know about my bears.

"Hey, all of you!" Touya barked. He had started working on the wyrms as we talked. "Stop yapping and start helping. Are you going to leave all the harvesting work to me?"

"I'm sure you can manage just fine on your own," said Jade.

"Keep up the good work," added Senia.

"Sheesh, come on," Touya groaned. "There's way too many of them. Help a guy out!"

Okay, maybe there were a lot of them. In total, there were about twenty wyrms lying on the sand.

"If we don't hurry up, they'll start attracting other monsters," said Mel.

"If we must," said Jade.

"Touya, you slacker," said Senia.

Touya blinked. "Wait, how is this *my* fault?"

Reluctantly, the other party members started to pitch in. They seemed to only be removing the mana gems, though.

"Hey, bear girl!" Touya called out. "Help us!"

"Me?" Hadn't expected *that*.

"We'll finish faster that way. Plus, we're splitting the mana gems evenly. You've gotta at least harvest your own."

"I'm fine," I said. "Don't need any, thanks."

Harvesting was just not something I did, period. That was why I brought monsters home to Fina, and even she probably wouldn't want to work with wyrms. No thanks!

"Oh, come on! You can't be serious."

"Well, I don't know how to harvest," I said, which prompted all four of them to stare at me in shock.

"You can't harvest them?"

"Aren't you an adventurer?"

"And you're so powerful..."

"You're pulling my leg, right?"

They were all giving me weird looks. Well, any normal, tender fifteen-year-old girl wouldn't know how to butcher monsters. Especially not a gross larva monster like a wyrm!

(Okay, to be fair, I'd come across a ten-year-old and seven-year-old who could, in fact, butcher monster corpses with the best of them.)

"I don't need the reward for slaying them," I said, "so don't make me join in the harvesting."

"In that case, could you burn the carcasses once we're done?" Jade asked.

"Burn them?" I repeated. "I've heard that sand wyrms are considered a delicacy to some people."

"No, that's just regular wyrms. Sand wyrms taste like garbage. Nobody wants to eat one of these things."

I hadn't known that. Maybe the wyrm I used to lure the kraken out had worked only because it tasted pretty good?

"But that doesn't mean we can just leave them. Other monsters are still gonna come by and eat them if we try that, so we've gotta burn anything that we don't use. Adventurer code."

"Also, we wouldn't want these getting in the way of other people who travel through."

Right, Sanya had also made sure the goblins were taken care of when I'd slayed those ten thousand monsters. Now that I understood why I needed to incinerate them, I joined Mel in casting a fire spell on the wyrms.

Since the four of them had worked on harvesting, we finished things up quickly. I guess to other adventurers, harvesting was an indispensable skill...and good for them, I guess, but that just wasn't for me.

"All right, if we loiter here for too long, we might run into more monsters. Let's head out."

Jade started giving instructions to the merchants. They immediately got onto their laggaroutes and prepared to ride off.

"What about you, Yuna?"

"I'm going to go on ahead of you guys." I didn't need to stick around, and Kumayuru would be much faster.

I turned to look for Kumayuru.

"Huh?!"

And what I found were Mel and Senia, latching onto my bear.

"Yuna, come with us, please."

"Yeah, please. I want to ride on your bear too."

"No. I'm riding my own bear," I said.

Wait a sec. What was going on here? Why had they assumed I'd be joining them?

"Would you be kind enough to let go of Kumayuru, please?" I asked.

"Actually, Yuna, didn't you have a white one too?"

"I heard you had a pair of them."

Were they even listening? I guess not. And apparently, they knew about Kumakyu too.

"Okay...I do have a white one," I admitted.

"I wanna see!"

"Um, I'm kind of in a hurry."

"Right, then I guess that means we need to head out."

For some reason, the two of them started clambering onto Kumayuru, who was staring at me with pleading eyes.

"Okay, you two have caused enough trouble for Yuna," Jade snapped, finally noticing what the pair were up to. "We're leaving, so hurry up and get on the laggaroute!"

Not that Mel or Senia seemed keen on following his instructions. "I'd much prefer the bear, thank you very much."

"Same here."

Seriously? Kumayuru was *my* mount...

"I don't care! Just hurry it up!"

"Okay, okay. Jeez."

"You're such a meanie, Jade."

They finally (reluctantly) let go of Kumayuru and headed to their own laggaroute.

"Sorry about those two," said Jade, but he didn't need to apologize. I mean, he'd just saved me! "We're going to take a rest stop at the next pillar. What do you say, Yuna? I'd like to split up the mana gems with you then too."

"Like I said before, I really don't need them."

"We can't have that, now. You're an adventurer, so take them. Otherwise, people will keep taking advantage of you. And it's not a lot. We're just splitting them evenly."

Well, I couldn't say no *now*, so I decided to travel with them up to the next pillar. I had Kumayuru run in the very back.

The party was guarding four merchants, each of whom apparently ran a different business. It seemed to be common for merchants to split the guarding fee when they traveled in a group. Quests at the guild often warned that there might be a change in the number of people who would need protection as well.

Jade and his party were silent as we rode along. Apparently, they were trying not to use too much of their strength. It was really hot, after all, so even talking probably wasn't fun to do in this heat.

The laggaroutes were much faster in the desert than I expected. I finally saw why people used them so often to travel in the desert.

Of course, Kumayuru was still faster.

After running along for a while, we arrived at the next pillar.

Everyone dismounted and started getting ready to stop. They got into the shade of the pillar and gave the laggaroutes water. Once Mel and Senia were done, they headed over to me.

"Your bear is so fast, Yuna."

"It's so odd to see a bear run through the desert."

Well, *I* thought it was even odder to see a giant lizard running through the desert, thank you very much. Not that I hadn't come to accept it by now. I mean, I was living in a world where monsters were real, after all.

"So, Yuna, where's the white one?"

I knew they'd both remember. Well, I was going to switch out my bears anyway.

I thanked Kumayuru and recalled my bear, which seemed to shock Mel and Senia. Then, I summoned Kumakyu.

"Wow, they really are summons!"

"It's a white bear. I've never seen one before."

This time, the two of them latched onto Kumakyu.

"How cute."

"It's so pretty and white."

"Don't bother them too much," I warned, but neither of them seemed to be listening.

I turned to look behind me and saw the merchants a little ways away from me looking super surprised. I guess it was pretty shocking seeing a white bear take the black bear's place—for them, at least.

"Here's your portion, Yuna." Jade made his way to me and gave me four mana gems. I couldn't refuse now that I'd already come all the way here, so I thanked him and took them.

"Looks like rumors of the white bear were true, then," said Jade, watching his two party members harass my bear. "Are you headed over all on your own, Yuna?"

"Pretty much," I replied.

"Yuna... Come with us, please," said Mel.

"With your bears too!" added Senia.

"True," said Jade. "It'll be safer if we all travel together."

"Does she really need us though?" Touya said. "Regardless of how she's dressed, we know just how powerful she is."

He was probably right. I didn't really need them as travel companions. In a way, I'd be safer traveling alone. I'd be able to flee monsters more easily if I couldn't handle it.

"But if we're all together, it'll be easier if anything bad happens."

"I agree."

Pat pat. Stroke stroke.

Pat pat. Stroke stroke.

"I'm starting to think you two just want to travel with that bear," said Touya, which was exactly what I was thinking too.

KUMA
KUMA
KUMA
BEAR

322
The Bear Reaches Dezelt

"**I**'M SURPRISED YOU'RE STILL wearing that getup. Isn't it hot?" Touya asked as he looked at my clothes.

I guess anyone would assume that, considering how fluffy my onesie was.

"You do look hot." Senia came by and pinched my clothes. "But you sure are soft..."

Did she have to put it like that? I didn't want people to think *I* was soft. Anyway, I gave them the same explanation I'd given everyone else for the umpteenth time.

"It's made a special way, so it won't be hot."

"Why'd you go through all that trouble of making something so weird so special?" asked Touya. "You're an odd one, miss."

I hadn't gotten myself a specially made bear onesie because I wanted it. The god forced it on me. So I wasn't the odd one—if anybody was weird, it was the god-dang god.

"Come to think of it, didn't you see Jade and Mel at the academy festival?"

"Yeah, I was pretty surprised to run into them." I'd bumped into them during the monster-harvesting demonstration.

"We were the surprised ones," said Jade. "Seeing Yuna was shocking enough, but that little girl who traveled with you really knew her stuff when it came to wolf harvesting. I still can't believe *you* can't harvest, though."

"Her dad works at the Adventurer Guild and taught her," I said. "I'm just a rookie adventurer, so I can't help it if my skills are a little lacking in some areas." I made sure to emphasize the word *rookie*.

Mel gave me a look. "A rookie. Right."

"What kind of rookie beats a black viper and a goblin king?" Senia asked, exasperated.

"And you defeated a golem that Babold's whole party couldn't take down."

Oh, right, I had. It hadn't been all that long ago, but it sure felt like a throwback. The golems had apparently disappeared from the mines after that.

"Speaking of which, are you sure you're still okay with us taking the credit?"

After I'd left for the capital, they'd been treated to a thank-you feast by the townspeople. Babold had gotten ahead of himself and talked about how much they'd fought against it. It was true that they'd fought the golem, though, so Jade's party hadn't been able to stop them.

"I'm fine with it." I didn't like people making a big deal about me, so that was actually ideal.

"But we did report to the guild that you slayed it."

Sanya had told me that too.

"I'd been so convinced you taught that girl how to harvest, Yuna," said Mel.

"I can't harvest monsters, so I leave that up to the guild and Fina."

"You know, you'll never learn if you don't try it yourself."

I knew that, but I just couldn't. Sometimes people have stuff they're great at and stuff they won't touch with a ten-foot pole.

"That's why we're making Touya do it."

"Yeah, exactly. We're teaching him."

"Uh, I already know how to harvest monsters," remarked Touya, "so I'm pretty sure you guys are just trying to skip out on the work."

Everyone laughed at Touya. Then Jade, who had been talking to the merchants, made his way over to us.

"We still have time, but don't forget to swap the mana gems," he said.

"Oh, I forgot all about that."

"Same here."

"I already did it."

Swap for what?

Mel and Senia were wearing mantles with hoods that hid themselves, but they started taking those off.

"It's so hot."

"Let's get this over with quick."

They took out some blue water gems and traded them with gems on the inner hood of their mantles, then they put their clothes back on again right away.

I guess that was what they meant.

"Ahh, that's nice and chilly."

"What are you guys doing?" I asked.

"We're switching out our gems. They'll stop working if we don't do it soon."

"Huh...?" Okay, so I understood they were swapping gems out since I'd just seen them do that, but...why?

"Wait, you don't know, Yuna?"

No, I really didn't. I had no idea what the two of them had been talking about, so I'd just nodded along.

44

"These mantles are treated with anti-heat measures. We use water mana gems to cool ourselves." Mel opened the front of her mantle and showed me the inner part of it.

Blue lines ran along the inside of it, spreading out toward the sides. *What's all of that?* They seemed to be connected to the water gems.

According to Mel, they attached water gems to the clothing and wove mana threads into their clothes. The cool water would then cool their body temperature, and that's what those blue lines were for. I wondered if it was similar to the mana lines that connected gems.

Basically, this was the equivalent of heat-resistant gear in a game. They found a way to make something like this without using science, which I guess made sense for a fantasy-style world.

"Would it work with ice gems, though? Maybe it'd work even better, right?"

"Wrong. You'd end up freezing if you tried that."

"Plus, it'd drain right away in the desert."

Okay, so that was a no-go. I guess it would've been kind of like leaving a fridge door open to cool yourself. Still, I learned something pretty handy.

A lot of the kids working at my shop looked awfully toasty lately, and I noticed a bunch of them sweating. I told them they didn't have to wear the bear uniforms if it was hot, but they wouldn't take them off. If I installed something like this in their uniforms, maybe that'd fix the problem.

I couldn't have them getting heatstroke, so I'd need to ask Tiermina and Milaine about whether that was possible after getting back to Crimonia.

"These are an absolute must for people going across the desert...or for *most* of them," said Mel, looking at my clothes.

C'mon, so what if I'm a bear?

When I'd met with Blitz and the others, they hadn't told me anything about this. Had they known? Or did they just assume everyone already knew about this stuff? Well, I told them that my bear suit kept me cool, so maybe they assumed I didn't need to know.

"Guys, I'm going to head out pretty soon," I told them.

"Yuna, are you really leaving?"

"I'm kind of in a hurry," I said.

It didn't seem like they were in an emergency yet from what I gathered in town before heading to Dezelt, but the king had told me to hurry. Since my bears were fast, I could get there a lot more quickly than normal people, but I still wanted to get there as fast as I could. Being late might have an awful cost, after all. I recalled Kumayuru and mounted Kumakyu.

"Yuna, once you're done taking the package to them, will you have some free time?" asked Jade.

"I'm planning on exploring the town for a while, so I think so," I replied.

I still had time until the work trip to the beach. Once I got to the town, I also need to check in with Fina. If I wanted to, I could even set up a bear gate and go home.

"In that case, let's grab something to eat when you're free, all right?"

"Yeah, let us treat you as a thank-you."

Jade and his party started promising me a meal. I didn't know what kinds of things Dezelt would have to eat, but I was relieved that they didn't eat wyrms. I wasn't familiar with all the cuisine in this world though, so I needed to be careful of what I ate.

"I'm looking forward to eating something good," I said.

After I left them, I had Kumakyu start running.

I continued through the desert without losing my way, thanks to the landmark pillars. Every once in a while, I'd see some merchants and adventurers, and I'd have to wait until we passed them by—not that we needed to work hard to overtake them. I stopped overnight partway there and caught sight of the town the next afternoon.

The town I saw from atop the dunes was enveloped by a wall. At the center of it all was a lake with a few surprising trees at the center, as if it was some kind of oasis.

Then, I caught sight of something else in an entirely different direction.

"Is that a pyramid?" It sure looked like one, at least, and it was just a little ways away from town. Since it was kinda far, I couldn't make it out for sure, but it definitely looked...pyramidal.

To think I'd end up seeing a pyramid in another world! A shut-in like me never would've even *dreamed* of seeing the pyramids or the desert in Egypt in my old world. Maybe I'd head over for some sightseeing after handing over the kraken's mana gem? Then again, could I even get into the thing? Would there be a mummy?

I directed Kumayuru to Dezelt, and we headed off. Let's see... How would I get into town? I'd scare someone for sure if I headed in on Kumayuru. But even if I walked in and they asked me how I traveled all the way there, how would I even reply?

After giving it some thought, I figured it'd be easier for me to just be upfront and explain stuff, even if I ended up scaring a couple of people. With my mind made up, I headed toward the town on Kumayuru.

Just as I'd thought, the people at the gate looked flabbergasted by my bear when I arrived.

"A bear?!"

"M-miss... Why is there a bear with you?!"

The two guards backed away. I guess this was a pretty typical reaction to seeing a bear for the very first time. It was kind of a relief, to be honest. It reminded me just how weird it was that Mel and Senia reacted like they did.

"This is my bear," I said. "As long as you don't attack them, they're harmless."

"Really?"

"They're a summons. I'll recall them."

I got off Kumayuru and recalled my bear to make them feel better.

"Whoa... This is my first time seeing a summons."

"I've seen one before, but not a bear."

They were still surprised, but I was in a hurry. "Can I head in?"

"Oh, sure. But no summoning the bear in town—you'll give people a fright."

I knew better than to do that, so I agreed.

I figured the first thing I ought to do was get a room at an inn. Then I'd head over to see Barlimer, the person who ran Dezelt. I'd be in trouble if I couldn't find a room, like in the last town.

"Excuse me, what's the way to an inn?" I asked one of the guards, who still seemed pretty bewildered.

"Oh, an inn? Right. There are a few, but the closest one is on this main road ahead. It's pretty big."

I also asked for directions to the town lord's house and the Adventurer Guild. It seemed that the lord's house was close to the center of the town, near the lake, and it was supposedly pretty big too—I'd know it when I saw it. They also told me that the Adventurer Guild was on the same road as the inn.

"Miss, I'm not sure why you came into town, but we're... going through some stuff here," said the guard. "I advise that you leave as soon as possible."

I assumed he probably meant the broken mana gem. Seemed like it really was an issue, then.

"Yeah, I know," I said.

"I see. All right, then. Also, miss, could I ask you something else?"

"What is it?"

"Those clothes you're wearing...what are they?"

"Bear clothes." And with that, I headed into town.

323
The Bear Makes a Stop at the Adventurer Guild

PEOPLE BUILT THEIR HOUSES around the lake in the middle of Dezelt. Since it was all the way out in the middle of the desert, I thought it'd be a lot smaller, but the city was pretty big and more populated than I'd imagined.

I'd go to deliver the mana gem after getting a room at the inn.

The guard had told me I'd find a large inn if I just went down the main road, but...where was it? As I walked down the path, I looked around and listened to the whispers. "What is that?" "A bear?" "There's a bear walking around." "Mommy, what's that?" It was just the usual stuff. People were staring at me out of curiosity. There was even a little kid pointing straight at me. Just more of the same. For the time being, I pulled my bear hood low over my head.

As I walked and searched, I came across the sign for the Adventurer Guild. Hmm...I kind of wanted to go inside for a bit. Maybe I could take a quick peek? Just a teeny little detour...

In games, after all, the types of monsters and quests you got varied by region. As a former gamer, I was so curious about the quests that I really couldn't help myself.

I was making excuses in my head as I slowly made my way into the guild, ever-careful not to draw attention to myself. Since I was so quiet, no one noticed as I entered. There weren't a ton of adventurers around, and most of them seemed to be hanging out and chatting.

I was trying to find the quest board when I overheard somebody—a girl.

"Please, could you take me to—Please?"

I looked around and found the speaker. The girl was red-haired and about the same age as Fina or Noa. She was talking to some adventurers.

"Please?" She bowed low to them.

"Sorry, you'll have to ask someone else." After the adventurer turned her down, she just went to the next closest adventurer and made the same request.

"Please?"

"You should ask someone at a higher rank."

Another adventurer. Another. And another again. But all they ever did was turn her down. I was curious about the girl, so I headed over to a woman at the front desk who was giving her a worried look.

"What's going on with her?"

"Huh?!"

The woman looked at me in surprise. Guess she didn't notice me come in.

"Um, Miss...Bear? What did you need? Did you come here to submit a quest?"

Because I was short and dressed as a bear, a lot of people thought I was younger than I really was, but it'd been a while since anyone had actually treated me like a child.

"Actually, I'm an adventurer."

"An adventurer?!" Her eyes went wide as saucers. Yeah, she wasn't buying it.

I ignored the woman's surprise and just kept asking questions. "What's going on with that girl? Couldn't she just put in a quest at the guild?"

Meanwhile, the girl was asking one adventurer after another for help.

"We did take her quest," the reception woman told me. "But no adventurers want to do it. She's been going around asking each one individually now."

"Is the payment too low or something?"

She was a kid, after all, though she looked pretty well dressed for a little girl.

"No, it's not a matter of money. The quest is simply too difficult. No one will take it."

"Please?" And still that girl was walking around the room, working as hard as she could to ask all the adventurers in the place, even though not a single one of them would accept it. Other adventurers turned awkwardly to look away from the spectacle.

"Is the quest really that difficult?"

"She wants someone to take her to the underground area of the Dezelt pyramid."

Right...probably the one I saw on the way into town. Wait, an underground area? Like a basement or something? I thought pyramids were for going up, not down.

"It's a dangerous place, and protecting her during the journey to *reach* the pyramid would be even more difficult, so no one will take the quest...especially considering who she is."

"And who is she?"

"Lady Karina, the daughter of this town's lord."

"The lord's daughter..." Didn't that mean I was about to visit her parents' house? "But why does she want to go there?"

The woman shook her head. "She only told us that she wanted to go to the lower levels, but we don't know why she made the request..."

The girl was looking down, her little hands balled into fists, and she bit her lip. She looked like she could start bawling at any minute. She didn't, though. Instead, she raised her head...and stared right at me. "A bear?"

Well, I was pretty curious about her too. "Hey. Did something happen?"

"No, nothing to tell a bear about." She immediately discounted me, bobbed her head, and went right back to the adventurers.

"I'm sorry," said the woman at the desk. "She's really not a bad kid."

I could tell. She wasn't looking down on me. Maybe she really did believe that a weirdly dressed girl like me wasn't exactly the right one to deal with...whatever she needed to deal with.

I looked at the girl absentmindedly as several adventurers entered the guild. I was pretty sure I passed by them along the way to town.

"This is the Adventurer Guild, eh? Bigger than I thought it'd be."

"Might be good to make some cash while we're around for a while."

"Town's pretty big too."

It seemed like they weren't from around here.

"Hear the town's having an emergency, though."

"If the going gets tough, we can just leave."

The little girl ran over as soon as she heard them, going up to talk to a man with a large sword—their leader, it seemed.

"Excuse me," she said, "could I ask you for something?"

"What do you want?"

"Please, just hear me out."

"I'm tired. Haven't got time to listen to some kid's story."

The man waved off the girl. It might've seemed like nothing to him, but it must've really wrecked her.

She collapsed to the ground. "P-please, wait," she said, managing to stand up and trying to grasp at them, as if to stop them from walking away.

He brushed her off again as she tried to reach out to him.

At that moment, I went on the move.

"Huh?" The man looked down at his arm...which I was gripping in my bear puppet's mouth. "A bear?"

"*The* bear?"

"Turning her down is one thing," I said, glaring at him, "but brushing her off like that? That's not okay."

At that moment, one of the adventurers with him let something slip. "Wh-why's the Bloody Bear here...?" He looked at me, surprised.

"Bloody Bear," huh? I hadn't heard that one in ages. I looked at the man who'd called me that, and he promptly took a step back to hide behind one of the other adventurers.

"You should get away from her," he said.

"What?" the leader barked. "You know this weirdo girl with the stupid outfit?" He strained against my bear puppet. My arm didn't move an inch.

"N-no, I don't know who she is," said the other man quickly, turning away.

Come on, he *definitely* knew who I was. He'd even called me the Bloody Bear. Actually...he was pretty freaked out, huh? Had I beaten this dude up sometime?

"How long are you gonna hold my arm for, little miss bear?" he asked with a smile.

"I guess until whenever a certain little someone loosens up," I replied, which made the man strain against me even more. But when he saw I wasn't even breaking into a sweat, that smirk of his disappeared real quick. As for the girl behind me, it seemed like she had no idea *what* to do.

"You should get away from the bear!" said the other guy—the one who'd called me the Bloody Bear.

"You heard the man," I said. "So. What's it gonna be, huh?"

The man squeezed out the last bit of strength he had, but he still couldn't move. In fact, I slowly brought his arm down.

The expression on his face shifted immediately. "Damn it! We're leaving. We report on the quest, then go out drinking, and that's that!" He shook off my hand and headed over to the front desk to make his report.

The man who seemed to know me passed by, cowering. I guess I'd punched that dude out some time ago, maybe? Eh, who could say?

"Um...?" the girl addressed me from behind.

"Are you okay?" I asked. "You're not hurt?"

"No, I'm fine. Thank you very much."

I was glad. Seemed nothing bad had happened to her. "If you want to ask people for something, make sure to take a good look at what kind of person they are," I advised her.

She stared at me. "Who are you?"

"Despite the getup, I really am an adventurer."

"An adventurer?" Of course she wouldn't believe it. She looked at me thoughtfully.

Suddenly, the woman at the reception spoke up. "Lady Karina, you ought to head home today. If an adventurer who will take your quest comes, I'll send someone over to tell you."

Wait, hadn't she just told me there wouldn't be any takers? Hmm...it kind of looked like she was just trying to get rid of the girl without causing a scene. Then again, what else was she supposed to do? No one could let the lord's daughter get hurt. It was a tricky situation.

"All right," said the girl after a moment of thought. "Thank you." With that, she bowed her head and left the guild.

As for me, I'd completely forgotten why I came to the guild in the first place. I followed her.

324
The Bear Follows the Girl

I LEFT THE GUILD to follow the young girl. She was staring at the ground as she walked. I could practically feel the sadness coming from her back, which made her seem even smaller than she already was.

Since I didn't know what to do, I decided to just... follow her for a while. She occasionally brought her hand up to her eyes. It seemed like she was crying.

Unfortunately, I just wasn't built to handle stuff like that. If she was the type to talk through her tears, like Fina, maybe I could help her. But if she just refused to talk to me at all, I'd be stumped.

While I tried to think of how to talk to her, the girl suddenly whirled around.

"Why are you following me?"

She'd noticed! Since my bear shoes weren't supposed to make a sound, I was sure she wouldn't. Maybe she'd sensed me?

Her eyes were a little red. Yep...she'd been crying.

"I'm surprised you noticed me there."

"Do you take me for a fool? Everyone around me kept talking about bears. Anyone would notice that."

I looked around. Okay, fair point. There were people staring at me and muttering their little ursine comments. I'd been so preoccupied sneaking after her that I hadn't noticed all the other people around me. Made sense, I guess.

"So, what is it you want? Why were you following me?"

"Uh...right. I came here to see your dad," I said, remembering that as I said it aloud. And hey, it *was* accurate, after all. I was supposed to go see Barlimer, her dad.

"You want to see Father?" She looked at me dubiously.

"I need to deliver something to Barlimer, as part of a job." C'mon, I was telling the truth here.

"You're really serious?" There was that suspicious look again—not that I could blame her for being a little uncertain about a girl in a bear onesie trying to follow her home in secret and asking to see her father.

Sadly, people really do judge books by their covers.

"Do you have proof?"

Maybe I could show her the king's letter? Though if she didn't recognize the crest, that'd put a quick end to the conversation. I showed her the envelope, hoping it'd be proof enough. It had an aristocrat's wax seal, like something straight out of a manga. The crest of Elfanica kingdom had been pressed into it.

"That crest..." She seemed surprised now. I saw a spark of recognition. "You do know forgery of a royal seal is a felony, don't you?"

"It's real!" Why was she assuming I'd faked it?!

"Perhaps, but I highly doubt that anyone from the royal family would entrust a job to a girl dressed as a bear."

Ugh, I didn't have a comeback for that. Even if I told her that I was the king's messenger, I knew I wouldn't be credible, what with the onesie and all.

Plus, she already had her guard up...which was weird, because I was dressed as a bear and there wasn't exactly anything I could think of to be cautious about. Maybe she was just really mature, as far as the kids out here went.

"What would I need to do for you to believe me?"

"Why don't you show me your guild card? You said you're an adventurer. If your rank is high, then I'll believe you."

"Um...define 'high.'" I wasn't anywhere near A-rank, that was for sure.

"I'd prefer B or above, but C will do."

Phew. I pulled my card out from my bear storage and showed it off to her. She scrutinized it.

"Your class is...bear?"

Why did people always focus on that part?

"That's not the part you were supposed to check."

She took another look at the card. "Adventurer rank C?!"

Right, there we go.

She squinted at the card. "You do know that forging a guild card is..."

"It's not forged," I said, which finally got a smile from her for the first time.

"I'm sorry. It was a tasteless joke. I believe you, Miss Bear—believe that you're an adventurer. You helped me out back there, and I could tell he was really fighting against you. I could tell you were trying to protect me too. But I just couldn't believe someone dressed as a bear could be an envoy from Elfanica."

"I think your father will believe me once he reads this letter," I told her. "At least...I hope."

The king hadn't told me what he'd written in it, but he assured me that I'd get an audience. Hopefully, it'd all just work out.

"All right. I believe you, Miss Bear."

"Thank you. But my name isn't Miss Bear. Could you use my name? It's Yuna."

"Yes, Yuna."

Yep, this was one good kid. I mean, some of them just wouldn't stop calling me "Bear" even when I asked them not to!

The girl then introduced herself formally. "You might already know my name, but I'll introduce myself regardless. I'm Karina, the daughter of the town's lord. Thank you for saving me earlier."

She was very polite as she introduced herself. She seemed well educated, just like Noa.

I introduced myself again too. "I'm Yuna, an adventurer. The king of Elfanica kingdom asked me to meet with your father. Would you bring me to him?"

"All right. I'll let Father decide what to do."

And so, I got my audience with Karina's father. My plans were going a bit out of order, so I decided to leave searching for an inn for later. We started walking to her father's house.

"Um... So, Yuna, why are you dressed like that?"

I knew it. She was a curious one. "It's because my class is bear," I said matter-of-factly, grinning.

That little joke got her to smile back. "Hee hee... Is that even a real class?"

"Isn't it?" I said, knowing it wasn't. I'd written it down as a joke when I registered at a guild, but Helen had actually entered it on my card. I wanted to give my past self a slap upside the head.

Well, it'd gotten a smile out of her, so maybe it was all right. Still, I never had a good answer whenever anyone asked me about that stuff. I really *wasn't* a swordsman or a mage. And the thing I was best at was, well, bear stuff. I hadn't changed much since then, either. Yeah...it seemed like I'd be stuck with this problem for a while.

"Did you come from the capital, Yuna?" Karina asked.

"Yeah, I did. I live somewhere else though, in a town called Crimonia. It's just a skip and a hop away from the capital, though."

"So, you came all this way? Wow... But you're only a little older than me."

Wait, how young did she think I was? It bugged me, but I pretended not to hear it.

"It wasn't that impressive," I said, ignoring the bit about my age. Besides, I traveled to the capital instantly through my bear gate and then rode here on my bears—that was all there was to it.

"How old are you, Yuna?"

"Fifteen."

"Huh?!"

Based on how she reacted, maybe she actually thought I was older?

"I thought you were a little younger."

I should've known.

"What about you, Karina?"

"I'm ten."

I was right—she was Fina and Noa's age. If she went to the academy, she might even end up in the same class as Noa. Then again, this town didn't belong to any country, so maybe that wouldn't even be possible.

"You're really level-headed," I told her. "You don't act like you're ten."

"I get that a lot," was her answer.

I felt a twang of despair rip through my chest from that response, though I didn't understand why. We were just talking about how we didn't look our ages, but...I felt like I'd lost a match or something. Anyway, I smiled—as maturely as I could—and resolved not to let my glass heart shatter at this setback.

Then, as I was taking in the streets of the town while walking with Karina, we finally made it to the lake where the mansion was supposed to be. I hadn't been able to tell from afar, but now I could see the water level was pretty low.

"There's not much water in there, is there?" Karina

commented when she saw me looking at the lake. "It used to be really big, to the point the water was almost over-flowing. That was even just a little bit ago. Kids used to play here too. I'd go with my friends a lot. But then one day, the waterline started to recede, and we're not even allowed to swim in the lake now."

"How did this happen?" I assumed it had something to do with the broken mana gem, but I asked anyway.

For a moment, Karina didn't say a word. She just stared quietly at the lake.

Then, slowly, she began to speak. "It's my fault."

That wasn't the response I expected. "What do you mean?"

"…"

It didn't seem like she was going to answer me.

So...that was that. She did something to cause it, somehow. That must've been why she was so insistent about talking to the adventurers about the quest.

But how could she cause something like this? Sure, I knew that the gem had cracked, but it wasn't like a little kid could do that. The things wouldn't break, even if you accidentally dropped them on the ground. Plus, I didn't see how hiring adventurers was going to fix the broken gem.

Yeah, I was still kind of confused. And if I asked Karina

how it happened, I didn't think she'd tell me. Maybe her dad would have answers?

"Yuna, let's get to the house quickly."

We walked the rest of the way in silence.

As we were walking near the lake, I caught sight of a building that was bigger than the rest.

"That's my house. Father will be there."

Standing out front, now I could see that the mansion was built similarly to the ones in the capital. A dark-skinned woman in her twenties was walking the grounds, looking like she was searching for something. When she caught sight of us, she ran over.

"Lady Karina!" she yelled and hugged Karina tight.

"Lasa," Karina said.

"Where in the world were you?! I was so worried."

"I'm sorry."

The woman gave Karina a tighter squeeze. "I'm so relieved. I was worried you wandered into the desert on your own."

"I'd never do anything as reckless as that."

"No, Lady Karina, I fully believe that you would."

"I just went to the Adventurer Guild."

"Still, I can't believe you left on your own. If you need to go there again, you can send me in your place."

"But I need to fix this. It's my responsibility."

The woman seemed genuinely concerned. She wiped away some tears and finally looked at me. "And who is this very cutely dressed friend of yours?"

"She's here for Father," Karina answered. "I ran into her at the guild."

"I'm Yuna, an adventurer." Since I was wearing the bear suit, I made sure to be as polite and proper as possible when I told her my name. I didn't want her suspicious of me too.

"Um…I'm Lasa, one of the people employed at the manor," Lasa said, but I could clearly see the confusion on her face.

Well, moving on… I explained how I'd run into Karina and that I was here to meet with Barlimer.

"So, you're an adventurer and you're here to meet his lordship?" She definitely looked suspicious now.

"Lasa, it's true. She showed me her guild card. And a letter for Father as well."

"Well, if you say it is so, then I suppose it must be, my lady," Lasa said.

Karina seemed to have convinced her. If I hadn't had the king's letter, things probably wouldn't have been this simple.

"He's right this way, so please come in." She led me into the mansion.

325
The Bear Meets Barlimer

"**L**ASA, is Father in his bedroom?"

"He's working in his office."

"Huh?!" Karina looked shocked. "You didn't stop him?"

"I tried to," Lasa said, "but he insisted he was fine."

Karina broke into a run. I followed right behind. She ran up the stairs, reached a room, and barged right in without knocking.

"Father! How can you work when you're injured!"

"Karina, don't forget to knock before entering," said a thin, middle-aged man sitting in the room. Piles of documents lay before him. If Karina was calling him "Father," then this was probably Barlimer.

"But, Father, when I heard you were working..."

"I should be fine now," the man answered. "I can't stay in bed in a situation like this."

"But..."

Karina approached him, looking worried. He didn't seem injured, but maybe he was covering a wound under his clothing.

"And who is that girl in the adorable getup behind you? Will you introduce us?" Barlimer stroked Karina's head and looked at me.

"She's Yuna," said Karina, "an adventurer sent from Elfanica for you, Father."

"For me?" Clearly shocked, he gave me a curious look.

"I'm Yuna, an adventurer. His Majesty sent me here. Just to be certain, you *are* Barlimer, lord of Dezelt, are you not?" I greeted him a bit stiffly, since I wasn't used to all the formalities.

"That I am. I am Barlimer Ishleet, lord of this town."

I handed him the letter. "This is a letter from His Majesty."

I figured it'd be quicker for him to read it than for me to explain. Besides, even if I did tell him that the king had sent me, he wouldn't believe me. I already knew that from previous experience and from my interaction with Karina.

"This letter has Elfanica's... You speak the truth, then?" He looked from the crest on the letter to me. Yeah, yeah, yeah. Girl in a bear onesie? An envoy from Elfanica? Wowzers, what a surprise.

"I believe the details are explained in the letter," I told him.

At least, I hoped they were. If not, I'd be going back to the castle for a word or two with His Majesty. I really hoped he hadn't, like, stuck blank paper in there as a joke.

Barlimer cut the seal and pulled out the letter. He pored over its contents, then looked to me. He seemed pretty taken aback. Still, it looked like the king had written out what I was here for...though I was kinda curious about what he'd written, specifically.

"Father, what does it say?" Karina asked in my place.

"It seems that she is indeed His Majesty's envoy."

It *also* seemed he was still dubious; letter or no. Bear onesies will do that to a guy.

"And he also wrote here that she brought a water gem to replace the one that has broken."

"She has?!" said Karina.

"May I take a look?" he asked.

I brought the kraken gem out of my bear storage and placed it on top of Barlimer's desk. "Here it is," I said.

"It's rather large..."

"Yeah, it really is..."

Barlimer picked up the gem. "You'll really give this to us?" He stared at the gem in disbelief.

"I think that's what it said in the letter," I said. Uh... probably.

"I just never expected to see a gem of this size. I have no idea how to thank you."

"Please; it's His Majesty you should thank." It was my gem, but I wasn't the one officially giving it to them.

"You've been of great help..." He sure didn't look happy, though. Maybe there'd been some other development, too?

"Father..." Karina stared down at the ground gloomily. Barlimer placed a gentle hand on Karina's head.

He looked up from the letter to me. Something flashed in his eyes then, as if he'd made a decision. "Your name is Yuna, you say?"

"Yes."

"His Majesty asked me to read this next letter if we're in any trouble."

He produced a second envelope from the first one. There were two of them in there? The king never mentioned that.

"He said that if the mana gem works without issue, to hand this off to you and take this to His Majesty. If we're in any additional dire straits, though, then he requested I ask for your permission to read this letter."

"My...permission?" I didn't follow. The king hadn't mentioned any of this to me.

"He says that it contains something that will help me trust you."

He'd written about me, huh? I hoped none of it was weird. I really wanted to tell him not to read it, but it seemed like Barlimer was in enough trouble that he needed help. If it wasn't serious, he probably wouldn't even dream of asking a beary odd adventurer like me for help.

"You're in trouble, then?" I asked.

"Yes, if I'm being honest. Though I'm not sure what His Majesty meant when he wrote this."

Who *wouldn't* think all of this was weird, though?

"But the king I know," he continued, "wouldn't do something without a purpose in mind."

News to me. I never saw the king actually working, personally. To me, he was that fancy guy who dropped by specifically to eat my food. The only time I saw him act particularly kingly was when we first met.

Barlimer looked like he was grasping at straws, trying to find anything that'd help him. I couldn't possibly say no in a situation like that, so I gave him my permission.

"Then if you'll allow me," he said as he opened the second envelope and pulled out the letter. Once he started reading, I could see the surprise on his face. He glanced up at me several times too.

"Father, what does the letter say?" Barlimer was covering it so Karina couldn't see. "Father?"

"Yuna, are the things written in this letter... Is all of this true?! I doubt His Majesty would lie."

"Err...can I see it?"

He handed the letter to me, and I glanced through it. It was basically a chronicle of everything I'd done so far. From the kraken I'd slain and the water gem that had been harvested to the black tiger and the black viper, it covered almost everything. He hadn't been explicit about the ten thousand monsters I'd slain, but there were little hints about *something* there too.

It also said that if Barlimer believed in me, he should ask for my help. If he did not believe this, though, then he was to say nothing of these things to me and to let me return to the capital. He even wrote that Elfanica would pay the fee.

Finally, it said that he shouldn't tell a soul about the contents of the letter, even if it was his own family. That was why he covered the letter when Karina had tried to look.

Something that kind of caught my attention as I read the letter, though, was that he repeated the phrase "despite how she looks" a lot.

No, I mean *a lot*. Like, the entire thing was about that! *Despite the getup, she... Although she dresses ridiculously...*

Of course, don't be fooled by her looks... He went on and on! To be honest, he wrote some pretty terrible things about me! Still, he *did* note at the end that I was a powerful adventurer. I knew he only wrote that in order to convince someone else I'd done all this stuff, but it still kind of hurt.

"It's true," I said. "All of it. But would you take me at my word?"

"I suppose I'm confused, really," Barlimer told me. "Had this been any ordinary letter, I would have thought it was a tasteless joke and ripped it to shreds. But His Majesty had you travel all the way here to deliver a valuable mana gem along with these letters. He would only do such a thing if he truly had faith in your power. At the same time, though it may be discourteous of me to say, you *do* rather look like an ordinary little girl dressed in bear clothes."

Yeah, couldn't blame him for feeling like that. Even the king's letter wasn't enough to erase every doubt.

"Would you allow me to inspect your guild card?"

"My guild card?"

"Yes. It should show a record of your accomplishments. I would be able to see the record of what you've slain, the quests you've fulfilled, and such. If you would be so kind, I would like to see that."

It would end up displaying all the same information that Atola from the Mileela Adventurer Guild had seen. I personally could only see the public-facing details on my card, so I didn't know all the private information that had been recorded on it. I had no idea what he would see. Honestly, there might even be things on there that I didn't want him to know.

"I won't tell anyone else what I see on it, of course," Barlimer said. "His Majesty has written in his letter that I should not."

If I wanted to leave without hearing him out, I could get away with not showing him. But curiosity was getting the best of me, especially since I'd seen Karina at the guild. Really, the thing that got to me most was that she'd been crying. I couldn't just leave after seeing that.

I didn't know whether Barlimer would ask me to do a quest for him or not, but I handed him my guild card anyway. He pulled a crystal panel out of his desk and placed the card on it.

Then my information popped up. I couldn't see it, though.

"Thank you," said Barlimer, returning the card. "Yuna, I have a request for you. Please, would you help us?"

And then Barlimer bowed his head to me, a girl in a bear costume. Which I guess meant he believed me, right?

"Um, if I can, I will." I didn't have any choice, considering I was staring at the top of his head.

"Thank you. Then I shall tell you all the details. I apologize for not offering you a seat earlier. Please, take that seat over there."

I took him up on his offer. Just as I did, the door opened, and a woman entered.

KUMA
KUMA
KUMA
BEAR

326
The Bear Learns about the Pyramid's Labyrinths
Part One

THE WOMAN STEPPED into the room, and I could immediately tell from her swollen belly that she was pregnant.

"Mother!" Karina ran over to her, looking worried.

Her mom was young, probably about twenty-five. Maybe people in this world didn't grow old that fast? And maybe that was why everyone thought I looked young? Yeah, let's go with that.

The pregnant woman's eyes swept around the room, stopping on me.

"My, so there really is a bear here." She sure didn't seem all that flustered, even though Karina looked worried.

"Listiel, what are you doing here? You should be resting."

"Ha ha, it's all right. Being cooped up in that room all the time is just as bad for my health. Besides, this is my third. I can tell how I'm feeling by now."

"If you insist..."

"Lasa informed me that Karina came home with a girl in a cute bear costume, so I just came for a look."

Excuse me? I'm not some kind of dancing bear sideshow...

Listiel looked me over and beamed. "You really are adorable."

"Mother, you must sit, please," said Karina.

"Oh, well, aren't you a little worrywart?" Still, she accepted Karina's hand and sat on a nearby chair anyway. "Thank you."

Karina's mother had somehow brightened up the depressing room. "Now, dear, who is this friend of yours?"

Friend? I don't know about *that.* I mean, I guess I did have some friends Karina's age. Fina and Noa, for instance.

"I don't have any friends who would dress up as a bear, Mother."

Ouch. Even if the same thought just ran through my mind, it felt a lot more cutting when someone else said it out loud. We only just met, so no, we weren't friends, but did she have to say it to my face?

"I'm Yuna, an adventurer. I came here under the king of Elfanica's orders."

"His Majesty?"

"Yuna brought us this big water gem," said Karina.

"Did she now?"

"Yes, it's true. She brought it all the way from Elfanica on her own. We should be able to fix the broken one now."

"You're sure that this bear did all that...?" Karina's mother looked at me in disbelief.

What, cross an entire desert on my own? Admittedly, I'd find it pretty far-fetched too if I had never met me before. I mean, if Fina popped up out of nowhere and insisted she crossed the desert on her own, I never would've believed her. In fact, I'd ask her who really brought her over.

Barlimer picked up the gem and attempted to stand, but instead ended up grimacing.

"Father!"

"My love!"

"It's fine. Just a little sting is all," he insisted.

He carried the gem to the woman, then he placed the kraken's gem on a table in front of him. Yeah, he was definitely injured somehow.

"Are you sure you're fine, dear?"

"Yes," he insisted. "Nothing to worry about." He sat down next to the woman in another chair, wincing as he settled in. "King Folhaut has trusted her, as an adventurer. Her skills are apparently top-notch, despite her...aesthetics."

Sigh. Fair enough.

"Lord Folhaut told me this in a letter," he continued, "and I saw it with my very own eyes on her guild card. There is a possibility he specifically sent her to us, knowing that our situation was this dire. So, I would like to tell her everything."

Surprised crossed the woman's face for a moment, but only for a second. She regained her poise immediately after. "Ha ha...all right, then. If that's what you've decided, it works for me."

"Thank you."

The two of them hugged each other gingerly. I was happy for them and how much they trusted each other, but all this matrimonial soppiness was kind of an eyesore for me and Karina.

"Um, so..." I couldn't have them flirting with each other all day, after all.

"My apologies, Yuna. Karina, if you could ask Lasa to prepare some tea?"

"Yes."

Karina nodded and left the room. I sat down in a chair in front of Barlimer.

"I am Barlimer's wife, Listiel," the woman formally introduced herself. "Um, may I call you Yuna?"

"Yes, please do."

"Now, please correct me if I'm wrong," Listiel said, "but it seems that you struggle with formalities?"

"Well..." Was it that obvious?

"Ha ha, I don't intend on keeping these up. Speak in whatever way makes you comfortable."

"In that case, I'll take you up on that," I said. I just couldn't get used to all the formal language, and I knew I wasn't any good at it. I gladly accepted the life raft Listiel tossed me.

"It's much easier to talk this way," Listiel said. "You were being so stuffy earlier, and it just didn't look right, considering how you're dressed."

"Listiel, that's how envoys are meant to act," Barlimer interrupted.

"Well, then *you're* too stuffy," she replied.

"And you're too lenient about these things."

"Um, I'd feel much better if you would also talk without all the pomp and circumstance," I said to him.

"Well... I suppose. It does feel a tad off-putting to speak to a girl dressed as a bear such as yourself with all the formality of a normal envoy."

I thought so. I was surprised he'd been able to address me with such a straight face, considering the impression I usually made at first. Most people would start calling me "miss" or "little girl" or something like that.

The king's letter must've played a big part in how I was being treated. The king really was pretty revered, wasn't he? Normally I just saw him as a regular dude who showed up to steal my food.

Just as we were about to get into the main topic at hand, there was a knock at the door and Karina entered.

"Father, I've brought the tea."

"What happened to Lasa?" Barlimer asked.

"She let me bring it instead," Karina said. "Father, please let me listen too."

She looked very serious.

"Father, please," she said again.

"Ahh... All right. Come sit here."

"Thank you, Father."

Karina looked happy as she set the tea down in front of me and sat next to me. I thanked her and took the tea. It was nice, cool, and thoroughly delicious.

"Yuna, how much do you know about the situation this town is in?"

"I know that the gem supplying water to the town broke and that you'll run out of water soon. That's why the king told me to hurry and bring the mana gem."

"I see. You're not wrong there. If we didn't have the water from the gem, this town would have become uninhabitable."

"But you should be fine now that you have the water gem, right?" He'd said earlier that it was big enough.

"Let's discuss the town before getting into that," he said.

Uh, really? That first? Well, I was curious about how things worked out here, what with them being a town with a lake in the middle of the desert. I wanted to know how all this stuff tied in with the water gem too, so I sat tight and listened.

"Several hundred years ago, this town was created by a certain party of adventurers. Did you see the pyramid?"

"I did, but only from a distance on my way here."

"The pyramid is divided into aboveground and underground levels, and the upper levels are a labyrinth. The labyrinth, in turn, is composed of a series of complex, booby-trapped mazes. This adventurer party was able to reach the final level several hundred years ago. Within that last level, they found a water gem and a magic ritual. This ritual amplifies the creation of water. When they used it on the water gem, it created a lake in the middle of the desert."

"And that's the town's lake, right?"

"Correct. Because they created the lake, travelers gained a place for reprieve in the desert. This steadily drew in more people, back in the day, until this town came into being."

Kinda sounded almost mystical to me, like a story right out of a fantasy novel. Seemed like the gems, magical ritual, and all that stuff were like a prize for getting through the labyrinth. Some ancient relic left behind, maybe.

"However, the lake's waterline has been receding because the gem cracked."

So, the lake was like that because of the mana gem breaking, just like I'd thought.

"But it can be fixed, right?" I asked. "You can switch out the gem." After all, that was the whole point of me bringing the kraken's gem here.

"Yes, we should be able to fix it. But we still need to get to the final level of the labyrinth."

"Uh...so you need to clear the pyramid in order to switch out the gem? Is that it?"

But that didn't make sense, considering what Karina had been saying before. The labyrinth was the top of the pyramid. Karina had asked to travel *down*, underground. I assumed at first that her goal had been to clear the pyramid so she could swap out the gem, but that didn't seem to be the case.

"Yes...and no."

"Uhh...?" I really wasn't in the mood for riddles. C'mon, answers please...

"I..." Karina looked down and bit her lip.

"The labyrinth had a map, in addition to the water gem," said Barlimer.

"A map?"

"Yes. It showed how to get to the last level."

I finally started to understand where we were going with this. Karina must've done something to lose the map. I looked over at her again. Her head was still down.

"On occasion, we used that map to check in on the water gem," Barlimer explained. "We realized during the last trip that the gem was broken, and so I asked Elfanica and Trifolm for a gem. But day by day, more water disappeared from the lake. I was hoping to buy us more time, even just a little. I gathered smaller water gems and went back into the pyramid...but then I got caught in a trap and dropped the map in a pit trap."

"No! Father, you can't lie like that. *I* dropped the map. I was so caught up in the moment that it slipped out of my hands..." Karina squeezed out the words.

"Karina..." said Barlimer softly.

So *that* was why she wanted to go down instead of up.

"You don't have a copy of the map?" I asked.

If they'd just made another one, they wouldn't have had to worry about losing the original, or about it catching on fire, or being stolen, or whatever. Then again, if it was stolen, they'd have no way of preventing anyone from doing something up to no good in those labyrinths.

Barlimer shook his head. "The labyrinth changes by the day. We need that map in order to keep from getting lost. We couldn't have copied it even if we wanted to."

It changed every day? And the map could keep track of that? The mystery just went deeper...

"If it changes all the time, then how would you use a map?" I asked.

"Because it's no ordinary map—it's a crystal panel. Channeling mana into it makes an image of the maze materialize."

Whoa, I hadn't realized that was a thing. I mean, crystal panels were pretty thin, but they could show maps now? It reminded me of a phone or a tablet.

"So," he concluded, "even with the water gem, we can't reach the furthest level."

"Pardon me for asking," I said, "but why would you entrust something so important to a young girl?" I didn't think it made sense to give something like that over to a ten-year-old.

"Well..."

"Dear..." Listiel gave him a small nod. "I'll explain the rest from here."

"Are you sure?"

"We already told her this much. There's no point to keeping it from her. Yuna, I do hope you won't spread what we are about to discuss."

"Am I allowed to know whatever this is?"

"Just as Barlimer says," said Listiel, "we really should tell you everything if we're to ask for your help."

I promised not to speak a word to anyone.

"Thank you."

Listiel then started to tell me everything.

"The panel found in the labyrinth is special in a certain way. The panel was discovered by one of the adventurers who founded this town, so it can only be used by the person who first channeled mana into it. It would not work for anyone else, no matter how much mana they fed into it. And so the adventurer decided to stay here and became the town's lord. That adventurer was my ancestor."

I nodded. "Which means the only ones who can use the panel are…"

"Yes, only the adventurer's direct descendants. Which means that the only people currently able to use it are me, Karina, and our three-year-old son."

"What about Barlimer?"

"I married into the family," he said, "so I'm afraid that makes me ineligible."

"And, considering my condition," said Listiel, brushing her hand against her stomach, "I decided to entrust Karina with it."

"It was my first time, so I was so excited," said Karina. "I wasn't looking carefully at the map. I took the wrong route, and we got caught in a trap. Father saved me, but he got hurt and I dropped the panel into the trap."

Aha. That explained Barlimer's injury and how it related to the missing panel.

"Um, so you're still pretty young, Listiel," I said. "What happened to your parents?"

"Well..." she said, averting her eyes. She seemed to have trouble saying it out loud.

I waved it off. "I'm sorry, I didn't know they'd passed away."

"Oh, I'm sorry. I've misled you. They're still alive."

Then what was she hanging her head like that for?

"Because my family needs to watch over the pyramid, we can't leave for long periods of time. They left me to serve that role and went off on a trip to see the world. Where they are now, I have no idea..."

Yikes. No wonder the situation was so awkward.

327
The Bear Learns about the Pyramid's Labyrinths
Part Two

I MORE OR LESS understood what was happening.

The gem had broken, they needed to go into the last level of the labyrinth to replace it, and they needed the crystal panel map to get there. Only certain people could use the panel, and Karina had dropped it in a pit trap. That's why Karina wanted to get to the basement of the pyramid, because she had to get that crystal panel back.

I followed the story up till now, but...did Karina really need to go into the pyramid herself? Sure, the map was a secret, but that didn't mean they couldn't just send in some good adventurers to get it on their own. Even if Karina felt responsible for what happened, she really didn't need to be there in order to find the panel in the first place, did she? In fact, she'd probably just be in the way.

"Why are you trying to go to the pyramid to get the map, Karina?" I asked. "You could just leave it up to the adventurers."

"What was that?" Barlimer scowled when he heard me.

"Uh, well, Karina was—"

"Y-Yuna..." Karina pleaded to me.

"Karina! Not another word," Barlimer ordered. "Yuna, please explain, if you could."

Oops, did I say something I shouldn't have? Then again, if Karina was putting herself in danger, I needed to stop her. I told Barlimer about what I'd seen at the guild.

After hearing my story, Barlimer broke into a frown. "Explain yourself, Karina!"

Karina's face had been turned down as she listened at first, but now she faced Barlimer with her head high and her voice firm. "Father, this is my responsibility! Besides, I know where I dropped the panel."

Wait, she knew where it was?

"That's irrelevant!" Barlimer was upset now, which was going to make it harder to ask about the panel.

Apparently, the original guild quest had only asked for an adventurer to retrieve an item lost in the lower level of the pyramid. They would have only explained what the object was to someone who took on the quest...but then

Karina had gone ahead and insisted that she'd go along with the quest takers too.

"Karina, is that why you went to the guild without telling us?" Barlimer asked, his tone slightly hard.

"Don't be so upset with her, dear. She felt that it was her responsibility."

"Regardless..."

"I can't go," said Listiel. "Karina must have felt obligated. We've told her about the role she would have since she was little, after all."

"Mother..."

Hmm...this sure was a tough situation. Karina felt guilty about what had happened. Not only did she feel responsible for her father's injuries, but she also lost an object passed down through multiple generations. On top of that, she herself might end up being the reason for the downfall of the town.

That seemed like a huge burden to bear for a ten-year-old. As for whether she was making the right decision now, though, that was...not so clear.

"And that's why you're trying to hire adventurers to search for the panel," I concluded.

"Yes," said Barlimer. "I'm not the sort of parent that would send my daughter into dangerous places."

"But all the adventurers already said no, regardless of whether Karina goes with them or not." I saw it myself. I thought at least a few parties would be interested.

"That's likely because of what's going on in the pyramid right now."

"Which is...?"

"Because the gem broke, there are a lot more monsters around it."

"I see."

Listiel sighed. "It's possible those monsters are propagating *because* the gem broke."

Oh, maybe that's what they meant at the entrance to the town. All this time, I thought they were just talking about the water gem being broken.

"Um, are there monsters in the pyramid too?" That'd make things a pain.

"Yes, there are, in fact."

Barlimer then told me that if you got caught in one of the traps in the upper labyrinth, you'd end up on a lower floor with monsters.

"And are these monsters strong?" I asked.

"Not from what I've heard," he said. "They're the same as the ones that appear in the desert itself. It's used as a hunting ground to make some money by any adventurers able to slay low-class monsters, such as wyrms."

"So, the issue is less what monsters are there and more how *many* of them there are, right?"

"Yes. There are many monsters near the pyramid, so there may well be quite a lot more within."

"Father, that's not the only reason that's happening," Karina piped up.

"What's that, Karina?"

"There have been some people claiming they've seen a large monster near the pyramid too. That's why no one would take the quest."

"I see."

So, there were a ton of monsters *and* some mystery giant monster that may or may not exist. Throw in an escort mission with the lord's daughter, and that was one tough sell of a quest.

They could've banded all the adventurers together in order to slay the monsters, but Jade had told me that most of the adventurers around here were just passing through on their own escort jobs. Plus, the escorts supposedly didn't need to worry too much about monster attacks because of the pillars. To put it bluntly, the escort jobs through the desert were safe enough that there weren't many strong adventurers around.

Also, I doubted anyone really great would come here voluntarily, considering it was so hot. Sure, I came out here for some sightseeing, but if anyone asked me whether I wanted to live here or in Crimonia, I would've gone with Crimonia hands-down.

"In that case, maybe it'd be better to ask one of the nations for help, rather than an adventurer?" I asked.

I was sure that the king would bring out everyone—soldiers, knights, and mages—if he knew what was going on. They would've been able to take down all the monsters near the pyramid in one go and gotten to the pyramid's lower level with no problem. Then they could've just had a ton of soldiers search together. It would've been easy to find the panel with bigger numbers.

The king had even said the town was important to them commercially, so I didn't doubt he'd lend them a hand if asked. Admittedly, the money would've become a problem, but...

Barlimer shook his head at my proposal. "We cannot do that."

"Why not?"

"Neither Elfanica nor Trifolm are allowed to dispatch troops here because of their treaty. Doing so, no matter the reason, would be seen as an act of aggression."

"Couldn't you just explain the situation?" I offered.

Barlimer shook his head again. "A treaty cannot be so

easily altered. No matter the reason, if any country gathered troops near their borders—whether they be soldiers, knights, or mages—it would appear to be a threat to other nations. One wrong move would risk a war in this town. That is precisely why we must abide by the treaty at all costs."

Okay, I got where he was coming from. Even if the nations were on good terms, they couldn't read each other's minds and know for sure that the other country wasn't going to attack.

I knew the king here personally, but not the royalty in Trifolm. Plus, I had no idea how they viewed Elfanica. If Elfanica did dispatch troops here, they might see it as an act of war no matter why they came. They might even think that the town was being used as a pretext for sending the military.

And it could go both ways. If *their* troops appeared here, it'd seem like a threat to us. And how could anyone guarantee that the troops would vacate afterward? This town was neutral and could exist like this with its standing because it didn't align itself with either country.

When you thought about it, political and military affairs always got messy, no matter the world. You can't just ignore them—not if you want to keep your home country safe.

"Also, if we were to ask for help from one country and not the other, that would show a lack of trust in the nation we did *not* contact," Barlimer continued. "If I asked only Trifolm, King Folhaut would surely feel uneasy. The opposite would hold true as well."

The two nations could have sent troops to work together, which would have worked out the best, but even that would take time.

This meant their only hope was the adventurers.

"That's why you're asking me," I concluded. Under any normal circumstances, they wouldn't be telling this to a girl dressed like a bear, like me.

"Yes, we would like you to go into the pyramid to find the crystal panel for us. Of course, we wouldn't have you go alone. We will make another quest at the guild, but without the requirement to guard Karina."

"Father! I must go too!"

"Unacceptable!"

"But I know where the panel is. I could tell them if I go."

"Wait... You mentioned that earlier," I said. "What do you mean by that?"

"Well..." Barlimer looked over at Listiel for approval.

She nodded, and he started his explanation.

"I told you that the only ones who are able to use the panel must share blood with the adventurer who first used it. Once the bloodline creates a contract with the panel, they cannot only use it, but can also generally sense the location of the panel. Their mana is connected to it, you see."

Got it. So *that* was why Karina was so insistent about coming along.

"Normally I would go, but..." Listiel touched her stomach again. Taking a pregnant lady over to monster city sure didn't sound like a good plan. She probably felt conflicted about not being able to go too. I bet she'd want to, if she could. As for Barlimer, he wasn't part of the bloodline, so he couldn't tell where the panel would be.

Karina truly was the only one who could do it.

"Karina, do you really know where it is?" I asked.

"Yes, I do. But only the general direction."

Well, that'd do just fine. "All right," I said. "I'll take Karina."

"Yuna!"

Karina looked ecstatic, but I could see her dad wasn't going to agree by the look on his face.

"But it really would make everything go so much faster," I said. Even knowing the direction to go would make a world of difference.

"But..."

But...a girl wearing a bear onesie wasn't the most convincing person on the planet, I know.

"You do believe in what the king wrote in his letter, don't you?" I asked.

"Of course. I do believe you are powerful, Yuna," Barlimer said. "But what will you do while you're fighting? Other monsters may attack during that time. Do you intend to have other adventurers protect her? If that were the case, the quest would be the same and we'd still have trouble finding people who would take it."

That wouldn't bother me, honestly. But I needed to make sure Barlimer had some peace of mind, so I silently stood from my chair and headed over to an open part of the room.

"Yuna?"

"Okay, please don't get all, uh, flabbergasted on me," I said.

And with that, I thrust my bear puppets out in front of me and summoned my bears.

"Bears!"

"...!"

"BEARS?!"

All three of them were, in fact, flabbergasted as they stared at my two summons. Barlimer winced, likely because he bothered his wound in his surprise.

"Father!" Karina ran to him in worry.

"Y-Yuna, what are these bears doing here?" Barlimer asked.

"They're my summons," I said.

"Summons…?"

"They'll guard Karina. They're more powerful than any common monster, so they'll be able to do the job. If worse comes to worst, they're fast enough that they can make a quick getaway. You really won't have anything to worry about."

"Please, Father," Karina said. "This is my responsibility, so I need to go."

"Karina…"

"Dear…" Listiel joined her daughter in staring at Barlimer.

Finally, he let out a small sigh. "All right."

He placed a hand on Karina's head and bowed his own deep and low.

"Yuna, I entrust Karina to you."

Karina had been the one insisting on going to the pyramid, but I saw the anxiety on her face at the prospect of going headfirst into a place with so many monsters. I decided I'd let her read the king's letter too, to give her some peace of mind. If that made her feel better, it was a small price to pay.

"A kraken… That's a big monster that lives in the ocean, isn't it?" she asked.

"Sure was."

"Then you obtained this mana gem yourself?"

"Mm-hmm. So you have nothing to worry about, okay? Just leave everything up to me."

"I will." And all the doubt disappeared from Karina's face.

328
The Bear Talks with Karina

AFTER THEY TOLD ME THE GIST of what was happening, I accepted the quest to look for the crystal panel that had a map of the labyrinth.

"Also, Yuna, I'd like to gather up some more adventurers now. Would you be all right waiting until after they're all assembled?"

I was fine waiting a few days, at least. I had plans to go to the beach, though, so I couldn't wait around for *too* long. Maybe it'd be best for me to check in with Fina?

"If it'll take a while," I said, "I can manage on my own."

"It should only be two or three days," said Barlimer. "I'd like just a little time to recruit them."

Two or three days was fine. Maybe I could explore the town while we were waiting.

"In that case," I said, "I'll come by again in two days."

"Oh? Where are you going?"

"I need to find an inn to stay at for tonight. As for tomorrow, I think I'll take a walk."

Since I was in a new town, my deeply ingrained gamer instincts were telling me to take a look around. Of course, if I were actually in a game, I would've been more likely to head over to a weapon or item shop, but these days I was more into finding some good snacks. Or hey, maybe I'd take a quick look at the pyramid.

"If you would like to," said Barlimer, stopping me, "you could stay with us while you're here."

Listiel nodded. "We really can't allow you to stay at an inn when you came all the way here to bring us the gem from the capital."

"Are you sure?"

"Why, of course. Karina, please inform Lasa and have her prepare a room."

"Yes, Father," Karina answered and left.

"And please take this gem back, Yuna." He took the gem from the table and handed it to me. "Listiel and I are in no condition to travel, so I think you will need to exchange the gem once you and Karina find the panel."

Listiel was pregnant, Barlimer was injured, and we knew that there were monsters gathering near the pyramid. There was no way the two of them could do it themselves.

While I could heal Barlimer with my magic, there was a chance he'd try to come with us and complicate things. I suppose my only option was to heal him later.

I put the gem back into my bear storage.

"Yuna, please take care of our daughter," said Listiel. "She can be reckless, but she really is a good girl."

I could tell Karina wasn't a bad kid. The worst thing about her was really just that she felt a strong sense of responsibility here. The way she tried to carry the world on her shoulders reminded me of Fina, back when I first met her.

"Don't worry. I'll make sure to bring Karina back in one piece."

"Ha ha, thank you. Then I'll head back to my room."

Listiel left and Karina returned in her place.

"Yuna," she said, "I'll take you to your room."

"Gotcha. I'll see you later then, Barlimer," I said. "Thank you for allowing me to stay under your roof."

"I'm sure you're tired from your long journey, so please, feel free to relax."

I started heading off, my bears following after me. I hadn't forgotten them or anything, but now I wasn't so sure about keeping them out like this. I recalled both of them.

"The bears are gone?" Karina's eyes went saucer-wide

with surprise. Well...yes, they were summons, so they'd naturally disappear when unsummoned, yeah? "Yuna, where did the bears go?"

"I guess they'd be in here?" I flapped the mouths of my bear puppets open and shut.

Karina looked puzzled. She touched the puppets, looking them over. "Those giant bears are in here?"

Yeah, even I was still a little confused by that. It was a mystery where my bears were when they weren't hanging out with me.

Karina pulled me away, guiding me out of the room and toward the guest room. The woman from earlier was there—Lasa, if I remembered correctly. She had fixed the room up for me.

"I've been anticipating your arrival," said Lasa. "Please use this room as you wish."

It was a pretty big room. Maybe they'd given me a really good one?

"Should you require anything, please inform me."

"Thank you. As long as I've got a spot to sleep, I'm good." The bed was big, so I'd be able to fit both my bears in their cub forms on it with me.

Lasa bobbed her head and left, leaving me with Karina in the room. Once Lasa left, Karina's expression changed.

"Yuna, you're not afraid of the quest? None of the adventurers would take it. We don't know what the lower level of the pyramid is like, or whether we'll survive coming back," she said worriedly.

Well, I assumed that most of the adventurers had refused because they were the type who only took relatively safe escort quests into the town. They were real cautious ones. Crimonia's adventurers would avoid more dangerous quests too, and a lot of them just wanted to make a living. I couldn't blame them for turning it down.

"I don't think I'm scared, really," I said.

Without my bear gear, though, that'd be a whole different ball game. I wouldn't dare to take on a quest like this without it. Honestly, I don't even know if I'd be able to *survive* in this world without my bear gear. But I did have it, and my bear skills, *and* Kumayuru and Kumakyu. And if push came to shove, I could use a bear gate to hightail it out of there.

There were tons of ways for me to deal with danger, so I could take on quests without a worry.

"You're very strong, Yuna. I know what I said in front of Father, but I was actually very frightened. I just want to run away from it all. If someone could take my place, I would gladly let them, but...this is all my fault. I'm the only person who can solve it..."

Karina's little hand formed into a fist. I could see her trembling, just slightly.

But she was only ten. Of course she'd be scared. Even adults were afraid of monsters. Karina didn't run because she knew it was her responsibility, her role.

Normally, a girl like her should have been consoled by a dashing hero in this situation, but that wasn't an option this time. What she did have was me—a bear. I crouched down and took her hand in my bear puppet.

"Yuna?"

"You're not weak, Karina. You're a very strong kid."

She didn't have OP cheater powers like me. She was just a normal girl, headed right into a den of monsters. That took guts. And I understood just how scary that could be. She wasn't insisting on coming with me out of ignorance, either. She knew exactly what kind of situation she was getting herself into, and how scary it would be. She wasn't faint-hearted in the least.

"But this all only happened because of me."

"Everyone makes mistakes," I told her. "That's how people grow."

"Oh, Yuna..."

"Besides, life would be boring if you couldn't make mistakes."

Even in the game, I'd made lots of blunders myself.

There were so many times I'd gotten a game-over screen again and again trying to reach a goal. Who would've wanted to play a game where you only got one try? The fun was in trying over and over again to win.

I couldn't imagine how boring an RPG would be if you had to start over from the beginning after failing once. But then again, games were different from reality. Yes, some mistakes could ruin your whole life or even kill you. But a ten-year-old girl was too young to have to deal with something like that. Plus, no one had died. She had another chance.

Kids grow by messing up from time to time. She could learn from those experiences...though if she didn't, she'd probably have some problems.

"But the panel is lost because of me," she said, "and Father is hurt too."

"And you'll find the panel, Karina. And besides, Barlimer isn't dead either."

"But Father looks like he's in so much pain."

"It's a badge of honor," I told her. "He saved his daughter. If you got hurt, I'm sure he would have blamed himself."

I could tell from our earlier conversation just how much Barlimer cared for his daughter. Yeah, he would've never forgiven himself if anything had happened to her. I could really see the family resemblance.

"So let's go find the panel for Barlimer and swap out the mana gem."

We could fix everything by doing that.

"Yes." Karina raised her head. All this time, she'd been staring down at the ground.

"And don't look so glum," I told her. "I promised Barlimer that I'd protect you, and I meant it. Also, they'll keep an eye on you too, so you have nothing to worry about."

I let go of Karina's hands and summoned my bears again.

"The bears..." She slowly approached them. "Do they have names?"

"The black one is Kumayuru. And the white one is Kumakyu."

"Kumayuru and Kumakyu then? Hee hee." Karina started to laugh.

"What's so funny?"

"Oh, nothing. I'm sorry. They just have such cute names. Kumayuru, Kumakyu, it's so nice to meet you."

Karina kindly patted Kumayuru and Kumakyu. They both crooned and nuzzled her.

We were called to dinner shortly after, but not before my bears played with her and got Karina to smile.

329
The Bear Encounters Curry

HEADED TO THE dining room with Karina.

"Yuna, please sit over here."

I did as I was told and took a seat next to Karina. She looked happy about that.

Once we got to our seats, the door swung open and Barlimer and Listiel entered. Listiel was holding a small boy's hand. Come to think of it, she had mentioned having a three-year-old.

"Mothaw..." he said, hiding behind Listiel the moment he saw me.

I probably scared him with my bear clothes. Well, bears are scary creatures, so it wasn't like he could've helped it.

"Ha ha, she's actually a very cute bear," said Listiel. "It's all right. Yuna, let me introduce you to my son, Norris.

Come now, tell her who you are." Listiel lightly pushed her son toward me.

"Nowwis." He said his own name in the quietest little voice, then bashfully hid behind Listiel again.

"Uh, I'm Yuna. Nice to meet you."

After we finished the introductions, Norris stayed behind his mother and only popped his face out every now and then.

"He's very shy, I'm afraid. I'm sorry about that." Listiel took Norris over to a seat.

Hey, I'm an understanding kind of bear, so that didn't bother me... Actually, to put it another way, I was kinda indifferent to the whole thing.

"Karina, did something nice happen?" Listiel asked as she looked at her daughter next to me. She probably looked a lot cheerier than before.

"Yes, I had fun getting to know Yuna's bears. They're so fluffy and soft to the touch."

Listiel smiled. "Well, isn't that nice! Yuna, thank you. She's been so gloomy ever since what happened."

I remembered just how gloomy Karina had looked when I met her. It was like her life was ending. Thanks to my bears playing with her, she seemed to have gotten her smile back. She was acting more like the little kid she was. The strain on her mind had softened a bit.

Once everyone took their seats, Lasa brought the food in on a pushcart...and a certain scent wafted over to me from Lasa's direction.

This aroma... Could it be? Had I really come upon it here, of all places?

Lasa placed bread, salad, and small bites down. Then she ladled an ochre soup onto our plates. The nostalgic aroma wafted up to me, hitting me right in the taste buds. It'd been months since I'd smelled this.

This was, without a doubt, curry.

I stared at the soup, which smelled like the same curry I'd had in Japan—or at least that's what the color and the smell made it look like. If it tasted different, I didn't know who I'd complain to, but complaints were going to be made! Admittedly, I didn't see any veggies or meat in it, but...

As I stared at the maybe-curry, Lasa addressed us. "Please dip the bread into it to eat it."

Once she explained how to eat it to me, she handed the soup to the others as well. After she'd served everyone, Lasa sat at the end of the table. Apparently, she ate with the family despite being a worker in their house.

"I hope that it's to your liking," said Lasa.

To my liking? The moment I was allowed to start eating, I was going to *inhale* this stuff. I was ready to dig in!

At Barlimer's word, we all started to dip the bread in what was definitely, absolutely, for sure curry. I copied everyone and picked up the bread, dipped it in, and brought it to my mouth. The sweetness that spread across my tongue reminded me of the good old days. Yep, this was that good old curry I remembered! I never would've dreamed of finding it here.

"Yuna, is something wrong?" Karina asked me as I basked in the joy of curry.

"Karina," I said, "what's this called?"

"It's curry," she said. "Do you not like it?"

"It's good!"

"Oh, good. I think it's very tasty too."

It was even named the same thing! Karina looked like she was enjoying her curry and bread too. I ate another bite of the curry-dipped bread. Delicious! I could make curry rice, curry bread, curry udon... Oh, the possibilities!

"Karina, do you know how to make this?"

"Um, you mean curry?"

"Yeah. If you know the ingredients used, I'd like to buy some."

They definitely had spices in this world. From what I understood, curry powder was made by mixing a whole bunch of them together. I knew about it generally, but I'd never made it from scratch before and doubted I could.

If they sold it though, I'd definitely want to buy it.

"Um, I'm sorry," Karina hesitated slightly before calling out, "Lasa!"

Lasa stood from her seat and walked over. "What is it, Lady Karina?"

"Yuna was just asking how to make curry."

"You would like to learn about curry?"

"I wanted to know about the ingredients. Would I just need to find spices? Where do they sell them?"

"Well, the spices are sold, but in order to make curry, many different kinds need to be mixed together. I have not seen it sold directly in stores in this form."

So it wasn't something I could just buy. I couldn't believe it. But I still had the option of mixing the spices myself.

"Could you tell me which spices I would need?" I'd made curry before but only out of roux blocks. I never used the individual spices directly. In fact, I didn't even know which types of spices I'd need or what kind of portions I'd have to use. Roux blocks were basically the be-all, end-all for me.

"This is a recipe that was passed down from my dear mother," said Lasa.

Her mother's prized recipe... Oh no.

"I'm so sorry," I said.

"Oh, no, I'm sorry. My mother is alive and well."

"She is?" Not again! They were really being misleading in how they phrased things. I was convinced her mom was gone. "But you're not comfortable sharing it because it's your mom's precious recipe?"

I could ask for it as a reward for Barlimer's quest, but that seemed unfair and manipulative. I wasn't willing to be an awful person, even for sweet, sweet curry. Were there other ways...?

Money? That seemed kind of cruddy too. You couldn't buy people off like that, not for something important to them.

This wasn't working. I was getting nowhere, but...I really wanted this recipe. But I *also* didn't want to force it out of her. And yet, if I could get the recipe, my culinary life in this other world would be transformed!

Ughhhhh, what was I supposed to do?!

"I understand that the recipe is important to you, Lasa, but would you be willing to teach it to Yuna still?" said Karina, throwing me a bone as I grappled with curry-related morality.

"Lady Karina, I haven't necessarily said that I wouldn't. She is, after all, a guest of his lordship. I would not mind telling her, but I would like her to teach me another recipe in return."

"Another recipe?"

"I would like another recipe to use for the family. Even one new dish would do just fine."

Trading recipes seemed like a fair exchange, but that meant she had to like my recipe too.

"You want a recipe you don't already know, then?"

"Yes."

"That might be difficult," said Karina. "Lasa has been studying all kinds of recipes, after all."

So any old recipe wouldn't cut it. Still, I had a ton of recipes to draw from. I knew about tons of foods that Lasa wouldn't, but there was also the question of her having the right ingredients and equipment for them.

That narrowed things down. The ones I could make right now were pizza, pudding, and cakes.

"Would something sweet be okay?"

"Yes, that would work."

"In that case, would you like to try it after the meal?"

"Um, would we be making it now?"

I shook my head. "I have some in my item bag, so I can get some ready right away."

Pudding would work as a dessert.

"And you were the one who made it?"

"Yep." I ate a lot of Morin's bread and Anz's cooking, but sometimes I made food myself. I made a lot of meals with rice especially. And sometimes, I'd make treats for Fina and the others. It was just such a pain to cook myself, though, so I didn't do it regularly.

"You're a very odd person. You're a powerful adventurer who wears bear clothes, and a cook on top of that," said Karina. She looked at the ground again, suddenly rather gloomy. "I can't do anything in comparison."

She was a kid, so that was normal. She had plenty of time to grow and learn.

"In that case," I said, "how about we make it together tomorrow, Lasa?"

"Are you sure?"

"If you okay it, then I'd still need to show you how to make it anyway."

I was planning on checking out the town tomorrow, but I would've been searching for curry spices anyway. I could do that after the quest. The time for curry was now. I needed to get this done before Lasa changed her mind!

I dipped the bread in curry again and ate it. Yum... I needed this recipe.

After finishing up our curry, I placed some puddings and spoons in front of everyone. I was sure she wouldn't know the recipe for this. Now I just needed to give some to Lasa and convince her that this recipe was worthwhile.

"Oh, I get one too?"

"Yes, please try it. If you think it's good, I bet it'll convince you to make the trade," I said.

"All right," she replied. "And I'll give you my impartial opinion."

"Lasa, have you seen anything like it before?"

"Not at all. This is my first time."

I should hope so! If she had somehow seen it before, that'd be pretty bad for me.

"This is..." said Barlimer, a glimmer of recognition in his eyes. "I believe this was served at the birthday festival banquet."

"You know of it, my lord?"

"Yes, King Folhaut served it for this birthday. It was delicious. Made quite the stir, it did."

Lasa looked surprised by that. Huh. So Barlimer had been invited to that banquet back then?

"And the recipe is supposedly a secret," he continued. "How do you have it?"

"Actually, I made that pudding," I said.

Barlimer looked even more surprised. "You made this?"

Now Lasa was looking at the pudding in shock. Then, finally, everyone started to eat.

"Mothaw, it's so good," Norris was the first to eat, and the first to smile after taking a bite.

"It's delicious."

"It's such a curious texture, and quite good."

"It tastes exactly the same as back then."

Karina, Listiel, and Barlimer had nothing but positive things to say.

"It really is good." Even Lasa, the one I was most concerned about, was all compliments.

Once all of their pudding cups were empty, it was time for the big verdict. "What do you all think?"

"This certainly passes muster."

And so, just like that, the deal was sealed.

330
The Bear Goes to Buy Spices

THE NEXT DAY, I was supposed to teach Lasa how to make pudding. I promised to teach Karina too, so we were all in the kitchen together. I also asked them not to share the recipe with too many people. Lasa had told me she only wanted to know in order to make it for the family, so she was fine with that.

The ingredients might've been an issue, but it seemed that they had birds around that could lay large eggs. I'd need to taste the pudding to know if they would work, so for the time being we just focused on the recipe. If it just didn't taste good with those large eggs, I could bring them kokekko eggs. Once the lake was back to normal, they'd probably be able to raise their own kokekko if they liked.

Still, I kind of wanted to see their big birds. What would they think at the orphanage if I brought a few back as souvenirs? I could just imagine the kids' surprise. If I could get my hands on some, I'd bring them back home.

It turned out that they had cattle too, though they seemed to be different from the ones I got cheese from. A quarter of the lake was used for agriculture and for grazing. Because there wasn't as much water here, though, both the agricultural and dairy farms were having a tough time.

They were able to grow crops and keep livestock in the middle of the desert because the temperature was lower in the area around the lake. Maybe it was because of the lake itself, or maybe the pyramid, but for whatever reason, it wasn't as hot here in town. I hadn't been able to tell because of my bear gear, but it seemed like the water gem had done a whole lot for them.

We really needed to find the panel so we could swap the gems and get the town back to normal.

"Are you sure about teaching me this?" asked Lasa. "This was served at the king's birthday banquet, after all."

"Like I said yesterday, I'm the one who asked the king to keep it a secret in the first place. No need to worry about that. And please, let Karina make it as well."

I remembered when the king barged into my house demanding I make the pudding, and how Fina, Morin, and Karin all refused to help, and I was forced to make all of it alone.

Today would be different. "All right, Karina, shall we?"

"Yes, I'll work so hard to help!" Karina brought her little fist up to her chest and answered with gusto.

I pulled some eggs out of my bear storage. I really wanted to use the large eggs, but we were in such a hurry that we hadn't been able to get any. Today we'd use the usual eggs for the pudding.

"Okay, you've gotta crack the eggs like so," I said. I lightly tapped the egg on the edge of the table, cracked it open, and poured out its contents.

"Yuna, you're so good at this," said Karina.

"Okay, you try too, Karina." I handed her an egg, depositing it into her little hand.

Karina copied me, looking hesitant as she tapped it against the table.

"You'll need to tap it a little harder for it to break," I told her.

"Okay, I will."

That time, she got it open. She got the hang of it in one try. Maybe she had the makings of a chef?

Lasa watched Karina with a smile.

"Lasa, don't just laugh," said Karina. "You need to help make it too."

"Lady Karina, I wasn't laughing."

"You were too." Karina pouted slightly.

Lasa started helping out as well, smiling all the while. We heated the sugar water to make the caramel sauce. Finally, we poured the caramel into a small cup, added the pudding mixture, and steamed it. Lasa took notes on what we were doing and how we heated the pudding.

"Then we cool it, and that's it," I told her.

"How long until it's ready to eat?"

"It'll be ready tonight, probably."

"I'm looking forward to it."

"Thank you so much, Yuna. But...is it really this easy?"

"That's what cooking's like," I said. The real issue was getting the ingredients.

I planned to buy the spices with Karina in the afternoon. Since Lasa needed to work, she couldn't come with us. Also, it seemed there were multiple servants at the house, but the rest commuted, so Lasa was the only one living here. That was why she ate with the family.

"Are you really sure you don't want me to come with you?" asked Lasa.

"I'll take her to the shops, so we should be fine," Karina replied. "You have work, after all."

"That is true, but..." Lasa seemed worried. She had already written down the recipe and the ingredient amounts on a piece of paper, so we just needed to talk to the people at the shop to buy them. As far as I was concerned, I just needed to know which spices to buy and where the shops were.

Karina and I headed off to the shop that was selling the spices.

We were walking along, with a glance here and there, and...

"A bear?" "A bear?" "Bear?"

We kept walking...aaaaand kept getting glances.

The people we passed were looking at us, and Karina had started to become aware of all the staring. "Um, Yuna... I know it's very late to be asking this, but do you always dress like this?"

"I do; why?" Look, you never know when danger might rear its ugly head! I was a weakling who lived cooped up in her home until now. Even Fina could probably beat me up if I didn't have my bear gear.

"I think it's cute, of course, but don't you think it draws a lot of attention?"

Of course it did, and of course that bothered me. But sometimes you just have to resign yourself to stuff, and so I'd resigned myself to ignoring the stares. In fact, if I let them get to me, I was basically losing!

Then again...the stares *were* bothering me, so I pulled my bear hood lower.

"If it bothers you, I can move farther away," I offered.

I was used to being alone. That being said, if I asked Fina if she wanted me to do that and she said yes, I'd be pretty bummed out. If she told me I was too embarrassing to be around, and that she needed some space, I'd probably mope in my room for a few days.

This was Karina, though, so I wouldn't necessarily be depressed if she told me I was embarrassing...although that was only because we hadn't known each other for all that long.

"I'm okay. I'm the daughter of the lord, so people stare at me all the time."

Karina blushed slightly and grabbed my bear puppet. Still, being stared at because she was walking with a girl in a bear outfit and getting stared at for being the lord's daughter were entirely different things. I appreciated the thought, though.

"Yuna, over here. Let's go." Tugging on my bear puppet, Karina led me over to a shop selling spices.

"Do you come here sometimes to buy things too, Karina?"

"Sometimes I go shopping with Lasa," she answered.

Then she tugged me along into the shop. At that moment, the fragrance of all sorts of spices wafted over to me. I looked at the shelves and saw rows upon rows of seasonings. But half of the shelves were also empty, as though they were sold out. Karina seemed to be staring at those empty spots too.

While we were looking around, a man in his mid-thirties made his way over to us.

"Why, if it isn't Lady Karina...and a bear?!" His eyes went wide with surprise.

Could people lay off with the staring already?

"Um, what brings you here today?" he continued. "Lasa isn't with you?"

Even as he talked to Karina, he kept stealing glances at me. If he was that curious, he could've just asked about why I dressed like this...not that I would've told him.

"Lasa isn't with me today. Yuna told me she wanted to buy spices, so I brought her here," Karina told him.

The man looked at me again.

"The shop looks less full compared to last time, though," she said. "Did something happen?"

"Well..." the man seemed to struggle to answer.

Right, so this wasn't normal. Now I knew that for sure.

"I...think we'd better focus on what you're here to buy," said the man, changing the subject and getting back to talking about what wares he *did* have.

I couldn't ask about it since we'd only just met, so I went down the list, naming the spices Lasa had written out for the recipe. To be frank, though, I couldn't tell what most of these spices were based on their names.

Obviously, I'd recognize "curry powder" and stuff like that, but that wasn't exactly something I could buy. I'd just have to rely on the shopkeeper.

"Uh, that one would be this here," he said. "And this, as well as this..." He pointed at several bottles filled with spices. "And how much would you need?"

"All of it," I answered.

"All of..." he paused and cleared his throat.

"All of it," I said again for good measure.

"Miss, are you sure you can pay for all of that? I'm not sure whether you're from a noble family, but spices are expensive."

Well, the prices *were* written on each type of spice, so I knew what I could buy.

"I have the money, so don't worry," I said.

"I see. That will be of great help," he said.

"Great help?"

"I was planning to leave the town soon, after all," he said.

"Leaving?"

The man paused for a moment, glancing at Karina again, but it was too late to take it back. He glanced to the right. To the left. And then sighed.

"I'm very sorry," he said awkwardly. "I'm sure you're aware of the lowering lake level, the monsters gathering at the pyramid, and the odd things happening of late. At some point, this entire town may be surrounded by monsters. If we tarry, it might be too late by the time we leave town. I talked it over with my wife, and we are planning to go sooner than later."

That also explained why his shop was half empty.

"Please, just wait," Karina begged. "The water will come back to the lake. So please wait just a little longer. Father will do something about the monsters as well."

"Oh, Lady Karina..." The man looked apologetic. "I'm afraid I'm not the only one who sees the way the wind is blowing. We might be able to fight off the monsters by hiring adventurers, but we are all powerless when it comes to the lake."

Right, he didn't know about the water gem. Of course he'd be anxious. Barlimer probably couldn't just tell people about it either, which would make things difficult.

If others knew there was a huge water gem fueling the lake, thieves would surely show up. If he'd been able to fix this earlier, the situation wouldn't have gotten to this point, but all of these problems had compounded and... here we were.

"I've lived here for a very long time," he said softly. "Neither of us want to leave either, but...we have children..."

Karina stared at the floor silently. I placed a hand on her head to comfort her.

"But that's not happening for a little while, right?" I said.

"Correct; we're just preparing right now," he confirmed.

"In that case, you won't need to leave town. The monsters should disappear in a few days, and the lake should go back to normal too. Right, Karina?" I gave her a smile.

"Father is dealing with the situation right now," she explained. "And I will work very hard as well. Please, just give us a little more time." She bowed her head low.

"Lady Karina, please raise your head. You're saying it'll be just a few more days?"

"Yes, I'm sure of it. We'll bring the lake back," she promised, her voice firm.

After I bought my spices, we left. Karina looked a little sad, though, even if it made sense that the man and his family wanted to flee town. The lake was keeping things cool. If it disappeared, the town would get way too hot.

"Karina, it'll be fine," I told her. "We'll find the panel and swap out the gems. That'll fix it."

"Oh, Yuna..."

Worst case, if we couldn't find the panel, I'd solve the labyrinth on my own and swap the gems for her. Those traps sounded like a pain, though, so it'd be much better to have that map.

KUMA
KUMA
KUMA
BEAR

331
The Bear Has Tea with Mel's Party

As I consoled Karina and we walked around town, I saw some familiar faces running over to us from up ahead.

"There you are, Yuna!"

"Mel?"

Mel locked me into a hug. Senia looked pretty exasperated when she saw us. I really wished she'd at least tried to stop Mel instead of just watching.

"You made it here too, huh?" I asked.

"Yeah. Just got in. Then Mel said she wanted to go looking for you."

"Well, Yuna *did* promise she'd eat with us."

True, but I'd technically only promised that to Jade. Actually, where was he? And Touya, for that matter?

"Where are the others?" I asked.

"They headed off to the guild to make their report, so we went off on our own mission: to find you. The gate guard said that you came by asking for directions to an inn, so we stopped by there, but nobody said they saw anyone in a bear costume. So we started walking around town looking for you. You do stand out with the way you dress, after all. And while we were wandering around, we started to hear people talking about a bear and stuff, saying somebody in a bear costume was walking about. We just followed the trail."

Made sense. I mean, who *else* was going to be walking around town dressed as a bear? Of course, that wouldn't work in Crimonia, with how some of the orphans liked to wear their bear uniforms around town.

"Um, Yuna, who are they?" Karina asked.

"Some adventurers I know," I replied and introduced all three of them to each other.

"The lord's daughter?" said Mel.

"Mm-hmm. I'm Karina."

"Well, aren't you a charming one," Mel said, which made Karina blush bashfully. "In any case, we've finally found you, so why don't we get something to drink together? And Karina is welcome to join us, of course."

They wouldn't take no for an answer, and they whisked us away.

Mel took us to an inn. This was probably the place I almost ended up staying at, actually. The first floor was a lounge where they served food. Mel and the others were staying here too, so Jade had told them to bring me over if they found me.

From there, Mel started to order from one of the employees and picked some random drinks off the menu.

"Where are you staying, Yuna? We all thought you'd be at this inn."

So had I, for a while. "Karina's family is letting me stay with them."

"Karina's family? You're staying at the lord's house?"

"I needed to take the package there," I explained.

"Oh, right, you did mention a delivery."

"Yes, Yuna brought us something very important," Karina chipped in. "So she's staying at our house while she's visiting." Of course, Karina kept mum about the important bits.

"How long are you hanging around, Yuna?"

"I have a job from Karina's dad, so I'll be staying put for a bit."

"A job?" As soon as I said that, both of them looked very curious.

"Sounds expensive," was Senia's only reply.

I had no idea whether I'd actually be making any money, but it was a difficult job for sure.

"Are you doing this job all on your lonesome, Yuna?"

"Oh, nah. I think there'll be a quest at the guild for it."

Lasa had told me Barlimer sent a messenger out with a letter to the guild just this morning. Lasa would've normally taken it over, but she needed to make the pudding and Barlimer had asked another servant to do it instead.

"Huh, I see... In that case, do you think we could take on the quest?" asked Mel.

"If it's from Karina's father," Senia mused, "then it's an aristocrat's quest. It'll definitely pay well."

"Do you really mean it?!" At that, Karina shot up from her seat.

"Karina?"

The two of them didn't know what to do. I tried to get her to sit back down.

"Um. I'm sorry," said Karina, sitting down again. "Just, uh... You'll really help us?"

"It'll depend on the type of job and the reward, of course," said Mel. "If Yuna will be part of it, I wouldn't mind a lower reward."

"How much do you know about the state of the town, Mel?" I asked.

"You mean the lake evaporating?"

Turned out they didn't know about the monsters gathering around the pyramid, so we filled them in.

"Monsters, huh? So is the job to slay them?"

"That's part of it, but we're also searching for something in the pyramid."

"You're looking for something?"

I didn't know how much I was allowed to say, so I couldn't give them other details.

"We can help out with monster extermination," said Mel. "Right, Senia?"

"Right."

"You can just decide like that?" I asked. "Don't you need to talk to Jade and Touya first?"

"If they say no, then we'll go help out on our own," said Mel, earning a nod from Senia.

"Are you really sure?" Karina asked. "There will be a number of monsters. None of the other adventurers would even take the quest. It's that dangerous."

"Are there really that many?"

"I haven't checked myself, but that's what it seems like," I said.

They hemmed for a bit before answering. "Well, I'm sure we'll be fine if you're around."

Senia nodded. "We might not even need to do anything."

Way to put me on the spot there, guys! Then again, the monster remains needed to be dealt with after they were slayed. If they could help with that work, that alone would be a huge help.

"Um, so is Yuna really that amazing?" asked Karina.

"I know all the rumors about her get to be a little much, but they're all true."

"Still, nobody would think a girl in such an adorable bear outfit could be so strong."

They were really laying it on thick, but it's not like I could tell them they were wrong.

"So you really do believe in her and how strong she is?"

"I mean, we've worked with her before, so..."

"May I ask more about what Yuna's done then?" Karina asked suddenly.

Why would she want to know? But the other two responded with grins I found, uh, *concerning*...

"Let us regale you with the legend of Yuna!" Mel said.

"The legend of Yuna?" Karina's eyes were glittering now.

Wait, what? The legend of *me*?! When had I become a legend? I had a bad feeling about this...

"Uh, Karina?" I said. "How about we get going soon? Mel, if you take the quest, I'll be much obliged. Thank you, bye now." Running was the way to go.

I stood up...and Mel and Senia pinned my bear puppet hands to the table.

"Uh... Why are you holding my hands?"

"The girl says she wants to know more about you."

"We're not letting you escape."

They were holding me prisoner. I could shake them off, but trying to do it by force might end in disaster.

"Yuna, am I not allowed to know?" Karina said. "I wouldn't want you to be upset..."

Now she looked apologetic. There was no way I could force her to leave with me after seeing that face.

I gave up and plopped right back into my seat. "But if you say anything weird about me, I'm leaving."

After that, Mel and Senia started up their "legend" about me. They started talking about when I'd beaten up an adventurer, the goblin massacre when I'd slayed the goblin king, the black viper, and how we'd gone to slay golems together.

"She can take out a rock golem with a single punch," said Senia.

"One punch?!"

"And that's not all..." added Mel, and Karina was hanging on to every word. "Yuna even defeated a golem that other adventurers—and even our own party—gave up on!"

Karina looked at me in disbelief.

"You'd never believe it, right? Because of how she dresses."

"I really wouldn't." She didn't even hesitate! But I'd already resigned myself to that stuff. Nobody would assume I was powerful based on my looks, after all. Honestly, I'd be freaked out by anyone who *did*.

"And she didn't even take credit. She gave it to us!"

"Really?"

"I just didn't want the attention," I explained.

"You say that, but look at your outfit. Not very convincing, I'd say." Yeesh, Senia, way to go for the jugular. If anybody knew how much attention I got, it was me! That's why I didn't need more.

"There are even rumors that she defeated the kraken," said Mel.

"Which is a little too much, if you ask us," said Senia, and they both laughed.

"But she really d—" Karina started to say, riiiiight before I clamped my hand over her mouth.

"What's the matter?" asked Mel.

"Nothing!" I said. "Nothing at all. *Right*, Karina?" I gave her a pointed look. She seemed to understand and gave me a little nod.

That'd sure been close. Just a little too slow, and word about the kraken would've started to spread too.

As everyone else had fun with the conversation (I, personally, did not), Jade and Touya walked through the door. Jade noticed us as well, and the two of them made their way to us.

"You found her?"

"We caught her while she was prowling around."

Just because I was *dressed* as an animal didn't mean they had to talk about me like one...

"Oh, right," Mel said. "Jade, Senia and I are going to help Yuna out with a job."

"A job?"

Mel started explaining to him.

"Ah, I saw that quest at the guild too. The guild asked us to take it."

"Really?"

"Seems like there's no lack of monsters though, just like you said, Mel," Jade continued. "I headed over on a laggaroute to take a look."

He'd gone all the way out there to check it out, then. Well, it wasn't the type of quest anyone would take on lightly. Maybe it'd be good for me to check it out before the quest too...

"Looked impossible to me," said Jade, "so I turned it down."

"Are there really that many?"

"Yeah, and you can even see them from afar. Tons of movement on those sands."

"We could've handled wolves," said Touya, "but wyrms'll be an issue since they're under the surface. But if Yuna's going to take it, I guess we might as well tag along."

Jade nodded. "If Yuna's there, we might be able to defeat them the same way as before."

"There are a lot, though," Senia noted, "so it's a matter of whether we can use the same strategy."

Mel looked to me. "Yuna, what do you think?"

"I'm not sure how many we're looking at, but if all I need to do is get them out of the sand, then that should be easy enough."

"That's normally the tough part," said Touya.

"So, Touya, could you run back to the guild and accept the quest?"

"Me? On my own? C'mon, let's all go together."

"Too much work," said Senia.

"You've got this!" added Mel.

The others were decidedly against his idea, which seemed to really bum Touya out.

Jade clapped him on the back. "I'll go with you."

145

"Jade..." Touya said.

"Hey, that's what a leader does."

"You all really do trust Yuna," Karina said, flabbergasted. Guess she hadn't expected that Jade would change his mind on a quest just because I was joining them.

"Yeah, I suppose most folks wouldn't trust a girl in a bear outfit like that," Touya said, giving a certain someone some pats on the head...that certain someone being me.

"I think it's really just the adventurers in Crimonia who'd have faith in her," said Mel.

"We've worked with her before, though. We even fought some wyrms with her on the way over here," said Jade.

Senia nodded firmly. "Yeah, we know Yuna's powerful."

Ehh... It was more the bear gear that was powerful, to be honest.

"Thank you, everyone." Karina got a little teary-eyed. Someone had finally, *finally* taken on her quest.

332
The Bear Heads to the Pyramid

KARINA SEEMED ECSTATIC that Jade's party was joining us. After we finished dinner, I cuddled with my bears in their cub forms and channeled some mana into my bear phone.

"Yuna? What is it?" It was the first time I'd heard Fina in days. It was so convenient, being able to talk to one another when we were so far apart.

"I was wondering how things were going over there. No news?"

"Yeah, everything's been, um...fine..." Things sure didn't *sound* completely fine.

"Did something happen?"

"Karin and Anz really didn't want to be measured, just like you didn't..."

Oh, okay. I kinda got how those two felt. Soon enough, Fina would get a bit older and start to worry about getting measured too. But Karin and Anz were also more grown up than me in a...certain aspect. That part I couldn't quite sympathize with.

"So, how'd that go then?"

"Sherry was on the brink of tears before they let her measure them."

Whoa, had Sherry learned the power of crying all cute-like? I didn't want her growing up to be a player, so I'd need to tell her not to go around pulling that one on guys.

"No, not like *that*," said Fina. "She was just very sad she couldn't do the job because you asked her to do it."

Fina had read my mind. I guess Sherry wasn't cut out for being a femme fatale—rather, she'd end up an over-zealous working adult. Now that I thought about it, that was *also* kind of worrying.

"Everything else is fine?"

"When we told the kids at the orphanage that they'd be going to the ocean, everyone was really happy. Mom and the headmistress had a lot of trouble getting some of the kids to quiet down."

I could hear exactly how hard it had been from the tone of Fina's voice. I was thiiis close to reminding Fina

148

that she was a kid too. Still, I was mostly just happy that the kids were getting hyped up about it. Their happiness was what mattered here.

"Did you find someone to take care of the birds?"

"Mom talked to Milaine. We think it should be okay."

One more problem solved, then. If I didn't have someone to look after the birds, I'd need to rethink my plans.

"How about the swimsuits?"

"Sherry was really excited, and that apparently became a whole thing."

"What kind of thing?"

"She liked making them so much, she started making designs besides the ones you drew. She's even thought about new colors and patterns to use."

Well, I *had* drawn everything in black and white and left all the details and stuff to Sherry.

"Come to think of it," I said, "do you know what's going on with my bathing suit?"

She'd only taken my measurements and hadn't asked me about the design. I didn't care too much about what I wore, but I hoped it didn't end up being weird.

"Oh, Yuna, I'm sorry. Mom is calling me."

"That's all right. I'll let you go. Let me know if anything happens. I have the bear gate, so I can come right back if you need me to."

"Uh-huh, I will. Please come back soon," she said and hung up.

Looked like we were making ample progress toward the beach trip. I'd need to finish up the quest pronto so I could get home and get the gears turning on that.

It was finally the day we'd head for the pyramid.

One other party had joined the quest, so it wasn't just Jade's group, Karina, and me. Before we left, we all gathered at Barlimer's house and got to know one another. I was there with Jade's party first, then the other party finally made their way over.

"It's the bear from earlier," a man said as soon as he entered the room and saw me.

Who was he? Had I met him before?

As I pondered over those questions, Karina whispered to me, "That's the adventurer who tried to push me away."

Oh, that dude... Which meant the guy hovering behind him, looking at me warily, must've been the one who called me the Bloody Bear.

After that, we introduced ourselves. They had a five-person party. Their leader was the pushy guy, and his name was Uragan. The others told me their names, but I forgot them. It wasn't like I'd need to memorize them or anything.

Barlimer checked in with them one last time to go over the quest requirements.

"Okay, all we've gotta do is escort the bear and the little girl to the pyramid?"

They brushed off Karina just days ago, but now they were escorting us to the pyramid? That'd apparently been what they negotiated with Barlimer, from what I gathered, but...ugh.

Anyway, Jade and the others would be heading into the pyramid with us.

"Are you sure you're willing to go into the pyramid with them to protect my daughter?" Barlimer asked them.

"Yuna is protecting her, so we're really just tagging along as extra help."

"Your aid is much appreciated," said Barlimer, seeming truly grateful.

Made sense, I guess. Only two parties had been willing to take him up on the quest at all, so I guess that was partly why he was so grateful.

Once we were done with the meet and greet, we left town. Everyone wore hooded mantles to combat the heat, including Karina. I was the only one dressed as a bear.

"Are you really sure you're not too hot?" Karina asked me.

"My clothes are also heat resistant, so I'm all right." I wasn't too hot or too cold. The temperature was just right.

151

"I see. Still, I feel hot just looking at you."

Yeah, I got where she was coming from. I had explained it to Jade's party once already, but Uragan's party was giving me weird looks.

When we were fully away from the town, I summoned my bears. I took Kumayuru, and Karina took Kumakyu. Jade's party had rented out a couple of laggaroutes, so Jade and Mel were riding one, and Touya and Senia were riding the other. Uragan's party rode on their own laggaroute mounts.

They were pretty surprised to see my bears. Even after Jade gave them an explanation, they looked kind of befuddled. I guess they accepted whatever he said, though, since they didn't ask me any questions.

Jade was a total lifesaver.

My bears really looked off next to the lizard-like laggaroutes, but it wasn't like I was going to ride any mounts other than my bears.

Once we got close to the pyramid, we could see movement in the sand. I used my bear detection skill, which showed a ton of sand wyrms there.

"Ey, that's a ton of wyrms..."

Uragan seemed bewildered, but everyone should've already known there would be tons. As for me, I could see even more than the rest of them…and there were far more wyrms than they knew.

"So, what'll we do?" asked Uragan. "Should we stick close and make a break for it to the pyramid?"

"Yuna, what do you think?" Jade asked me.

"Why're you askin' the bear, anyhow?"

"Barlimer told us to follow her instructions as much as we can."

Uragan snorted. "Oh, c'mon, why's a C-rank party leader deferring to some girl dressed as a bear? Are you kidding me?"

Right, they probably didn't know my rank. Uragan's party was D-rank but getting close to C.

"Of course I would. She's the strongest out of all of us."

"You *gotta* be pulling my leg."

"If you actually knew how powerful she was, you'd say the same."

"What, you really think I'm gonna risk my life listening to some weird bear girl?"

"If you need to, you can just run away if things get tough. We've got permission from the client."

Barlimer had even permitted us to retreat if things got too hot.

"Okay, okay. We'll hightail it outta here it if that happens."

They could do just about anything and I wouldn't care one way or the other. My job was to protect Karina.

"So, Yuna, what'll it be?" Mel was asking me now.

How was I supposed to know? Hmm... I used my detection skill and thought it over.

"I think it'll be a pain to run for it, so why don't we just slay them all?"

I had no idea what the inside of the pyramid might look like, so we could end up in more trouble if the monsters followed us in. Taking them out now would make things safer inside *and* make the trip home easier.

"Come on, are you serious?"

"We need to slay them sometime, don't we? And it'd be easier now than later too. Why put it off?"

"Sheesh, you make it sound so easy. You see how many are out there?"

"As long as you put in the work, it'll be fine."

"Are you serious?" Touya was looking at me in disbelief.

"Ey, tell us what's going on! Come on!"

I would drive out the sand wyrms and everyone else would finish them off. Easy-peasy.

Jade explained that to Uragan's party for me. Again, I was so grateful for Jade. He'd been staying ahead of any potential problems. Come to think of it, he'd been great at handling the bozo rangers too. Maybe he just knew how to deal with people?

"Are you for real?" Now it was Uragan's turn to be surprised.

"We guarantee it'll work," Jade said. "The issue is whether we can get all the sand wyrms before they burrow back into the sand or not."

"Heh heh. If she can really pull it off, we'll finish off those wyrms real quick."

According to Jade, the sand wyrms weren't that powerful individually. The problem was when they were in the sand. It seemed that Uragan knew that, and he was just waiting to see whether I'd be able to deliver.

Which I would.

"Right, then. This bear girl's supposed to be getting the sand wyrms out of the sand for us," said Uragan. "It's our job to give them a poundin'. That's all there is to it. Don't let a single one of 'em escape, you hear?"

Uragan's whole party answered back in the affirmative. It was easy for him to get so cocky about it when he didn't know just how many there were...which was way, *way* more than any of them thought.

"So, how're we divvying this up? We got more in numbers, so I suppose we'll take on more of 'em."

"I don't need any share," I said, "so you can tackle my part."

"Right, we're heading to the pyramid after slaying them. If you can do the harvesting, you can have half of our share."

"Looks like we got ourselves a deal."

Uragan grinned. Jade did too. Wait, who had won that negotiation? Uragan was happy he'd be getting more of the reward, but Jade seemed happy that they wouldn't need to do any harvesting.

I guess there'd be a lot of wyrms for their reward, which meant they'd get a lot of gems, so...it was just good all around? Maybe Uragan would be sorry for taking up the harvesting later, but he sure wasn't now.

"Karina, it'll be dangerous," I said, "so you stay with Kumakyu over here. And under no circumstances are you to leave Kumakyu's side, you hear?"

"All right. Please, Yuna, you be careful too."

"It'll be fine. We'll slay them really quick, and then we'll be right back. Kumakyu, you keep an eye on Karina. And head back to the town if anything bad happens, got it?"

Kumakyu let out a slightly sad croon in response. Watching over Karina seemed fine, but Kumakyu didn't like the idea of leaving me.

"I'll be fine, okay?" I insisted. "Worst case, we'll leave Touya as bait and run off."

"Seriously?!" Touya groaned.

Ugh, *classic* Touya, eavesdropping on my very important conversation with my magical bear. I ignored him and kept talking to Kumakyu.

"Okay, I'm leaving Karina in your hands." I gave my bear a pat on the head, which got me another croon. Then I got on Kumayuru, and for whatever reason, Mel joined me from behind. "You'll need someone who can use magic behind you, right?" she asked, though I was pretty sure she just wanted to ride on Kumayuru.

"Mel might get hurt while we're waving around our swords," said Jade. "So please, if you could let her stick with you..."

Well, *now* I couldn't say no to Jade.

"I'll push you off if you start horsing around," I warned her.

"I'd never," she said, latching on to my clothes.

And then Senia claimed she'd be protecting Karina, hopping right onto Kumakyu's back. Though it sure looked like she just wanted to ride Kumakyu...

"Not to worry! I'll protect Karina," she said.

Well, I guess I'd feel better with her being with Karina? Sure, she was kind of weird, but Senia *was* great with a knife. Sand wyrms would be nothing to her.

Once we were all ready, we started up our plan of attack. Kumayuru would lead us. Jade and Touya would be behind and to the right riding laggaroutes. To the left, Uragan's whole party would be following on their mounts.

I started firing air shots from my bear puppets, which brought out sand wyrms the size of wolves. Jade and Touya shredded right through them. Behind them, Uragan and his party seemed shocked. But there was no time to hesitate.

I fired off air shots to the right and to the left. Right and right again, then to the left. Each time, the sand wyrms flew up into the air, dropping right down onto the sandy surface. They writhed like fish out of water and tried to burrow back under, but Uragan's party dealt them deadly blows right away. There was no escape. Mel was hitting them with her spells too, tearing into the wyrms' bodies.

All things told, this was going well.

"All right, I'm going to speed up now," I said and drove Kumayuru to run faster.

"Seriously?!"

"Wait, you bear!"

"Rubbish!"

I pretended not to hear them and brought up one sand wyrm after another. They really did look more like giant fish than wyrms...

"Damn it!"

"Hey, don't let them escape into the sand!"

Uragan seemed to have given up trying to reason with me and had gotten back to focusing on the monsters. If they really couldn't do it, I could join in myself.

I could see five motionless wyrms a ways away. I hit them all with a giant air shot and sent them flying up into the air. I would've been happy about the perfect shot if they hadn't been wyrms. I just really couldn't get into the idea of fighting bug monsters, you know?

I used my detection skill to continue focusing my shots on spots where a lot of them were gathered. We left a trail of sand wyrms in our wake.

KUMA
KUMA
KUMA
BEAR

333
The Bear Slays Sand Wyrms

WHILE URAGAN and the rest of his crew were making a whole scene behind us, we were all working to slay those wyrms.

And it was going great. I lobbed another air shot at the ground, and sand wyrms soared out of the sand and into the air. They fell down like fish blasted out of the surf onto the turf, at which point Mel bombarded them with magic.

Mel was on her knees atop Kumayuru's back, using one hand to steady herself against my shoulder and the other to blast away. She looked at where my bear puppet was pointed and aligned her spells to hit the sand wyrms right where it mattered, then Jade and Touya dealt the finishing blows. We kept doing that for a while.

Thanks to Mel's support, Jade and Touya were saving some of their stamina.

"Yuna! Are there more?!" Jade asked from behind me. He sounded out of breath. Though Mel was helping a ton, they were still steadily running out of steam.

I knew there were about half as many wyrms compared to when we started. We defeated a lot of them, but there were plenty more left. The pyramid had brought together a real glut of monsters.

"We still haven't gone over in that direction," I said, "so we're not done yet."

I could see exactly where we hadn't gone yet by looking at all the carcasses we left behind. Some of the wyrms had come to us, mistakenly thinking we were food, but there were still a lot around.

"Uragan! Are you all right?"

"O-obviously we're fine," said Uragan firmly. "Who do you think you're talking to?" I could see right through his bluff, but I still liked it better than his whining.

Guess it was time to take him for his word and get back to de-wyrmifying the desert.

"I'll run support," Mel said to the group from behind me.

I kept blasting out more and more wyrms. It was kind of boring, to be honest. I mean, it would've been one thing if they were *actually* fish, and like, edible or something? But nope! Wyrms. Nasty.

We kept at it for a while.

"Hey, you! Bear!" Uragan yelled at me from behind. I pretended not to hear.

"C'mon, you there in black!"

My name wasn't "you there," thank you very much.

"Are we...still going...?" His voice was getting softer and softer. "Yuna, behind you..."

"Just a little more," I said.

"Please. Please stop..."

"This is the last bit," I said. I launched the final air shot. After that, all the sand wyrms in the area would be goners.

When I looked behind me, though, I saw that literally *everyone* had collapsed and were panting on the ground. Even though he'd been whining toward the end, Uragan seemed to still have it in him, swinging his sword around even as he gasped.

The rest of Uragan's party was spread out all over and staying put, groaning to themselves.

"Damn it all! I haven't been this active in a long time."

"I can't move another inch."

They lay there, out of breath and lying against their laggaroute mounts. I was still impressed they'd managed to keep up until now, though. If they really couldn't keep going, I would do it all alone.

And while I thought that Jade's party would be fine...

"I don't wanna move ever again."

I saw that Touya was slumped over and complaining too.

"I didn't think we'd have to fight this many sand wyrms," said Jade, looking around at all the carcasses.

It was already more than a hundred—in fact, maybe it was *several* hundred. Which was a lot, probably? Not much compared to the ten thousand monsters near the capital, of course. More importantly, we were basically done slaying the sand wyrms near the pyramid now. Even after I used my detection skill, I could only spot a few wyrms here and there. We could probably leave those without issue. Plus, it'd be a real pain to track them down.

"We should be able to go into the pyramid now," said Jade. He gave the exhausted Uragan a rather merciless smile. "As agreed upon, we'll leave the harvesting to you."

"Y-you can't be serious! You're leaving all these with us?!"

"An agreement is an agreement. You said you'd do the harvesting in exchange for Yuna's share, and half of ours too." Jade gave Uragan a look.

Wait... Had Jade known how many sand wyrms there were? Was that why he'd agreed to the trade?

Either way, Jade and his party had to go with me and Karina into the pyramid and the sand wyrms really did have to be disposed of. Maybe I was overthinking it, but it sure seemed like he'd given up half the share in order to avoid any harvesting.

"Well, we did say that, but I..." Uragan looked over the many dead wyrms on the ground.

Could they get it done in a day? Unlike wolves, sand wyrm parts weren't all that useful, so they could just take their gems and get rid of the corpses to make sure that they didn't attract other monsters. No, it wouldn't take much time to take care of a sand wyrm...but there were a whole lot of them. *And* they were in the middle of a desert. It wasn't exactly the best spot for a really long harvest sesh.

"Just break it up. Think of it as multiple jobs."

"Fine, damn it. We'll do it, all right. But we're taking our rightful share."

Yeah, this really was a lot like several jobs in one. Once Uragan made peace with that, he reluctantly agreed with Jade. Their leader had agreed to it now, so the rest of Uragan's party didn't complain. Then again, if they didn't take care of the wyrms, even more monsters would show up.

We headed back to Karina. Our actual goal was to get Karina into the pyramid, after all, and now we could do that without worrying about the wyrms.

As we approached Karina, Kumayuru looked to our right and crooned. "What is it?"

The sand shifted. Another sand wyrm?

Kumayuru crooned again, this time seeming on guard. I activated my detection skill. It said there was a sand wyrm there, but...nah, we'd be fine leaving just one around here.

"Kumayuru, it's all right." If it approached, we could take care of it then. It wasn't like we had to go out of our way for one measly sand wyrm.

But as I was thinking that, the little dune started to approach us rapidly...and a whole lot more sand started to move too. Now everyone had picked up on whatever it was.

"What is that?"

Just as I saw a small ripple in the sand, it expanded upward, and a *gigantic* sand wyrm appeared from the sand.

"What *is* that?!"

"There was a big one around too?!"

It was about as big as the wyrm I'd fought off near the capital.

Okay, *that's* why Kumayuru had been so on guard. I was convinced it was just your everyday sand wyrm, but nope. I mean, even my detection skill had said it was a normal one. Looked like my skill couldn't tell the difference between bigger and smaller versions of the same monsters, just like before with the wasps. The skill really wasn't too useful in situations like these, huh?

I faced off with the gigantic wyrm.

Was this, like, the parent or something? Maybe the normal-sized wyrms had gathered around mama wyrm? Or was this their spawning ground? Either way, the bigger they were, the more room they had to be as ugly as hell. The worst part was *(ugh)* their sticky drool.

"Yuna!"

"Damn it, let's scram!"

"Yuna! What should we do?!" Mel yelled from behind me.

Uragan's party was starting to make a break for it. Jade looked between me and Uragan, as if considering his options: fight or flee.

Obviously, it'd be *much* better to slay this thing now instead of putting it off. Otherwise, it'd definitely get in our way as we headed to the pyramids.

"I'm going to fight it off," I said. "You all head over to Karina." It'd be easier to take this thing out without having to worry about the others.

I got off Kumayuru's back. I didn't want this to become more trouble than it already was, so I planned to finish it up fast. I did already have experience fighting off a giant wyrm, after all.

"Yuna, I'll go too," said Mel.

"Can you go with Kumayuru over to Karina?" I didn't want her getting too close and being caught up in the crossfire.

"Are you really sure you'll be okay?" asked Jade.

"I'll be fine, promise," I replied, then ran off toward the wyrm on my own. The sand wyrm saw me, decided I was food, and drooled from its gigantic maw. It slithered over to me.

Wait...did it think I was a real bear? What a matchup: Bear vs. Sand Wyrm.

I cast a fire spell, trying to make sure I had the wyrm's attention. Just as I'd expected, I hit the wyrm, but it was far from being a fatal wound.

Still, it was fine as long as I could keep its attention on me. The worst possibility would be if it headed off toward Karina. She'd be able to escape on Kumakyu, but Jade and the rest might not be so lucky with their laggaroutes. If they tried to run to the town, then that worst-case scenario was them bringing the sand wyrm along with them. So yeah, I had to keep the sand wyrm's focus on me.

It whirled its head around to face me after my spell hit—good. The sand wyrm came at me, and I kept my distance, trying to time things just right. The best way to defeat a giant monster is to destroy it from within. It's easy *and* effective, though it doesn't work if you want something from inside of said monster. But I didn't, so that wasn't an issue.

I dodged the sand wyrm's attack and waited for the perfect time as it turned its maw toward me. I was waiting for this.

The distance, the timing—

There!

All at once, I unleashed the mana I had collected in my hand. Small flame bears appeared in a row in front of me. "Go, bears!"

I lifted my arms in front of me, and the bears leapt right into the sand wyrm's gigantic mouth. The sand wyrm drooled as they rushed right in. The bears traveled through the monster's gullet, burning it from the inside out. I saw it writhe, banging against the ground again and again. Normal magic wouldn't have been enough to do this, but my bears wouldn't extinguish so easily. No, they traveled right on through its body.

The wyrm twisted and turned and smashed against the ground for a while longer. I waited. Eventually, the sand wyrm stopped moving, and our foe was quashed.

Right as I thought that, though, the wyrm writhed again and launched itself at me. I hadn't thought it would attack anymore, so I was slow to respond. I quickly guarded with my bear puppet, but it sent me flying.

I rolled and tumbled over the sand. Again, and again, and again...

When I tried to stand, I staggered a little. My vision swam, but only a little, and I was unscathed. Wow, the bear gear sure did work wonders for me this time. That was what they meant about never letting your guard down. And there I was, thinking I'd good as won.

Still, it seemed like that had been the wyrm's last sliver of strength. It started to slow down more and more, then it fell over quietly to the ground and stopped moving completely. I used my detection skill to check that it was really dead. No surprise attacks this time—the thing was finally dead.

I looked over at Jade and the others to tell them...only to see Karina racing over to me on Kumakyu.

"Yuna!" Karina leapt off of Kumakyu and ran into my arms. "Oh Yuna, oh Yuna!" She held me tight with those little hands of hers, clutching at my clothes as she kept saying my name.

Her eyes were red. Had she been crying? I very gently stroked her hair.

"Did Senia do something mean to you?" I asked as I stared at Senia, who was still on Kumakyu's back.

Senia gave me a sour look. "Me? *You're* the one who made her cry, Yuna."

What on earth was she talking about? When had I done anything to make Karina cry? Until now, I'd just been fighting the sand wyrm. I hadn't even been *near* Karina. But Senia had been right there, so she had to be responsible.

"Y-Yuna..." Karina sobbed into my chest.

I gave Senia a look, as if to say, *why did you do this to her?* I didn't know how to comfort her if I didn't know what Senia had done.

"You headed off to face down a giant sand wyrm on your own, Yuna," Senia said. "Karina got so worried that she started sobbing. You scared her, and that made her cry."

Ohh, so that was why Karina was so upset. I must've really worried her, then.

"And when that wyrm sent you flying, she was positively beside herself. It was so bad. She even said it was all her fault."

Right, that's probably how it looked from far away. Uragan and the others fled when the giant sand wyrm appeared, I headed off to the wyrm on my own, and she saw me get tossed into the air.

I must've looked like a goner, even if it hadn't really been that dire from my point of view.

"Sorry for worrying you," I said. "But you know how strong I am. Something that small isn't going to take me out."

Karina knew about the kraken. A giant sand wyrm shouldn't have been any cause for concern.

"It's different knowing about it and seeing it happen. I can't believe you would face off against a giant monster like that alone..." She turned up to look at me with bright red eyes. "I th-thought you would be eaten, Yuna."

Agh. The teary puppy-dog eyes...!

"Wh-when it hit you and blew you away, I thought you were really gone."

She just wouldn't stop crying.

I took a handkerchief out of my bear storage and wiped away her tears for her. It looked like I'd made her really, *really* worried. "Thank you for caring so much about me, Karina."

I stroked her hair, trying to calm her down. After all was said and done, even though she felt a strong sense of duty, Karina was still a normal ten-year-old girl.

Jade and Uragan came over as I comforted her.

"Did you really slay that thing?" Uragan looked between me and the wyrm a couple of times, then went with Jade to check out the carcass and poke around at it.

"Unbelievable," muttered Jade.

"I know exactly what you mean," Touya agreed.

"Anyway, I'm gonna store it away for now," I said.

I wasn't about to just leave it hanging out here, and I really couldn't force Uragan's party to deal with the giant wyrm, so I put it into my bear storage. There was a chance I'd be able to use it later, like when I'd caught the kraken. Still, a sand wyrm wasn't the same as a regular wyrm, so I wondered if it'd be tasty to monsters. I could try testing it out by using it as bait sometime. If it didn't work, I'd just throw it in the sea.

Uragan's eyes went wide when he watched the gigantic wyrm disappear. He seemed to want to say something to me, but he didn't, so I just ignored him.

Jade started to explain to Uragan when he noticed that.

"The giant sand wyrm... It just... Her bear hand...and it..."

"Just give up," Jade said.

Wait, give up on what? I kind of wanted to ask Jade what exactly that was supposed to mean.

334
The Bear Enters the Pyramid

"**G**UESS WE BETTER get in the pyramid soon," I proposed after getting Karina to calm down.

Uragan rested a bit before heading off to harvest sand wyrms, complaining all the way. Jade and the others were going to enter the pyramid with me. They were resting in the shade of a giant rock to recuperate a little.

"You all right, Karina?"

"Yes, I am," she said. "Um...I'm sorry for crying earlier."

"But hey, now you know that I'm pretty tough, so there's no more need to worry about me, okay? I'll protect you no matter what."

"Yes."

Still, I really hadn't been expecting to make anyone cry just by fighting a sand wyrm. Fina and the others had never seen me actually fight a giant monster before... How

175

would they react if they did? Noa would probably look at me with a sparkle in her eye and tell me how great I was. On the other hand...would Fina worry?

Anyway, guess I needed to be careful about fighting anything in front of Fina and the others. Even my OP gear is useless against the power of a crying kid.

"But, Yuna, are you sure that you're all right? The wyrm did hit you."

True. I went down for a tumble and rolled around for a while, but...

"It'll be fine. I guess I got a little dizzy, though."

I pretended to stagger a bit. That got a laugh out of Karina.

"Hee hee! You got dizzy!" she repeated.

I hadn't said that part to make her laugh. I guess it was funny, though?

"You really didn't seem like you'd survive after you got hit and flung around and rolled like that. But you're not hurt at all."

"It's really true," said Mel. "What's your body even made of?"

Mel had come over during her break, and now she was starting to poke and prod at me. I really wished she'd keep her hands to herself. Since I really didn't like all that, I ran away from her.

Man, I wish she wouldn't give me that weirdly longing look! I got into a stance to defend myself.

"You said you have the blessing of the bears, right?" Mel mused. "I don't really believe that's a thing...but then I see you, and I've got to wonder."

Blessing? I guess, but it was a curse too. Didn't change the fact that thanks to my blursed bear gifts, I was living it up in this other world.

"She's been blessed by bears?" asked Karina. "If I can get the same blessing, would I be as strong as her? Oh! And could I summon Kumayuru and Kumakyu too?"

"I dunno," I said, gesturing at my outfit. "If you got it too, you might be forced to dress like this."

For a while, Karina just stared at my bear outfit. "I... think it's cute, actually," she said finally.

But why would she... Well, there was a *second* there where—

"I'd be so conflicted," Mel broke in. "I mean, summoning bears? So tempting."

What, did Mel want to dress in a bear onesie? How would she look in one, anyway? Senia was shorter, so she seemed like she'd look good in it. As for Mel...

"Yuna, did you have something to say?"

"No, nothing at all..." I replied, a little awkwardly. "More importantly, shouldn't we be heading off soon?"

I turned away and hopped onto Kumayuru. Mel seemed like she had something she wanted to tell me, but she obediently got ready to head out too.

Karina got onto Kumakyu, and Mel and Senia got on their laggaroutes, though they'd tried to get on Kumayuru and Kumakyu. I had politely and firmly told them no. We really didn't need them riding on my bears this time.

The sand wyrms were all but gone, and we weren't going to be attacked on the way to the pyramid, so all we were doing was running past carcasses. Hmm...yep, they still looked like giant bugs to me. Riding past them was an absolute parade of nasty. I hoped Uragan and his buddies cleaned these guys up fast.

He said hi as we rode by—they were hard at work harvesting.

"The quest was to escort you to the pyramid," said Uragan. "I take it that's not necessary anymore?"

"Yeah, most of the sand wyrms are gone. You've done your job already."

Our path to the pyramid was completely safe, so Uragan and company had fulfilled their duties.

Karina looked over at Uragan and bowed her head. "Um, thank you very much."

Uragan looked at me and snorted. "We only helped out because the bear over there said she could get the wyrms out of the ground. It's nothing to thank us for. This is our job. Your dad's payin' us, so don't worry about it. And you're gettin' in the way of work now, so git!"

Maybe it was all in my head, but did he seem a little bashful? Even though they'd been hired to do it, you still thank people who do a good job. I couldn't exactly fight them on that now, though, so I just moved along to the pyramid like they'd told us to.

We finally reached the entrance. The looming opening seemed to beckon to us, almost like the opening to a labyrinth level in a video game. I imagined monster rooms, rooms with flames you had to avoid, and your standard death pit... Ahh, talk about old school.

As I was inspecting the entrance, Jade called me over. He was near a hut thingy right next to the entrance. It looked like it'd been made through earth magic.

"What's this for?"

"It's a place to tie up the laggaroutes," said Karina. "Father and adventurers come here often, and this gives them a place to safely hide from even small wyrms that might attack."

Jade and the others took the laggaroutes inside and placed water buckets and food for them. We didn't know how long we'd be in the pyramid, so we had to make sure they were fed.

As I watched, Touya brought some rope over for me. *What is this for?*

"This spot's open," he said. "I'll tie them for you."

He tried to throw a rope over Kumayuru. My bear, on the other hand, lightly stepped back to avoid it. Touya then lost his balance, toppling to the ground. Kumayuru placed a foot lightly on Touya's back.

"Fmgh?!" He let out a strange little sound.

"Touya, what are you playing around for?!" Mel snapped.

"I was just trying to get a rope around the bear!"

"You should already know that her bears wouldn't need to be tied up." Mel then placed her own foot right on Touya's butt, all while Kumayuru was stepping on him.

"We're about to head into the pyramid, so I was joshing around a little to lighten the mood! Why're you guys stepping on me?"

"I can't believe you'd pretend to tie Kumayuru up as a joke." Mel started putting more pressure on Touya. Kumayuru copied her.

"Wait—that's too heavy. Too heavy! Can't...breathe! I'm sorry. I won't do it again! Get off!"

He started to struggle now. Mel took her foot off then, and Kumayuru did the same.

"Sheesh, that was heavy. You've gained weight since last—"

As he tried to stand up, Mel put her foot on him again. "Fmgh?!"

This time the sound he made sounded a little more like a frog getting crushed. Or what I figured that'd sound like, at least. You would've thought the same thing if you heard it.

"How about we tie *Touya* up instead?" Mel declared. "He can have the same feed the laggaroutes eat."

Senia raised her hand in agreement. Even Jade came over to us. Right as I thought things would get out of hand, Jade stopped the two of them. Touya ran behind Jade's back after being saved.

This sure was an entertaining party.

At long last, we entered the pyramid. Karina took off her hood and put it in her item bag, and the others followed suit.

"It's not too hot inside?" asked Jade.

"That's right," Karina said. "You won't need a hood from here."

"That'll be nice. It's hard to move with one on."

After they all finished putting away their hoods, they made their way into the dark passageway. It was a lot wider in there than I expected. We could even all walk side by side if we wanted. The ceiling was super high too, so it didn't feel claustrophobic at all.

Jade and Touya led us, followed by Karina atop Kumakyu with Mel and Senia walking beside her. Finally, I guarded everyone from the back.

I used my detection skill just in case. No monster signals nearby. Still, I didn't know what would be there, so I didn't want to let down my guard. I'd done that with the sand wyrm and got blown away, so I didn't want to do anything that'd make Karina worried again.

"It's really bright in here," said Senia.

"Father said there's something inside the pyramid that creates light. I've only been here in the middle of the day, but it's supposed to get dark at night."

Whoa, that was an interesting setup. In games and manga, you usually had torches that some mystery person had set up, or places that were lit up even though there was no light source. I remembered making jokes about who could've set up all those torches and candles, especially while somehow navigating all those pathways into darkness. Honestly, it was hard not to make a joke about the pyramid as well. Anyway, I was glad to have some light.

For a while, we plodded along in silence. It was a lot prettier than I'd expected. Maybe it was a little weird or inappropriate, but I was kind of excited to be here.

"Looks like there aren't any monsters around," I said.

"You're right. There were so many outside that I thought there would be some in here too."

That seemed for the best.

"So, Karina, all we need to do is take you to the very last level of the pyramid?"

"Why do we need to take you specifically, though?" Touya asked.

"Did you not listen to anything we talked about?" said Jade with a sigh. "Her mana reacts to the thing we're trying to find and can tell us which direction to go."

"So it's, like, some sort of magical device we're looking for?"

"Yes, and it's a very important one."

"It should be easy enough to find if we know which direction to go."

They were all talking about it like it was some normal magical tool. It seemed almost like lying, so I felt bad. I guess it wasn't *technically* a lie, because it *was* a magical device, but...

We kept going down the long passageway. Was the ground sloping down, or was it just me?

After a while, we got to a wide, round area that looked a whole lot like an arena.

"What's this for?" I asked.

"The stairs going up to the labyrinth levels and down

to the lower level are here," said Karina. "Could you check the top of that staircase?"

I looked where Karina had told me. Next to the stairs leading underground, I saw a set that went up instead. Instead of stadium seats, I saw something that looked like an entrance or a hole. It was only big enough to let one person through.

Except...that wasn't the only hole, not by a long shot. The circular arena was completely lined with them. There might've even been a hundred.

"Those are the entrances to the labyrinth," said Karina.

"Wait, you mean all of them are?"

"Yes."

Uh, this really felt like we were being set up to fail. And this labyrinth was supposed to change by the day, which would make the place impossible to map. If this were a video game dungeon, I'd label it downright impossible. And there's nothing worse than a game that's impossible to beat.

We *really* needed to find that panel.

335
The Bear Heads to the Pyramid's Lower Level

"**I**'D HEARD ABOUT all these entrances, but seeing them is really something else," said Mel, gazing at the many, many holes leading down into the labyrinth.

There were a ton... If this had been in a game, there'd be an avalanche of complaints, along with a flood of troll posts about it.

"Nobody would try to delve into the labyrinth like this."

"On top of that, someone already got through it hundreds of years ago. There really aren't a ton of people interested in trying it anymore. Some people say there's still treasure inside, but who wants leftovers? And the risk of going through the whole labyrinth to find nothing at the end...it'd be a total waste. Nobody's dumb enough to try going through it knowing how low of a chance they've got."

It definitely would be a waste of time to get through a labyrinth like this only to realize there was nothing at the end of it. I wouldn't have put in all that effort either if I knew I'd end up with nothing to show.

"Yuna, we're going to take a look around, so just wait for us for a bit."

Jade's party scouted the area, making sure it was safe. I'd used my detection skill, but I didn't see any monsters on this floor. I'd learned from my time in the mines with the golems that my skill only worked for the floor I was on. If there were monsters beneath us, I wouldn't know about them.

"Still, Karina, I'm surprised your ancestors got through this place," I said as I looked up at the many, many entrances.

Her ancestors must've been amazing. I was surprised they even bothered trying to get through this brutal pyramid at all. If I tried, I probably would've started smashing through the passages to brute force my way to the destination. Then again, there was no guarantee the pyramid would always be the same shape. There was a chance it'd even wipe away all traces of anything left in it. But as long as you get to the treasure, it's always worthwhile.

"Apparently Lord Mumulute, an elf in the party, did a lot to help them with the labyrinth."

"Mumulute?" That sounded like a familiar name. Hmm...but where had I heard it?

"And the traps were undone by Lord Kodielko, a dwarf. My ancestor helped with getting through the labyrinth too."

I didn't know anything about this Kodielko fellow, but Mumulute sure was a familiar name. Where had I heard that before? I *knew* I knew it...

Hmmmm. I frowned, thinking it over.

"Is something the matter?"

"No, it's just that name. Mumulute. I feel like I've heard it before."

"Lord Mumulute?" Jade repeated. "Did he get through any other labyrinths or something?"

No...if there were any legends about that kinda stuff, I didn't know them. I must've heard the name somewhere else.

When it came to elves, there was Sanya. Then Luimin. Their mother Talia, and their father—

"Oh! I remember now." I clapped my hands together. It was their grandpa!

Sanya's grandpa was the head of the village. Mumulute.

I finally remembered and felt a lot better now. Not that I'd forgotten about him or anything. His name just slipped my mind a little. That happens to everybody now and then, right? I had a ton of excuses like that ready to go.

"You remembered something?"

"This Mumulute, he's an elf, right?"

"Yes."

"And I'm guessing he's a man?"

"Yes, that's what I've heard," said Karina.

"Then I might know him."

"What...?" Karina looked at me in disbelief.

Not that I could blame her, given I was telling her I was directly acquainted with someone who had gotten through this very labyrinth several hundred years ago.

"I know an elf named Mumulute who's the head of a village and has grandchildren, so I think he's probably about the right age."

I was pretty sure he was a few hundred years old. And yeah, maybe he was just someone with exactly the same name, but there was a good chance it was him.

I had my bear gate, so I could actually just go for a quick visit to ask. If he remembered, I could ask him all kinds of stuff about the labyrinth... Well, *if* he remembered those days. It had all happened a hundred years ago.

Maybe some things had fallen through the cracks of his memory.

"I'll ask next time I see him," I said. "It'd be amazing if it was the same guy."

Karina's face clouded for a moment when I said that. But then when I looked at her again, she was smiling. "Yes, please. I would like to know more as well."

Weird. I must've imagined that look on her face...

Jade and the rest of the party came back from scoping the place.

"I don't see anything particularly dangerous," said Jade.

"Which means we just need to go down, right?" I confirmed.

Our goal wasn't to clear the labyrinth, after all, but to get the panel that had fallen into the lower level. We just needed to go down far enough to find it.

We headed down the stairs. As we went, the architecture of the pyramid shifted from man-made structures to the old, natural stone of a cave. A vast space opened up once we got to the bottom of the stairs, and bluish-white lights illuminated the cave. Again, we wouldn't need any light magic.

Huge, stalactite-like pillars hung from the ceiling. I wondered if we'd end up caved in if those broke... Yeah, I'd need to be careful if I was going to use magic here.

"So, where do we go?"

We all looked at Karina. From here on out, we'd be following Karina's directions. She closed her eyes for a couple of seconds, then slowly opened them.

"That way," she said as she pointed. "But I feel it from below."

"So you're saying we need to go deeper, then."

It was exactly as Karina had suspected. I kind of felt like digging...but I didn't know in what direction to dig. If I did, I could've made, like, a pipe, and we could've slid down it like a slide to get there directly.

I'd put that aside for a last resort, maybe. For now, we headed off in the direction Karina indicated.

I used my detection skill. I didn't know how they'd gotten in here, but I spotted sand wolves and sand wyrms. Well, Jade and his party were here, and the monsters weren't that powerful, as far as those things go.

"Yuna, do you really think we'll be able to find it?" asked Karina. She seemed worried.

"We should be able to if you just know which direction it's in." Worst case, there was always my pipe method.

"Do you think there'll be monsters?" she asked.

There would be, a little farther ahead. We kept going through the cave, which was filled with craggy rock faces with small openings.

"I heard that adventurers would come to hunt monsters down here," I said. "Do you think there really are any around?"

"Ahead, maybe," Mel answered, looking down at a piece of paper. "Supposedly, monsters fall from above in this area."

"They fall? Like how?"

"I'm not sure. I heard at the guild that the monsters drop and that's why this place is used as a hunting ground."

We kept heading forward to where the monsters would apparently drop.

"According to the map, it's up ahead."

Jade held his arm up to the side at the front in order to stop us.

"Sand wyrms," he said.

I asked Kumakyu to protect Karina and checked it out from atop Kumayuru. Jade was right. There were sand wyrms. I could see about ten of them writhing around, but the ground wasn't made of sand, so they couldn't burrow down into it.

"But how do they drop?" Mel murmured, and at that moment, something fell from above.

It was a sand wyrm! A sand wyrm had dropped down— were they falling down from the sand above, then?

I looked up, but the ceiling was so high that I couldn't see what was up there. When the sand wyrm fell and hit the ground, it just writhed around like nothing had happened.

"The sand wyrms are definitely falling from above," I said.

"I don't think adventurers are the only things that hunt here..." said Jade.

Sand wolves appeared from farther back.

"Looks like they think we came here to steal their prey," said Mel.

"Karina, which way's the object we're looking for?" Jade asked, and Karina pointed past the wolves.

"Then we'll cut our way through!" said Jade, and everyone readied their weapons. "Mel, can I leave the sand wyrms to you?"

"If they can't burrow into any sand, they're basically sitting ducks," she said.

"Gotcha. Touya, Senia, and I will handle the wolves," Jade said.

"Uh, what about me?" I asked.

"You can protect Karina, Yuna. That's your job, isn't it? We can handle some weak monsters," said Jade, and then they headed off to do just that. Mel pelted the wyrms with spells from a safe distance.

Before I knew it, Jade and the others had taken care of the wolves. As Mel fought, more sand wyrms dropped from above. This kind of seemed like the perfect spot for infinite resource grinding.

Once we were done, we headed forward, delving deeper and deeper until we reached a fork. We all looked at Karina.

"I feel it that way." Karina pointed, and we headed that direction. Mel marked any forks on her map.

The path sloped downward and still we delved deeper. Whenever we came across monsters, Jade and the others slew them. It was pretty easy. I just got to ride Kumayuru and didn't have to do anything.

At the front of our group, Jade stopped. "The bridge is broken."

Someone had made a wood-and-rope bridge, but now it was half-collapsed. I wondered if there was a cliff below. Mel investigated the bridge, looked down, and visibly twitched. She stepped back a little.

"That is extremely gross," Mel said as she looked down.

Curious, I took a look too...and regretted it. Sand wyrms were packed tight like sardines, wriggling down at the bottom of the pit. They were like real worms in a bucket, waiting to be used as bait or a snack for other animals. I really wanted to use my magic to burn them all away. Bear flames would do the trick...

193

While I pondered that, another sand wyrm fell from above to join its crew. So *that* was why there were so many down there. Maybe this was where the sand wyrms of the desert gathered...

"Looks like the sand wyrms destroyed the bridge as they fell," I said.

"What should we do?" wondered Jade.

"I'll make a new one." I got off Kumayuru and used earth magic to make a new bridge. Just for fun, I made a roof for it too. If anything fell from above, they'd hit the roof and wouldn't get on the bridge itself.

"You've got a ridiculous amount of mana."

"All thanks to the blessing of the bears," I said, using my secret technique to explain it away. It would've been too much of a bother to get into the details.

Since the bridge was done, we could keep going without looking down at the wyrms below.

"Karina, no looking down," I said.

"Um...too late. I saw them from on top of Kumakyu. I'm scared...what if I fall in there?"

If I fell into a pit of wyrms packed together like a bucket of actual worms, I think I would've gone nuts. Nope, I *really* did not want to fall into that.

"Oh, you children," Touya said. "Can't handle a couple bugs. This is nothin'. But then again, *I'm* all grown up."

Touya walked ahead of us. Was that an invitation to push him down? It was, wasn't it? I really wanted to give his back a shove.

While I was thinking that...

"There you go," Senia actually did push him.

"Ahhhh!" Touya lost his balance and started to totter. "I-I'm gonna fall!"

The sand wyrms below waited for him, open-mouthed. He somehow got his balance back, though, and kept making his way across the bridge.

Aw, what a shame.

"So close," Senia said.

"Close to what? I was close to falling!"

"But you're so mature, Touya. You would've been fine even if you fell down."

"Fine? I would've died!"

"I thought you liked the wyrms. Since I'm such a baby, I much prefer a fluffy bear over some gross wyrms." Senia hugged Kumayuru.

For once, I agreed with Senia. Mel and Karina nodded along with her.

"Jade!" Touya begged for help from the party leader.

"I'd prefer Yuna's bears over wyrms too." Even Jade had abandoned Touya? Ice cold.

We kept heading forward, leaving Touya, who looked

pretty gloomy, behind. I guess everyone else was pretty sick of him too.

"W-wait up!" Touya cried as he followed after us.

336
The Bear Fights Scorpions

WE KEPT HEADING FORWARD after we crossed the bridge above the writhing sand wyrms.

"This sure is a lot bigger than I expected." I mean, it would've been normal in a game, but in reality? It was something else entirely. If anyone told me we had to go down a hundred of these levels, I'd probably snap and just start digging. Even if there were only fifty of these, there was about a twenty-five percent chance I'd get right to digging.

"Almost there. It's really close," Karina said, her eyes closed. We took her at her word and headed off where she pointed.

We went pretty far down.

"What's this doing here?"

It was...sand? Even this far underground, sand was falling from above. I checked my bear map and saw that we weren't directly below the pyramid anymore—we were off by a little. Was this falling from the desert above?

"Hey!" said Jade, looking over the ground ahead. "I think there's something here."

I agreed. I used my detection skill and saw a name I'd never seen before pop up: scorpions. I guess they were a monster version of the real thing.

"Yuna, can you see anything?" Mel asked.

Oops—Kumayuru was supposed to be the one who could see this stuff. I'd been pretending that my bears were the ones that sensed monsters, so that's what I did.

"Kumayuru, what do you see?"

"Cwoon." Kumayuru, always the brilliant actor, pretended to see something and crooned.

I fired off an air shot in the direction of the scorpions. One of them broke from the sand—a scorpion roughly the size of a wolf with dark coloring. Man, why did it have to be so big? Fantasy settings and their constant surprises...

Jade's party immediately readied their weapons, but the scorpion burrowed back down.

"Your bear really is amazing, Yuna," he said.

Mel agreed. "Scorpions are pretty terrible to deal with."

"What'll we do?" asked Touya. "Run past it?"

Jade shook his head. "Too dangerous."

The scorpion still hid beneath the sand. I didn't know what they were like in this world, but in my game, they were smarter than wyrms, and they usually stayed still until you got close enough to aggro them. When their prey approached, they'd stick them with their tails, paralyze them, and gobble them up while they couldn't move.

I used my detection skill and saw that the whole place was swarming with scorpions. I could dig them out like I had with the wyrms, but I didn't know whether Jade's party could deal with them as easily. If just one of them took a long time to defeat, the other ones might start attacking too.

"Jade," I said. "I can dig them out. Would you be able to fight them off easily?"

"Can't say. Haven't fought scorpions before. They only live in a certain part of the desert, so we don't encounter them very much. Their shells are supposed to be thick, so Senia's and my weapons should be able to pierce them, but Touya's sword wouldn't be able to crack into them too easy."

Touya seemed to want to say something, but he kept quiet. In other words, he was useless right now.

"And if Senia got close enough to use her knives, I'd be afraid of her getting stung by their poisonous tails," Jade added.

Yeah, she'd need to get in close to gank them with her knives. Plus, the scorpions I'd seen on TV were pretty fast with their tails.

"What about Mel's magic?" I asked.

"I'm sorry. I've never tried magic on a scorpion, so I'm not sure if it'll work."

So that was that. In other words, Jade was the only one with a chance at fighting them.

"But they're weak to water," Mel said, "so you might be able to help."

"Water, huh?"

"Yes. If you get them wet, I hear scorpions stop moving. You can use that moment to take them out."

"And their bellies are soft too," Senia added.

So, we'd need to flip the scorpions over? Hmm, what would make sense here?

"Could we have her make another bridge?" Touya proposed.

"Their stingers can fire off a poison sting as a kind of ranged attack," said Mel, shooting Touya's idea down in a flash. "Too risky."

Well...I could just make a bridge with walls, but it was pretty far over there. It wasn't totally off the list, but it'd probably be better to just slay them. There was a chance they'd attack us once we got to the other side.

Let's see...the scorpions would freeze if we got them wet. They had soft bellies. They liked hiding in the sand. Finally, they could shoot their stingers.

Hmm, what to do...?

After hemming and hawing to myself for a bit, I spoke up. "I'm going ahead. Alone."

"Yuna!"

"Yuna?!"

"That's too dangerous!"

They all seemed shocked by what I'd just said.

"If we don't fight them," I said, "we're putting Karina in danger."

"But why do it on your own?" asked Mel. "We can help you."

"Yeah, not like we can't deal with them," Touya said.

"No, it's fine," I said. "I'll finish them off real quick."

I understood how they felt, honestly. This was Jade's party, and they meant every word they said. Still, this was dangerous stuff. I wouldn't be able to sleep at night if they got hurt right in front of my eyes.

"Real quick? You make it sound easy," said Jade. "Are you sure you'll be okay?"

"There's something I want to try out. If it doesn't work, we'll think of something else," I said. Plus, I could just make a bridge if I really had to.

"Yuna, please be careful," Karina said in a worried voice, looking at me with wide eyes.

"I'll fight them off and come right back," I assured her.

The moment I stepped onto the sand, the stationary scorpions started sneaking silently. I could see them with my detection skill—it made sense that they were quiet. Probably helped them hunt.

I pulled out the cheap throwing knives I'd bought when I'd arrived at Crimonia, imbued them with mana, and threw one at a scorpion lying in wait under the sand. The scorpion crawled right out of the sand, the knife jutting from its back. Just one knife wasn't enough to inflict a mortal wound, huh? I threw another one, aimed at its face. That seemed to do the trick.

"Yuna, how do you know where the scorpions are? You're not next to Kumayuru..."

"My mind is connected with my bears," I said. Both of my bears crooned in response.

Anyway, it looked like I could get through their shells using mana. I could still take advantage of their soft bellies and water weakness, but this worked well enough for now. The important thing was to slay them...but when I pulled the knives out of the scorpion, the blades fell apart. Looked like these were one use, then. Must've been the mana infusion that broke them.

Well, I bought them for just that and I hadn't found any other use for the things, so I didn't mind. And if I used magic and made a mistake, the other scorpions would notice me and probably start swarming. If I attracted them, that'd put Karina in danger. No, I wanted to pick them off one by one with my knives, and I wanted to do it carefully.

I walked toward the scorpions lying in wait and started throwing the mana-imbued knives. I had a hundred, so I knew I'd probably have enough.

I pulled out more, imbued them with mana, and checked in with my detection skill. Then I sent the blades whooshing through the air at the scorpions, again and again. It took two or three knives for each one, generally, and I always kept an eye on their stingers.

Every once in a while, they would try to blast me with a ranged stinger attack, but I already prepared some earth spells that covered my blind spots.

The problem was that now I was out of knives, and there was still one more scorpion. Left with no other choice, I whipped out my mithril knife and threw it at the last one, imbuing it with my mana.

One mithril knife did the trick. Talk about an upgrade, huh? Ghazal the dwarf had made that knife, so what had I even been thinking? When I pulled it out, it didn't have even a single scratch on it. The blade was still beautiful. It felt unfair to compare it to those cheap knives, but Ghazal's craftsmanship was just so impressive.

After I finished all the scorpions off, I collected their corpses as I made my way back to Jade and his party.

"All finished," I said.

When I got back, Touya and Kumayuru ran over to me. Uh, what?

"Careful!"

Right as Touya had been about to grab on to me, I took a few steps to the side and dodged him. What was that about?

I immediately found out.

As soon as Touya passed by where I'd been, a scorpion fell down right there from above. I was so surprised that I was late to respond—but Kumayuru crushed the scorpion under their left foot at once, pinning its tail with their right.

"Kumayuru!"

I came back to my senses right away and used the mithril knife in my hand to cut off the scorpion's tail, then stabbed it through its shell. It stopped moving.

I broke out into a cold sweat. Needless to say, I was a bit flustered.

I looked over at Touya and saw that his head was stuck in the sand. "Uh, you okay?"

"Yeah, I'm fine." Touya pulled his sand-covered head out and stood up.

"Uh...thanks," I said.

If Touya hadn't done what he did, I probably would've been attacked by the scorpion.

But then Kumayuru gave me a look, as if to say, *That's not true. I would've protected you.*

"Thank you too, Kumayuru," I said. I gave my bear a pat on the head. Kumakyu would sulk if I only pet Kumayuru, so I made sure to fairly distribute the head pats. "Thank you for protecting Karina, Kumakyu."

"Yuna, are you okay?" Mel ran over to me.

"I'm fine," I said. "Touya yelled to warn me, after all."

"I'm still surprised, though. Touya, how did you know?"

"I was looking at Yuna when I noticed something making a sound from right above her. I looked up and saw it coming down. It wasn't like I was staring 'cause I was jealous of her mithril knives, though, okay?"

So...he *was* jealous of my mithril knives, then. Still, that jealousy had saved me.

"I ended up being faster than your bear," Touya boasted.

Kumayuru let out a forlorn cry. Jeez, Touya... Even if it's true, it's a childish thing to say out loud! I wasn't so grateful anymore. If he'd only bitten his tongue before saying that last bit, I would've liked the guy a whole lot more.

"So, Yuna, about that knife..." said Senia hungrily. Her too?

"I saw you fighting with a knife a while ago, and that's when I knew I wanted to have mithril ones made for me," I said.

Senia blushed slightly, flattered. She was a dual-wielder and looked pretty cool whenever she got into a fight.

I had actually gotten the mithril to make Fina a harvesting knife, but I ended up with a lot more mithril than expected, so I had weapons made too.

"May I see?" she asked.

I handed the mithril knife to Senia. She looked it over from blade to hilt.

"Wow, it's beautiful. This is a truly wonderful weapon."

"I had Ghazal, a dwarf in the capital, make it," I told her. "I could ask him to make some for you too."

"Ghazal..." Immediately, he started looking for something on the knife. "There. Found it..."

"What is it?"

Senia used one of her short fingers to point at a spot near the blade. Something had been engraved there.

"The sword master Ghazal always puts his name on the weapons he puts a real effort into forging...and it's such a rare occasion that he's famous for it. I'm jealous."

No kidding? Ghazal hadn't told me about that at all. I wish he'd at least told me.

"And he even added a bear crest," she said.

"He said he did that because he was bored," I offered.

"I can't believe it."

Well...he told me that he did it because I took too long to come back to get the knives. What else could I say?

"Damn it. Maybe I'll go to the capital to have a mithril sword made after this quest."

Touya, that sounds like a death flag in a game...

Anyway, we all headed onward after I defeated the scorpions. According to Karina, we were almost there.

KUMA
KUMA
KUMA
BEAR

337
The Bear Discovers the Crystal Panel's Location

"IT'S AHEAD," Karina said. "We're very close." She rode along on Kumakyu happily.

At this rate, we'd be able to retrieve the map without issue, then use it to swap out the mana gem in order to complete the quest.

"I was wondering how the rest of this would go when we were fighting the sand wyrms," said Touya, as he walked ahead of us for some reason. "Looks like the job is going to be easier than expected."

"What are you talking about? We fought the sand wyrms, but Yuna still had to make that bridge," said Jade.

"*And* she took care of all those scorpions," said Senia.

"We've been letting Yuna do all the worst parts of the job," said Mel.

Touya shrugged. "I guess so, but we've been fighting too."

"What we mean is that even though the job *seemed* easy, things would've been a nightmare without Yuna."

"If I'd had a mithril sword, I could've at least helped with the scorpions," said Touya.

"You're right," said Jade. "Let's buy you a mithril sword once we get back to the capital, like you mentioned. It'll strengthen our party."

"Good point," said Mel. "That'll lessen the burden on you too, Jade."

Senia nodded. "No objections here."

They told Touya he wasn't ready for one yet during that time with the golem, but I guess Touya had grown since then. Because they all gave their permission, Touya seemed to be on cloud nine.

But suddenly, he looked a little conflicted.

"What's wrong, Touya?"

"I...don't have the money for it."

Everyone groaned at once. "Seriously?!"

Even I was close to making fun of him now. He'd just said he was going to buy one himself. Why would he have said that if he didn't have the money? I had countless questions about whatever was going on in that brain of his.

"Unbelievable."

"Touya, you're the absolute worst."

"I told you to save up your money so many times, didn't I?"

"B-but..." Touya stammered. "You all kept saying it was too soon for me, so..."

He tried to make excuses, but Jade slapped him on the back.

"I'll chip in to help, at least a little," Jade said.

"Jade!" Touya looked overjoyed.

Jade was so kind. Mel let out a sigh as she watched the two of them.

"Well," she said, looking exasperated, "I guess I'll lend you some money too, then."

"I'll lend you some, but you better pay me back," said Senia, whipping out her knives. She swiped them right in front of Touya's face. "Or else."

"Aww, you guys...thank you..."

They made fun of Touya a lot, but really, the party seemed to be on good terms.

I had some extra ore from defeating that mithril (plated) golem a bit ago. Jade's party had helped me a ton back then too, so I could've just given them some. But Touya seemed happy already, and they were all smiling too. Yeah, I didn't need to go out of my way with the generosity here. They had this covered.

All we needed to do now was find that panel, hopefully without any more problems. I was tempted to agree with Touya that there was a good probability we'd get out of here without anything else happening.

We kept heading down the slope.

"It's just up ahead," said Karina. If she hadn't been riding Kumakyu right now, I was sure she would've been running up ahead of us. We cleared the slope and kept walking through the passageway.

Soon enough, the passageway opened up.

"This place is…"

It felt like we were standing over a void. We looked down, and the scene spread out before us was shocking. We were speechless.

"What the heck is this…?"

A vast scorpion nest filled our vision. In the middle chittered a mind-bogglingly gigantic scorpion. Its shell looked hard, and its pincers were large enough to hold a person with ease. Its gigantic stinger bobbed in the air.

The wolf-sized scorpions we already dealt with seemed downright minuscule now. This thing must've been over ten meters long. And the color—it looked just plain *sinister*. It was pitch-tar black. Even the color almost made me shudder in horror.

Jade's party seemed surprised too.

"What is with that giant scorpion?"

"It's huge."

"You've gotta be kidding me...!"

"I've heard of those before, but I've never seen one."

They fell quiet again. We needed to observe this thing before acting.

I used my detection skill. All it said was "scorpion," plain and simple. *Seriously?* Since it was obviously different from the other scorpions, the skill could've called it a big scorpion, or a dark scorpion because of its color, or even an obsidian scorpion! Something cool like that. Even "scorpion king" would've worked if it was their leader or something.

"There's...no way we can beat that thing."

"And the other little ones around it are going to be in the way. We can't fight it."

"We don't need to fight, though," said Senia. "We just need to pick up the lost item."

She was right. Our actual goal, in the end, was to get the crystal panel and not to fight the scorpions. We didn't need to fight the big guy, or the thirty little guys around it either.

"So, Karina, where is it?" Jade asked.

If it was here, all we needed to do was pick it up. I just hoped there wouldn't be any scorpions near it.

Karina closed her eyes and searched for the panel. Then she slowly opened them.

"There's no way... There's just no way..." she whispered.

Karina got off of Kumakyu and looked at the giant scorpion in disbelief.

"No... Why? We've come so far!"

"Karina, what's wrong?"

"Oh, Yuna..." Karina looked at me with tears in her eyes. "Th-the panel... It's inside that big monster."

"You're kidding me...right?" Jade muttered.

"There's no way we can beat that thing," said Touya.

They stared up at the giant scorpion.

"Trying to find an opening to grab the object is entirely different from having to fight a monster like that," said Senia.

She was completely right. If the panel had just been on the ground, Mel and I could have used a spell to draw away the scorpions' attention in order to make an opening. But if the panel was *inside* the big scorpion, we had to beat it.

"If we're going to try this, we need to bring in more adventurers," said Mel. "High-ranking ones too. Otherwise, this is impossible."

"You don't think you would be able to defeat it?" I asked.

Mel gave my question some thought. "Hmm...it'd be really tough, at least. If we put our lives on the line, we might be able to win. But we would need to be prepared to make sacrifices. Someone might die if we attempt this battle. At the very least, someone could get maimed."

"Even then," Mel broke in, "we'll never beat it if all the other scorpions are there. The small ones will get in the way."

The small ones (and by small, I mean wolf-sized) would mean trouble, just like she said. They'd definitely swarm us if we had to fight. Even if we got rid of the small ones first, there were tons of them to get through, and we couldn't just expect the big guy to sit around and watch.

"We should temporarily retreat and ask Barlimer what we should do," said Jade.

"You're right. We should avoid battles that we wouldn't win," said Mel.

"Let's head back, then," said Senia conclusively.

"If only I had a mithril sword..." Touya groaned.

I'm sure he'd wanted to lighten the mood, but no one bothered to make fun of his last remark.

Karina stared at the giant scorpion. Hmm...was there a way for us to beat that thing, though? Just as Mel had said, even the little ones would be an issue. Without them, we'd still be lucky even with a close fight. Maybe we could attack the little ones from above to slay them first...

As I thought of a way to defeat them, everyone decided that they would be heading back.

"Are you all right with that too, Karina?"

"Yes..." She bit her lip, not looking very *all right* at all. Since she'd agreed to go, everyone started heading back where we came from.

But I didn't move.

"Yuna?"

"Karina, you go ahead. Go back with Jade and the others."

Everyone seemed shocked when I said that.

"Yuna, you're not going to fight that thing, are you?" said Jade.

"Scorpions aren't the same as sand wyrms, you know," said Mel. "They have thick shells, and they're really fast. They're dangerous beasts."

"This isn't the time to push yourself," said Senia. "We still have time. We can talk to Barlimer."

They all tried to stop me, but our goal was right there, ready for the taking. We wouldn't be able to defeat the scorpion with just our group. We wouldn't be able to do it with every adventurer in Dezelt. And it would take time to call powerful people from the capital or from other countries.

Most importantly, I had OP bear powers. If I didn't fight it now, when would they be able to fight it?

I patted Karina on the head.

"Yuna..."

"It'll be fine. I'll make sure to get the panel, okay?"

Karina shook her head. "No. It'll be dangerous. It's okay. I'll tell Father what happened, and...you already got me here. You did everything you promised, but this is too dangerous. You're strong, but...you can't win this."

"No. I haven't finished the job," I said. "I'm supposed to get the panel and to bring you home."

"Y-Yuna..." Karina grabbed on to my bear clothes with her little hands.

With my hand still on her head, I looked over at Jade and the others. "Keep an eye on her."

"Are you really going to fight it?"

"Then we'll lend you our strength," said Mel.

I shook my head. "Your job was to get us to the right place, Mel, but it's *my* job to keep Karina safe. You've already fulfilled your duties. The rest of them are mine."

"Then you should come back with us, Yuna," said Senia.

"That's right!" said Mel. "No matter how important this panel thing might be, it's not worth risking your life over it."

Senia and Mel were both trying to stop me out of worry, but I wasn't trying to risk my life on this at all. I was fighting because I had my OP bear powers. And my gamer instincts demanded that I go through with this. I mean, I couldn't just leave this boss unfought, you know? It'd be shameful.

"If I don't think I can win, I'll run for it," I told them. "It'll be okay."

"You really won't push yourself too hard?" said Karina.

"No. If something happens to me, I know you'd feel responsible. I wouldn't want that," I said, placing a hand on Karina's head again.

"Yuna..."

"All right, then," said Jade. "We'll take Karina up to the surface. We better see you there soon, eh?"

I wish they wouldn't spout lines like I was walking into a death trap or something. They were basically jinxing it! I wasn't planning to die. If things didn't work out, I'd run, just like they asked.

"Kumakyu, you take care of Karina, okay?"

"Cwoon." Kumakyu nuzzled up to me.

"I'll be back later, and we'll sleep side by side, y'hear?"

"Cwoon." Kumakyu headed off to Karina and crouched. Jeez, Kumakyu was being such a good bear today. I'd need to spend a lot of time with my bears once we got home.

"Don't push yourself too hard, now."

"I won't," I answered.

Everyone headed back into the passage we came in from as I created a wall using earth magic to block the way.

"Yuna!"

"Yuna, why did you block us out?!" Karina called from the other side.

"I wouldn't want the scorpions to get out and attack you guys," I said. Just seeing me might get them to start climbing all over the place. If that happened, there was a possibility I'd get stuck up here.

Most importantly, this would stop anyone from the party coming back to get me. I didn't know how the fight would go, but I couldn't get them caught up in any of the dangers, especially if there was a cave-in. There was a possibility that I'd need to push my cheat powers to the limit to win this, and I didn't want any of them to see that.

Also, I really didn't want Karina to see me fighting and cry again. If I sealed the opening, they wouldn't be able to come back.

"I suppose, but..."

"Yuna..." Karina sounded like she was about to cry again.

"Don't die... Please don't die."

I had my bear cheat powers, so I'd be fine. If I was really in an emergency, I'd use my bear gate. But I couldn't use that if everyone was with me.

"Miss," said Touya, "we've gotta grab some good grub when you're back."

"Sure," I said, "but you're paying."

"And when you get back," said Mel, "you have to let us ride on Kumayuru again."

"Only for a little bit, all right?"

"And let's have a duel with our knives."

"Please go easy on me, though," I told her.

They were acting like this would be the last time they saw me alive. I wish they'd cut it out. I was still alive, and I'd be coming home.

Karina and the others finally left.

The battle was about to begin.

338
The Bear Fights the Giant Scorpion

NOW THAT I WAS ALONE, I turned my sights on the giant scorpion.

"All right, Kumayuru. I'm on my own now, but...how should I handle this?"

"Cwoon." Kumayuru made a face that said *I dunno!*

Hmm. Indeed!

"Maybe I can use my bear flames on them?" I mused.

I imagined it. Let's see... Even if their shells were impervious to the heat, their insides wouldn't be. It's like how heat travels through pots and pans into what they're holding. Maybe I could steam my way into those shells of theirs.

I looked at Kumayuru, who just crooned and shook their head.

"What was that?"

Kumayuru got up and patted their stomach.

"You have a stomachache?"

"Cwoon." Kumayuru shook their head again. Okay, so that wasn't it.

Kumayuru dramatically moved their head to look at the giant scorpion.

"The scorpion?"

Kumayuru's stomach... Scorpion... Which meant... uhhh... Aha! Okay, I got it.

"You mean the panel!"

At that, Kumayuru crooned happily—bingo! So Kumayuru was signaling the scorpion's belly rather than their own.

It was a good point. I didn't know how sturdy the panel was. Would bear flames destroy it? That spell was pretty toasty, after all. What if the flames turned the panel into ashes? Now that I thought about it, I was sure fire would be a bad idea.

But that meant electricity magic was also out of the question. I had no idea what havoc that could wreck on the scorpion's insides, so it'd probably reach the panel and sizzle it too, somehow. Really, any magic at all that might affect the scorpion's insides was a no-go.

Water, ice, wind, and earth magic...all of them were usable, but none of them would deal a killing blow. There

I was thinking that my OP bear skills would make this a breeze, but I hadn't even considered the problem of the panel being *inside* the monster. The more I thought about it, the more I was starting to regret this whole thing.

I gave Kumayuru a pat on the head as a thank-you for reminding me.

Before I battled the big scorpion, I needed to figure out how to get rid of the little ones.

From several dozens of meters above, I aimed down at where a scorpion was skittering along and launched an ice arrow. The arrow skewered the scorpion right through its back, but...it kept walking about like nothing had happened.

Was its shell too hard to penetrate at all? Or had I just not put enough force into it? Either way, this didn't seem like a good way of attacking them. Maybe I underestimated the little ones a little? It seemed like I needed to make the arrow stronger, sharper, and quicker.

Suddenly, the scorpion I'd pierced with the ice arrow pointed its tail up and fired a stinger right at me. I quickly ducked to dodge it and crawled forward to look down again.

That's when I saw that the scorpions had started to gather.

What the—these guys were fast! All I'd done was fire one measly ice arrow. For the first time, I found myself wondering how good they were at working together. But I knew I'd be safe up here, of course.

Aaand that's about the point when the scorpions started to scale the freaking walls!

"You have *got* to be kidding me."

Worse yet, they were lightning-fast. Sealing off the entrance earlier had been the right call. If things went sideways, at least they wouldn't be able to reach Karina.

I shifted so I was right above one of the climbing scorpions. The thing was still scaling the wall on instinct. Now that I was right above it, the sucker was basically calling for me to hit it right on its defenseless little head.

I aimed at its clicking mouth as it scurried upward, and I fired a hard, sharp, and quick ice arrow straight into its gullet. The ice pierced straight through, and the scorpion fell to the ground, motionless.

Like any living creature, its mouth was a weak point. As long as something doesn't have teeth to block attacks, shooting anything in the mouth basically scrambles its insides.

I aimed at each of the scorpions' mouths like I was playing a shooting game, and they dropped like flies.

There may have been a lot of them, but I was steadily picking them off.

Just when I was starting to think I could take out all the scorpions easily, the giant one began to stir. Its massive head lurched in my direction, and its eyes— its pitch-black eyes, just like a doll's—swiveled right at me. *Apex* nastiness.

It raised its gigantic tail high in the air and turned the tip toward me. I quickly ducked my head and took cover as it fired off one stinger attack after another.

The stingers impaled themselves on the wall that the smaller scorpions were trying to scale, as well as the wall behind me. Part of the cavern came crashing down on itself, knocking a few of the smaller nasties off the wall.

Each stinger was the size of my arm, with a sharp point on the end. I kind of doubted my bear gear would survive a hit from one of those. Maybe I'd withstand the sheer force, but those points made me nervous. My bear clothes wouldn't tear if I got hit by them, right? And yet I couldn't imagine what *would* happen, and I wasn't eager to find out.

The giant scorpion wasn't letting up either, blasting another stinger barrage straight at me. The little ones were still trying to scale the walls, even after all of this. Not good. Trying to fight off both the big guy and grappling with the little ones at the same time was getting to be a huge pain. I could use a few less of the little guys right about now.

I attacked the smaller scorpions as I called Kumayuru over. I was just about to recall my bear to keep them out of harm's way—not that I doubted Kumayuru's prowess in battle, of course. But I didn't want them to get caught up in my own attacks or hit by any of the scorpions.

Kumayuru seemed to be having none of it, though, and crooned in response.

"I'll be fine."

"Cwoon."

I tried to pet Kumayuru, but my bear still seemed unhappy.

"Please, it's going to be dangerous," I said.

"Cwoon!"

"I'm sorry. Once the fight's over, I'll call you back."

With that, I recalled Kumayuru. I was happy that my bear was so worried about me, but I was just as worried about them. If anything happened to Kumayuru, I would be beside myself. I mean, I wouldn't even be able to forgive myself. My bears were family.

And so, I faced off against the giant scorpion on my own.

"All right, time to shake things up!"

Taking care to watch for more giant scorpion stingers, I got to work steadily picking off the smaller bugs. Soon enough, there wasn't a single scorpion clinging to the wall. I'd probably gotten through seventy or eighty percent of them, total. The rest were crawling along the ground.

I gripped my two mithril knives. The black one was the Kumayuru knife, and the white one was the Kumakyu knife. I couldn't think of good names for them at the time (really not one of my talents!) and Ghazal had made these based on my bear puppets. That's why I named them after my bears.

I leapt several meters into the air, running at the smaller scorpions. Then I blasted them with a water spell. They flinched as the water reached them, and *swoosh*—I sliced off their tails with my Kumayuru knife, following up with my Kumakyu knife to stab them right in their buggy little necks.

After I got through two or three, the giant scorpion started to move in. It aimed its tail straight at me and fired a few stinger shots in rapid succession, just as I expected.

"Huff..."

I jumped away to the side to dodge, then I ran around the right side of the giant scorpion and stopped the smaller ones in their tracks with a few more blasts of water, finishing them up with a few stabs from my Kumakyu and Kumayuru knives as I went.

I was really glad I had everyone leave. If they saw the true extent of my powers, I think they would get freaked out. Most importantly, I couldn't let them see how I fought in this bear onesie. It'd just look too weird to believe.

I ran around the giant scorpion, taking out scorp after scorp, and all the while the big boy kept trying to nail me with stinger shots.

Too slow!

But I still needed to get rid of the smaller ones at my feet, and I couldn't just ignore the giant one either. The giant scorpion swiveled around and used the centrifugal force of its tail.

Okay, *that's* fast!

Its tail thundered toward me. I leapt up, and with breakneck speed, the tail came crashing down right where I was split seconds before. The small scorpions in its path were thrown from the ground and crashed into the wall, heaving their last breaths before falling still.

I could see just how much force had been in that swipe—the scorpion carcasses were practically pulp. This wasn't fun and games. Even if it didn't actually injure me, I didn't want to end up on the receiving end of that.

At least there weren't as many scorpions now. The other tiny ones made a break for it to nest holes on the side.

Great, I guess? I mean, at least I wouldn't have to worry about my surroundings as I fought the giant scorpion.

The real battle began now.

I created a giant water bubble and tossed it at the giant scorpion. It swiveled around and smashed the bubble into droplets. Even though that water splashed against the scorpion, it didn't slow down one bit.

This thing wasn't like the little ones.

Next up, bear cutter. It stopped that with its giant pincers. I got maybe a little nick in it and that was all. Big scorp was too sturdy, I guess.

Next up, gigantic boulder. I tried to whip it around at the thing, but the scorpion protected its face with its pincers. The boulder did dent the scorpion's shell a bit, so physical attacks were at least a little effective.

All the while, I couldn't help but worry whether these attacks could break the map inside of it. I couldn't attack it with everything I had and risk the crystal panel, could I? Plus, this was a small space, so it was pretty hard to fight in here. I couldn't get any distance away from the scorpion, and that was giving me trouble.

The scorpion tried to pursue me now. It attempted to grab me in its large, right pincer. I went left, and the scorpion swiveled its whole body around.

I jumped to get away and landed on the platform of the entrance. I took a breath and tried to think of what I could even *do* now, but the scorpion wasn't going to give me the time. More stingers hurtled through the air. The wall behind me started to crumble away from the force of the attacks.

C'mon, all I wanted was a second or two to think...

If only I could use fire or electricity. I wanted to burn it from within and really give it a pummeling. I was starting to get stressed out. It kind of felt like a really weak opponent getting ahead of themselves and trying to push the attack.

Well, I wanted to show it what was really up.

I landed on the ground and faced the scorpion head-on. It had a scary mug now that I was staring directly at the thing. A truly nasty experience.

It crawled closer, bringing down its pincer. I leapt to the side and jumped forward. Then I landed on its head and leapt onto its colossal back.

This was the perfect way of winning. I channeled mana into my Kumayuru knife and brought the blade down, piercing its shell. Looked like my knives would work.

I started hacking away at its back with my two knives. I wasn't drawing anything that looked like blood though, likely because I hadn't been cutting away enough. The shell might've been too thick for my knives to get all the way through. Maybe a longer sword would've worked better for this? I really would've liked to hit it with some magic where I'd damaged the shell, but there was that dang panel in there! Not an option.

While I was trying to figure out what to do, it attacked me with its tail. With a flash of my Kumayuru knife, I cut it right off. The tip of its tail went soaring across the chamber. Now it wouldn't be able to fire stingers at me!

...Which I enjoyed for about two seconds before its tail bulged and a new tip appeared at the end. I guess this meant I needed to cut off its tail at the base.

What to do...?

KUMA
KUMA
KUMA
BEAR

339
The Bear Slays the Giant Scorpion

THE SCORPION STARTED attacking me even as I stood on its back. I leapt to dodge it, but jumping was a big mistake. The tail swung back like a pendulum and whacked me away in midair. I tumbled all the way to the wall.

At least I hadn't been distracted that time. In a way, it felt like I was playing a game: Even when you take damage, you can use a recovery item. That's why being a little aggressive wasn't such a big deal.

Still, this world didn't have recovery potions, at least as far as I knew. Just in case, I needed to fight a little more deliberately.

I used my bear puppet hand to steady myself, trying to stand up, but there was a puddle right there and my bear puppet sunk in. Huh. I'd been blown right into some water. If my bear gear hadn't been given to me by a god, its white belly definitely would've gotten grunged up.

Wait, what was water doing here?

I looked around. There were water puddles all over now, but there hadn't been any at the start. They'd probably formed because of the water spells I'd used earlier. And if the ground was made of bedrock—which it sure seemed to be—then the water had nowhere to go. No drainage meant puddles.

I managed to find a great way to win against the scorpion. If I just... Hmm.

Well, it'd take a little too much time to use just one. No, I needed to make several.

Yeah. This could work.

I created five bear golems of earth, lining them up in front of me. Then I unleashed them on the scorpion. Instead of having them attack, though, I had them run around and distract the giant monster.

All the while, I ran along the walls, closing up the holes in them as I ran. Sometimes I'd see a small scorpion and that'd spook me, but I'd end up just sealing off that hole anyway.

Meanwhile, the golems ran circles around the scorpion. The scorpion would grab them in its claws or break them with its stingers, but I just kept on sealing the holes even as my golems were getting destroyed.

Finally, the scorpion picked up the last one and crushed it in its pincers. Even if they were made of earth, I felt sick seeing my bears destroyed. But thanks to the bear golems, I was able to seal off this whole cavern. My preparations were complete.

This thing was going down.

I could've just gone straight for the kill, but I wouldn't feel satisfied with just that. I wanted to get back at it for blowing me away earlier and breaking my bear golems. Plus, when I get payback, I make sure to collect interest.

I made one last bear golem and had it run in front of the scorpion. While the scorpion was distracted, I approached it from a blind spot and got onto its back. It noticed and tried to sting me, but I dodged and ran over to the base of its body. Now I was in a spot where it couldn't get me with its tail or its pincers.

I pierced through the base of its tail with my Kumayuru knife, but the tail was still too thick to just slice off. I tore my knife out of it and stabbed again, but the scorpion flipped around and tried to buck me off.

Yet again I stabbed with my Kumayuru knife, hanging

on tight so it couldn't shake me off. The scorpion skittered around and around, but I wasn't gonna stop. With the Kumakyu knife in my left hand, I stabbed again and pulled the knife toward me. The tail finally started to come apart.

I stuck my bear hand into the wound. It felt disgusting, but I held on fast. The scorpion screeched and flipped around, trying to shake me off, but I was holding on to its tail with my left bear puppet—no way was it gonna get me off.

I gathered mana into my right puppet and unleashed a bear cutter.

Bear cutter, bear cutter, bear cutter, bear cutter, bear cutter!

The scorpion shrieked some more. It froze for a moment, and that's when I cut off its tail all the way. The centrifugal force sent the tail—and me along with it—flying toward the wall.

It clicked its mouth and swiveled its eyes around to see its dismembered tail. Aww. You mad, big guy? Well, that's what we humans like to call payback.

Normally I would've gone in for a round two, but there was still the panel to worry about. No, I'd leave it at that.

It got up and charged at me with ferocious speed.

I braced my bear feet and leapt, nearly reaching the ceiling. The scorpion couldn't stop—it bashed itself head-on against the wall.

And now, finally, it was bleeding from the head.

I used earth magic to create a foothold near the ceiling for myself. The scorpion seemed even angrier it couldn't find me. Even if it did spot me up there, it didn't have a tail, so it wouldn't be able to sting me.

Time to put this thing to rest.

I made the foothold larger for myself, then created some bear gates—yes, plural. I lined them up and created ten in total. Then I used one to head to my bear house in Mileela.

It'd been a while since I'd been there, but I couldn't stay long.

I went outside and saw several new buildings outside. They'd progressed with development, but the land was bare near my bear house, as if they were avoiding it.

Wait, were they? Uh, no time to think of that. Taking care not to get seen, I ran down the hill, jumped over a fence, and—still making sure no one caught me—headed to the outskirts of town. From there, I ran off toward the waterfront to a secluded spot where I knew I wouldn't see anybody.

Maybe this was far enough? I headed close to where waves were lapping at the shoreline and dug a hole about two meters deep. Then I created one gate outside the hole and nine inside. Finally, I connected them to the gates in the lower level of the pyramid.

I went through the last gate outside the hole, went back to the pyramid, and looked down at the scorpion. Yep, it was still angry.

Time to cool that hothead down a bit.

As a finishing touch, I used magic to move the sand away from the gates so nothing was protecting them from the water.

The nine portals opened like floodgates, with huge bursts of water through them like waterfalls, all coming down on the scorpion.

It gets pretty dry in the desert. Staying hydrated is important, you know?

The scorpion's shrieks grew even louder, even angrier, but this was the end. I was going to drown it in the seawater.

I was worried it would try to crawl up the wall, but it only wandered around on the ground level below. Maybe it was too big to climb up like the others? If it tried, I would've smacked it back down, but it seemed like my worries were unnecessary.

The water level kept rising as more flooded in. I suppose I'd need to wait a little longer.

I summoned Kumayuru to keep watch for me. My bear nuzzled me right away. "Cwoon, cwoon, cwoon."

Wait, was Kumayuru scolding me?

"I'm sorry for worrying you."

"Cwoon."

"But it's all okay now."

"Cwoon."

I patted Kumayuru, hugged them, and they finally forgave me. I was happy that Kumayuru cared so much about me, but I hoped they understood how I felt too.

"Okay, I'm going to rest up for a bit. Let me know if the giant scorpion does anything,"

Kumayuru crooned happily now that they had a job to do. I leaned onto Kumayuru's belly and listened to the waterfall for a while as I rested. As I lay on my side, hugging Kumakyu, I felt more and more comfortable. The sound of the waterfall was pretty nice too.

Most importantly, Kumayuru was just super comfy.

For a long while, I was on the verge of nodding off, somewhere between reality and dreamland.

Huh? I opened my eyes to Kumayuru shaking me.

"Kumayuru?"

"Cwoon."

I could see that the waterfalls were still going, and I could hear them too. I was surprised I could nod off at all, considering all that noise. Maybe I was just super tired?

"Something happen?"

"Cwoon."

I got up and looked at the scorpion. There it lay at the bottom of the cavern, motionless. Maybe it was dead? I used my detection skill—the scorpion didn't have any kind of signal. I'd slayed it, then.

Once I thanked Kumayuru, I went to the beach through my gate to stop the flow of seawater. I made an earth wall to stop the water flowing in from the gates, closed them, and then withdrew the gates.

It was a chore, but I headed back to my bear house in Mileela and used the gate there to get back to the cave. Finally, I withdrew the gate in the cave too, and that was that.

The last issue was how to get the scorpion out, but I already thought about that.

I couldn't dig a hole to the side, since that'd take forever to drain. Plus, I'd need a place for all that water to go.

I decided to leave the seawater as it was and just get the scorpion out of there.

I used wind magic to whip up a bubble of air, an idea I came up with when I was trying to find a way to fight the kraken. It wouldn't have let me fight it properly, but I could've used this to dive underwater for a while.

Of course, I didn't use it back then—the air wouldn't last long, and I could only stay under as long as the air in the bubble held up. Pretty obvious stuff, because breathing used up the oxygen pretty quick. Still, it'd give me enough time to get the scorpion.

"And that's the plan," I told Kumayuru. "You wait here."

I headed into the water. The bubble sank down to the gigantic scorpion. Once I got there, I reached out and put the whole carcass in my bear storage.

Mission complete! I also collected the tail I'd cut off and the smaller scorpions from the start before returning to Kumayuru. Now I just needed to get back to Karina.

Except...I had no way out. The passageway I'd come through was underwater now. Well, if I didn't have an exit, I could just aim for the surface and dig. I decided to make a staircase for myself. I had made that tunnel between Mileela and Crimonia before, and it had been a piece of cake.

I dug through the rock face, plowing through the sand, and made my way upward. After a while, I finally made it to the surface. Wow, it was pretty bright out here! I pulled my hood low over my face to block out the sun.

I was finally out of that pyramid.

I ended up leaving the seawater down there. The water would probably be discovered later by adventurers. Researchers in the future would analyze the underground seawater, wondering where all the fish had come from... but none of that was my fault, okay?

KUMA
KUMA
KUMA
BEAR

340
Karina Worries about the Bear

SHE WAS AN ODD GIRL, the one who dressed like a bear. But she was also kind, cute, and didn't seem like an adventurer at all. By the king's command, she'd brought a mana gem all the way across the desert. Right when my heart felt like it could take no more, she'd offered me her hand.

Everyone else had told me it was impossible, but she accepted my quest with a smile. She fought off the sand wyrms and brought me close to the crystal panel.

And then she had said she would face the unfathomably large scorpion on her own.

I stared at the wall. Yuna and Kumayuru were beyond it. I didn't care about the panel. I just wanted her to come home safe and sound.

"Cwoon."

Kumakyu nuzzled me as I worried. I think the bear was trying to comfort me. I gave Kumakyu a pat on the head. Kumakyu was so kind, just like their owner.

"Karina, we need to go," said Mel as I stared at the wall.

We couldn't stay here forever, so we prepared to leave. I rode on Kumakyu. Though it pained me to leave this way, Kumakyu started to walk onward.

"Yuna will be all right," said Mel gently.

"But she's facing such a large monster all on her own."

"You saw her go up against that giant sand wyrm, didn't you? Yuna is actually a very powerful adventurer. I'm sure she'll be able to defeat it."

"And Kumayuru is with her," said Senia from the other side of me, "so she'll be fine." But that just meant that both she *and* Kumayuru might die.

If I were in her shoes, I would've been too scared to move a muscle.

"Most importantly," said Mel, "Yuna said that she wanted to fight it, so we need to respect her wishes."

"That's what it means to be an adventurer," said Senia.

Was it really? I would never be an adventurer, then.

"But I've never seen a scorpion that large before," said Touya from behind us. "Can she really handle it on her own? And there were tons of smaller ones swarming around too."

I agreed with him. I just couldn't believe Yuna was fighting all those monsters on her own. It didn't seem possible.

"Yuna took out those smaller ones easily," Senia pointed out.

"But in a small space like that? And you gotta remember, there's a giant scorpion hanging around. Last time, she faced them one at a time. If she went in there, they could've all swarmed her..."

"You have a point," Mel admitted, "but still..."

Did that mean that they couldn't be defeated?

"Yuna said she wanted to stay behind," Mel continued, "so I'm sure she has a strategy. She defeated the golem on her own too."

"I was surprised to hear about that," said Touya. "Everyone else had gone home to drink, and the next day, the little gal comes back from the mines claiming she slayed the golem."

"I haven't seen Yuna fight all too often, but anyone would admit she's defeated some formidable monsters. Her rank in the guild proves it. And if she finds out she can't fight it, she'll know when to scram."

She was fifteen, and yet she was supposed to be a C-rank adventurer already. That was amazing. And she'd even defeated a kraken!

"She wouldn't say *how* she defeated them, though," said Mel. "Maybe Kumayuru actually did it."

"In that case," said Touya, looking at Kumakyu, "maybe this bear is way strong too."

Was that powerful bear blessing Yuna was talking about from these bears themselves? Kumakyu crooned very cutely, like they knew we were talking about them.

"She's an odd one," Touya said finally.

"Ha ha, truly. Yuna is *such* an odd girl."

"We have no idea how powerful she really is."

Just like everyone said, she was very mysterious.

"But most adventurers haven't seen her fight, you know," Touya continued.

"She probably doesn't want anyone to see."

"She could've taken on those sand wyrms in the desert all by herself too," said Senia. "She tried hiding it by having us help."

Whoa. Was that really true...?

"She can defeat scorpions hiding in the sand, after all," said Touya. "If I had that kinda power, I'd show that off for sure."

From what they were saying, Yuna was super powerful. If she'd really defeated the kraken, she *had* to be really strong. Still, when I saw Yuna's cute bear clothes and her fighting the sand wyrms and scorpions, I just couldn't believe it.

"But aren't you curious about how she does it?" asked Touya. "And doesn't it worry you?"

"Of course it does. We did leave a sweet girl like her all alone."

"In that case, maybe we should've stuck around..."

"I want to see Yuna fight," said Senia.

"Then let's go and check it out," Touya agreed. He tried to turn around, but Jade stopped him.

"Our job is to take Karina outside. Senia, don't listen to Touya."

"See, now Jade's mad at us! This is all your fault, Touya."

"How's it my fault?"

The party started to laugh.

"Also, if we go back, we'd just hinder Yuna."

I wanted to go back, but Jade was right. I couldn't fight, so we'd just get in the way. We headed back to the surface, passing all the scorpions that Yuna had cleared out of the way for us, along with the bridge she'd made.

The trip back was so easy thanks to her. It reminded me just how powerful Yuna was.

We reached the pyramid's exit safely. When we headed outside, I realized that although I was still worried, some of the tension had disappeared. Maybe I'd been even more worried than I'd realized.

Jade and the others checked on the laggaroutes. I stayed at the entrance with Kumakyu and waited for Yuna to come back.

"Oh, Yuna..."

"Are you that worried?" As I said Yuna's name, Senia and Mel came up from behind me.

"Didn't you go to check the laggaroutes?" I asked.

"We're your guards. We need to be here if a monster attacks."

"Cwoon," Kumakyu crooned next to me.

"Hee hee, of course!" said Mel, giving Kumakyu a head pat. "We trust you, Kumakyu."

Apparently, Kumakyu wanted to show us that I didn't have to worry while they were around. I was so impressed! To think that Kumakyu could understand what we were saying...

"Ah, I'm so jealous of Yuna," said Mel. "I want some cute summons too!"

And so did I. It'd be *really* nice if they were bears like hers.

"Also, they have a connection with Yuna, so Kumakyu might know if something happens to her."

Oh! I remembered Yuna saying that. "Kumakyu, do you know how Yuna is?"

"Cwoon."

I didn't understand. But if something happened to Yuna, maybe Kumakyu would know.

While I waited near the entrance, Uragan came by. I looked around and saw that the others were harvesting the monsters. Apparently, that was what they'd been doing all this time.

"Ey! You're back?"

"For now."

"Did you find the thingamajig?"

"Umm, we did...but to be honest, we didn't retrieve it."

"How does that happen, eh?"

Just like Mel said, we had found it, but we hadn't been able to actually get it back.

"What does that mean?" Uragan repeated.

"Apparently...a monster ate it?"

"Then just slay the thing," he said with a shrug. "You just ran all the way back here?"

"Don't be ridiculous," said Jade. He'd come back from the laggaroutes, and now he was explaining the whole situation. "It was a giant scorpion."

"A giant *what* now?"

"You must have heard the stories. Sometimes giant monsters appear."

"It was super huge!" Mel held out her arms and tried to show him. It had been even bigger than that, though.

251

"You're pulling my leg, right?"

"You wouldn't expect it, right? But it's all true."

"In that case, did you give up? That why you guys are back?"

Mel shook her head. "Yuna stayed behind on her own to fight it."

"Hey, wait a sec... You left her all alone?!" Uragan's eyes went wide.

"Yes," Mel said.

"Seriously?!" Uragan angrily grabbed her by the collar.

At once, Senia put her knife to his throat. "Let her go."

"Damn it!" Uragan threw Mel aside.

Fighting was supposed to be bad, after all.

"I thought you guys were better than that," Uragan fumed. "No matter how strong that girl is, you shouldn't have left her alone with monsters."

"Yuna said she wanted to stay behind, so we couldn't do anything about it."

"We wanted to stop her too," Touya said. "But Yuna said she was going to fight them alone, so that was that."

I'd wanted to stop her as well, but I hadn't been able to.

"Did she really defeat the black viper and tiger wolves on her own?" asked Uragan.

"You know about that?"

"One of my party members knows about her. He told

me some. I laughed at first," Uragan said. "He kept telling me she was too dangerous to get near and to steer clear. And then he kept spouting stuff that sounded like a joke when I asked him why. I was surprised when she was there after we took on this quest. But it seemed like you guys trust her, and then I saw her slay that giant wyrm and stuff, so now I know it's true. Even after seeing it with my own eyes, I can still barely believe how strong she is." He laughed.

"Then what can we do if Yuna says she's going to fight the monsters?"

"True enough, but you didn't have to come all the way back here," said Uragan. "Should've stayed, just in case. Common sense."

"Ha ha." Now it was Mel's turn to laugh.

"'Scuse me, something funny about what I said?"

"Well, I didn't think you'd be so worried about her."

"Hmph! Ain't like that."

Everyone laughed as though there was something funny about what Uragan said.

Yes, he was scary the first time we met at the guild. But he remembered who I was and apologized when I saw him at my house. I thought it might've been because I was the lord's daughter, but maybe he was just a kind person...even if he had a scary face.

253

"So, what're you lot doing now?"

"We're waiting for Yuna."

"Then I take it you have nothing to do," said Uragan. "You can help with the harvest." He pointed behind him with his thumb. Uragan's party members were out on the sands, working. "It'd help if we had a mage around. 'Course, we'd recalculate how much you get too."

Jade and Mel looked at each other before nodding.

"All right. I'll head over. Senia, you keep an eye on Karina."

"You've got it," Senia answered, then hugged Kumakyu.

Mel looked fed up, but Jade and Touya followed her to do the harvesting work.

"Kumakyu, let us know if anything happens to Yuna."

"Cwoon!"

I just hoped that Yuna would come back safe and sound.

341
The Bear Obtains the Crystal Panel

LOOKED AROUND when I got to the surface. "Uh, where am I?"

I spun all the way around and found the pyramid behind me. I didn't see the entrance, though. After checking the bear map, I realized I'd emerged *behind* the pyramid.

I sealed up the opening I came out of and rode Kumayuru toward the front of the pyramid. As I made my way around the pyramid to the entrance, I saw something fast and white heading right for me. It was a bear—no, it was Kumakyu!

No, it was Karina *on* Kumakyu, raising up a dust storm behind them as they rushed over. I could see that Karina was trying her darndest not to fall off. She wouldn't fall even if she didn't hold on tight, but she wasn't thinking about that right now.

I got off Kumayuru. At the rate they were going, my bears would've run right into each other!

"Kumakyu, stop, stop, halt right there!"

Kumakyu slowed down and nuzzled me. "Cwoon, cwoon!"

"Kumakyu, I'm back." I gave my bear scritches under their chin and around their face. Kumakyu seemed happy about that. "Did you protect Karina while I was gone? Thank you, Kumakyu."

"Cwoon."

As I was praising my bear, Karina's face popped up from behind. She was still holding on for dear life.

"Y-Yuna?!" Karina got off and held on to me. "Yuna, you're safe! I was so worried about you."

"Cwoon." Not to be outdone, Kumakyu nuzzled me some more. Karina also came to me.

"Calm down, you two."

"Yuna!"

"Cwoon."

I couldn't keep standing and fell right over. I could've pushed them back, but I couldn't do that to Karina and Kumakyu.

When I fell, they piled on me. Kumayuru was looking at me too.

"Kumayuru, heeelllp meee!"

Kumayuru crooned at me but didn't come to my aid. Meanie. Anyway, I pushed past the two and stood up again. Yeah, they both were worried for sure.

"I'm so glad you're safe." Karina had tears in her eyes.

As I stroked her hair to comfort her, Jade and the others arrived on laggaroutes.

"Yuna?!"

"Kumakyu started running over suddenly, so we were trying to figure out what had happened."

"I was so surprised when Kumakyu took off."

Mel and Senia were with Jade. I saw no sign of Touya.

"Um, well, I'm back!" I offered.

"Why are you outside, Yuna?" asked Jade. "We were waiting for you at the entrance."

"It was too much work to go back the way I came, so I used a teensy bit of magic to dig a hole, and I ended up here."

"A teensy bit, you say?"

Mel and the others looked flabbergasted. I felt like we'd had this conversation before.

"So, did you defeat the scorpions?"

"Pretty much."

They all looked surprised again.

"So...I actually wanted your help," I said. "Could you do the harvesting for me? And I'll give you a thank-you, of course."

I couldn't harvest, after all, and it wasn't like I could head home to Crimonia to ask Fina to do it either. I could've gone back to the town and asked Barlimer to find me someone, but then they'd see the scorpion and it would be a whole *thing*. If that was the case, I figured I might as well have Jade's party do it. They'd already seen the monster, after all.

"You don't need to give us anything for it. Getting experience harvesting one of those monsters is enough for us."

"Even if we do get experience harvesting one of these, we might never harvest one again. It's a once-in-a-lifetime experience."

They happily agreed to my proposal.

We headed back to the pyramid's entrance for the harvesting. When I tried to get back on Kumayuru, Kumakyu gave me a sad croon.

Kumakyu wasn't leaving my side. My bear wanted me to ride them.

"Kumakyu was okay at first," Karina told me. "But then they started to miss you."

I'd asked Kumakyu to guard Karina, after all, so I hadn't ridden on them in a while.

"Karina, would you be okay with riding on Kumayuru?"

"Y-yes, I can. Thank you, Kumayuru."

"Cwoon." Kumayuru did as I said and let Karina on.

I was glad Kumayuru was listening. Even if both of them wanted me to ride them, there was only one of me, after all.

My bears both listened to me, which was good. When I got onto Kumakyu, my bear happily burst into a run.

"P-please wait." Karina followed behind on Kumayuru, with Jade and the others following after. Once we got to the pyramid's entrance, we found Touya standing there all by his lonesome.

"How could you? You left me behind!"

"Well, what were we going to do when Kumakyu ran off like that?"

"You shouldn't have been sleeping in the first place."

Mel and Senia were being pretty mean to him. Then again, why had he been sleeping while I was fighting? Then again *again*, I was sleeping earlier myself, but I wasn't about to admit that.

"I couldn't help it. I was tired from all the harvesting."

"Everyone was!"

"Jade!" Touya looked to the party leader for help.

"Sorry. I forgot about you too."

"Jaaade!" Touya's wail echoed through the desert.

Anyway, I decided that was enough of Touya and looked around. "Uh, where are Uragan and the rest of them?" I looked around, but I didn't see Uragan or the others.

"They headed back to town after the harvesting was over. They wanted to wait for you at first, but they were so tired that we had them go back."

"We helped them too," Touya added. So *that* was why he'd been tired enough to sleep in the desert.

He also fought plenty of monsters, so maybe he was so amped up that he crashed. Thinking about it that way, I was impressed by Jade and the others.

"Well, let's finish harvesting and then head back too." I pulled the scorpion out of my bear storage.

"You really did beat the thing, huh?"

"Wow, it really is massive."

They all gathered around the scorpion.

"No tail, though. You cut it off?"

"I see traces of a knife cutting the back too," said Senia from atop of the scorpion.

But even that had barely damaged the thing.

"What was the finishing blow, though?"

"The tail, I'm guessing?"

"If you could kill it just by doing that, it wouldn't be difficult to fight."

"Then how did you slay it?"

They all turned to look at me.

"I just, y'know. Dealt with it real quick."

"..."

They were all silent, boring holes into me with their stares. I couldn't exactly tell them I drowned it with seawater via bear gate. Fortunately, putting it into the bear storage hadn't brought any of the seawater with it, so it wasn't wet or anything. Still, there was a chance there was still water inside of it.

Imagining the bear god that had (probably) brought me into this world, I prayed that none would come out... not that I really thought it would work.

"You really managed to beat this giant monster, Yuna..." Karina cautiously approached and touched the scorpion. I kinda felt like teasing her when I saw that.

I quietly snuck up behind her, got right up to her ear, and went "Boo!"

"Eek!" Karina yelped and fell on her behind.

"Are you okay?"

"Y-Yuna..." She looked close to crying as she stared up at me beseechingly.

Maybe I'd overdone it. "Sorry."

"You're a big meanie, Yuna," Karina replied. "You scared me so much."

"Sorry! I'm really sorry! I saw you so hesitant to touch it, and you were so cute! I couldn't help it!"

"You totally could have helped it! You really shocked me. I thought I was going to die right then and there."

"Oh no," I said quietly. "Did you pee a little or something?"

Karina turned bright red right in front of my eyes. "O-of course I didn't! I don't want anything to do with you anymore!"

I guess I made her angry. I was only kidding around, but I knew I really blew it.

"Karina, I'm sorry. You're just so cute..."

"You're one to say that in that outfit," Karina harrumphed without bothering to turn around and face me.

I really didn't know how to deal with ten-year-olds. What was I like at ten? I tried to remember. Hmm, I think I was pretty cute, right? No, seriously, I was.

"Could we get started on the harvesting soon?" Jade and the others didn't look too impressed with our shenanigans.

"I'm so sorry."

"Sorry..."

Karina and I apologized, bobbing our heads a little for good show.

"So, we just need to get whatever it is you're looking for out, right?" asked Jade. "Karina, where is it?"

Karina approached the scorpion, made a loop around it, and then stopped. "Around here."

It was toward the back, near the tail.

"Here? I guess we'll need to get the shell off. Touya, let's get it done."

A scorpion's shell was connected the same way as a crab's was, or like a shrimp's when you flipped over the tail. They all had gaps where the shell met the body.

Jade ordered everyone to help him take the second part of the shell off from the back. He and Touya produced knives that they stuck into the seam of the scorpion.

"It's pretty sturdy."

"Senia, Mel, a little help here?"

"If we must."

All four of them worked together to pull off part of the shell. Looking at it again, it was pretty thick. Jade dug into the spot that Karina told him to, and soon he unearthed a blue crystal panel.

"This it, Karina?"

"Y-yes!" She happily ran over and took it.

Mel cleaned it off using magic, of course. I was glad that there wasn't any seawater around too, because I had no idea how I would've explained that away.

"All right, quest complete!" said Mel.

"This shell sure is tough," Touya said as he knocked on it.

"You're right. It's harder than iron. Might make a great piece of armor."

In the game, I had definitely made armor out of monster parts without a second thought. But looking at a huge monster piece in front of me, I wondered how anyone could turn this stuff into armor. Still, they kept talking about it...

"Right. I don't like wearing protectors, so I'd prefer gauntlets."

"And it's pretty light, which is nice."

"Go ahead and take the shell you pulled off," I told them.

"Are you sure?!" Touya seemed super happy, maybe more so than Jade.

I really didn't need it.

"No, no, we can't accept this," Jade said. "You fought it, Yuna."

"Jade, c'mon! The gal's saying she's gifting it to us," said Touya. Man, he really wanted this.

"Then...let's call it hush money," I said.

"Hush money?"

"I'd prefer it if you didn't spread word of this around."

"You're not reporting it to the guild?"

"It'll be a pain," I said, "so I'm not planning on it."

"I don't get it," said Touya. "If I were you, I wouldn't be able to *stop* telling people about it."

"You don't need to bribe us to keep quiet, Yuna. If that's what you want, we won't tell anyone."

"Yeah, we won't."

Everyone looked at Touya.

"Err, totally! I mean, even if you didn't give me that shell, my lips would be sealed..."

Uh...for some reason I really felt like I couldn't trust Touya's words there, even though everyone else seemed perfectly trustworthy.

Jade was thinking something over. "If you want to stop anyone from talking, you'll need to get Uragan's party too."

"Wait, they know I was fighting the scorpion?"

"Yeah. They asked where you were, so we told them."

I should've hushed them up before letting them go. If Uragan knew, I'd need to keep his whole party quiet too. It'd be bad if they started rumors.

"We'll figure that when we get back to town."

I stored everything, including the bits of shell, in my bear storage. Now all we needed to do was swap the gem, but the sun was already sinking.

First, we'd go report to Barlimer.

KUMA
KUMA
KUMA
BEAR

342
The Bear Reports to Barlimer

ONCE WE WERE BACK at the mansion, Lasa welcomed us back.

"We're home, Lasa," Karina said.

"Lady Karina...you've made it back safely." Lasa gave Karina a hug. After all, she was a ten-year-old who'd gone with a bunch of adventurers to a place crawling with monsters. Just about anybody would be worried. Lasa looked like a concerned older sister as she hugged Karina.

"Lasa, I can't breathe," Karina said.

"I'm very sorry. The adventurers who came earlier talked to us, and I was so very worried."

Who had come earlier? Oh, maybe she meant Uragan's party.

"I was okay with everyone there," Karina insisted.

"But there were so many sand wyrms, they lost count," said Lasa. "And there was a huge sand wyrm too. I almost fainted from shock when they told me."

Uragan had *definitely* stopped by to make a report, then.

"Yeah. But Yuna and the others slayed them, so I was okay."

"Indeed, I heard that you all worked together."

"Yuna did most of the work, though."

Mel and the others smiled slightly as they listened.

Uragan and the others had worked pretty hard fighting the wyrms I'd dug up. Only Jade's party and Uragan himself had been able to keep up at the end. They'd also done the wyrm harvesting, which had been a huge help.

"Yuna was so cool too," said Karina. "She beat a wyrm this big." Karina held up her arms to demonstrate. Then she posed like she was firing off a spell. I guess she was copying me? Did I really look like that in action?

"Ha ha, well, that is amazing."

"Oh, Lasa, you don't believe it, do you? But it's true! The wyrm was this big!"

"Hee hee, I do believe it. I heard from the other adventurers."

"Then why are you laughing?"

Probably because Karina looked adorable as she tried to explain it all. Karina pouted when Lasa smiled.

But then Jade interrupted, somewhat apologetically, "Karina, we need to make our report to Barlimer."

"I'm sorry," said Lasa.

"Me too," said Karina. "Lasa, I'll tell you more later."

Lasa took us to his office. Inside, Barlimer gave us a surprised look.

"Karina?!"

"I'm back, Father." Karina ran to him as soon as she got to the room.

"Karina, you're not hurt, are you?"

He tried to hug her, but then his face twisted in pain.

"Father!"

"It's fine. Just a little sting. Such a pity that I can't hug my own dear daughter."

"You shouldn't push yourself while you're hurt," said Karina. "You can hug me after you're better."

"Then I'll need to heal sooner rather than later."

Barlimer stroked Karina's hair instead. Then he looked over at the rest of us.

"I received a report from the other adventurers. I hear that you all defeated a horde of sand wyrms, including one colossal wyrm. You slew all the monsters near the pyramid, even though it wasn't part of the quest. I don't know how to thank you all. We will, of course, give you additional compensation for all of this."

"Don't worr—" I started to say.

"Thank you very much," said Jade quickly.

"Yes!" Touya said. "Mithril sword, here I come." Mel and Senia seemed happy too.

That sure was close. I almost turned him down! Jade was just replying as any adventurer would—who wouldn't take a reward for all that hard work?

If I had come back alone, I would've just said, "Don't worry about it," or, "Those monsters just happened to be in the way, is all." Something like that. I almost stopped them from getting their extra pay.

"I also heard that there were scorpions in the lower level and the object was inside of one of them. Is that true? Uragan told me that you would have more details." Barlimer sounded anxious.

Since Uragan only knew what Jade had told him, Barlimer had to press us for more information.

"Father, it's all true, but we are fine. Yuna fought the giant scorpion and got the panel back." Karina pulled the panel out of her item bag and handed it over.

"Thank you, everyone," Barlimer said.

"Well, it's not really everyone you should be thanking," said Mel. "Yuna did all the work."

The other adventurers nodded. "We really didn't do much."

They really didn't need to say all that, though. Mel and the rest of the party had helped me out tons. Karina seemed to understand that, so she started speaking up for them.

"That's not true at all," she said. "Yes, Yuna fought the big scorpion, but Mel and Senia stayed with me and protected me. Touya was behind me too, keeping me safe, and Jade was up front to fight off any monsters. They all made sure that I could get to the underground level."

"Ah ha ha! Oh, Karina, thank you," said Mel. "You have no idea how happy I am to hear you say that."

"It's just as Karina has said," Barlimer replied. "You all contributed. I'd like to thank you again. You have my deepest gratitude. Please, come and have dinner with us. We will prepare you a meal."

"Woo-hoo!" Touya sure seemed happy.

Mel elbowed him in the ribs. "Thank you," she said, representing everyone.

Barlimer nodded. "Please rest until dinner is ready."

With that, Jade's party thanked him and left the room.

"Karina," Barlimer called to his daughter just as the two of us were about to leave the room.

She slowly approached him. "Father?"

"Please take this," he said.

"But this is..." she trailed off.

"I'm sorry, Karina, but you'll need to go into the pyramid again."

Right, of course. Only Karina and Norris could use the panel, along with their mom, Listiel. Listiel couldn't go since she was pregnant, and Norris was much younger than Karina, so he was out too. Karina was the only one who could go into the pyramid right now.

She stared carefully at the panel. Then she slowly reached out to take it.

"Yes, Father...I understand," she said. "I'll take it."

She cradled it preciously in her hands.

Once we were done talking with Barlimer, we headed over to Uragan and the rest of his party, who had gotten back earlier. In one of the large rooms within the estate, they were lounging on sofas and chairs, relaxing.

One of them let out a frightened whisper. "The bear's back..."

Uhh...but I hadn't done anything to him?

"Looks like you made it back in one piece," said Uragan.

"We just came back from reporting to Barlimer," I said. "I didn't know you were still here."

"When we came back, he told us to refresh ourselves in this room. Then he said that he wanted us to stick around to check in on you guys if you didn't return."

Right, he wanted someone around to make sure his daughter made it back safely. And it was a lot easier getting Uragan to check up on her than to go through the guild again.

"Hey, you beat that giant scorpion that Jade and crew talked about?"

"Of course she did," said Mel proudly, as though she herself did it. Not that I minded.

"So the rumors are true, then?"

"Rumors? What rumors?"

"That's for us to know," said Uragan.

I didn't mind rumors about other people, but I hated rumors about me going around. They were probably all about that bear stuff, and maybe that *other* bear stuff, along with the other, *other* bear stuff.

"Ah, right. Yuna was asking about whether you could keep her battling the scorpion a secret," Jade said in my place.

"Why would she want that?"

"She, uh..." Jade coughed. "She wants to...keep a low profile?"

The whole room stared at me.

Yeah, yeah. I knew what they all wanted to say, but standing out because I was dressed as a bear was totally different from standing out because I took down a giant monster.

If rumors spread, I wouldn't know what to do! People might start asking me to do a bunch of exhausting tasks for them and stuff. I didn't mind it when I was choosing to involve myself, but it was another matter when people were pushing work on me.

Uragan stared right at me and burst into laughter. "Ah ha ha ha!" He just laughed and laughed, and his party started chiming in (save for one guy).

C'mon, did he need to crack up at me to my face like that?

"Everyone, you've gotta stop laughing!" the one guy said. "Never make fun of her! Knock it off!"

Um, whoa...that one was downright terrified of me.

"Ah, right. You guys, you knock it off. Still, you took the thing down, huh? You really are one ridiculous girl. I don't mind keeping silent about it."

"You don't?"

"Yeah, just give me a look at that scorpion. I'm an adventurer too. I'd like to see how big this thing was if it made Jade's party run away."

"We didn't exactly run from it. We just did what Yuna asked."

"Same thing," said Uragan. "If you really did slay a monster as big as that, I'd like to see it, as a fellow adventurer."

This was a weird trade. He'd tell people if I didn't show him the scorpion. Then again, who would believe him if he blabbed? Maybe people from Crimonia would. Yeah, all in all, it'd be easier to just show him.

I looked at Jade, who didn't say anything. It seemed like he was leaving the decision entirely up to me.

"Okay, I'll show it to you, so you better keep it under wraps. If you tell anybody, you might end up like *him*," I said, pointing at the terrified adventurer for good measure. (I didn't remember the guy, though. Like, at all.)

"I'll never tell anybody," he said, faster than anyone else in the room.

Maybe he was one of the guys I beat up in Crimonia when I first arrived? To be blunt, I couldn't remember any of the faces I'd punched.

"Yeah, all right, you got a promise. You all better keep to your word too," said Uragan, and everyone nodded along.

"But where should we go for you to see it?" I asked. This thing was pretty big, and I didn't want anyone else to see it either. There weren't a lot of places that'd work.

"Would the back garden do?" Karina proposed. She had been silent up until that moment. "It's large, so I think it should be good."

KUMA
KUMA
KUMA
BEAR

The Bear Makes a Deal

SINCE I WAS GOING to show the scorpion to Uragan's party, we needed permission from Barlimer to use the back garden. Karina had sulked a little bit already about giving us the okay, but we really needed to make sure to ask the owner of the house. He allowed it, fortunately, so we headed off to the back garden.

It was pretty big. Very fitting for the lord of the town.

Both Jade's and Uragan's parties had gathered in the garden. Karina and Barlimer had also come in order to observe.

"Okay, move back a little," I warned everyone as I produced the scorpion from my bear storage.

THUD!

Unlike a normal scorpion, the thing was gigantic and tar black. I heard gasps from Uragan's party and Barlimer.

"That's huge. To think you managed to slay this..."

"Whoa."

Uragan's party seemed impressed. And honestly? The scorpion looked even bigger than before, somehow. A normal scorpion was already big in my eyes, so this thing was ginormous.

Jade's party, on the other hand, didn't show as much surprise. They had already seen it.

"And the panel was in this thing, was it?" murmured Barlimer.

"Yuna said that she was going to fight it, so I was so worried," said Karina. "I was so, so, *so* scared, right up until Yuna came back. No matter how long we waited, she hadn't returned."

That was because I'd taken a nap on my nice, fluffy mattress, also known as Kumayuru.

"And then she came back like nothing had happened."

"Would you have preferred she come back battered and injured?" Barlimer asked gently.

"I-I didn't mean it like that..."

"Then you should just be happy she made it back in the first place. I'm sure you were very worried, but Yuna risked her life to fight this giant scorpion. Remember to think about who she fought it for...who she was risking her very life for."

"Father..."

He was lecturing her, albeit gently. "I think you can see how dangerous fighting this monster was based on its size, yes?"

"I do..." she said.

Uh, I kind of felt like this was being blown out of proportion. Yeah, I fought the monster for a bit, but in the end, I just decided to drown it and take a nap on Kumayuru.

"Yuna is doing her best to pretend nothing happened in order to keep you from feeling worried," said Barlimer.

That wasn't true. While she was worrying, I was just catching some Zs.

I couldn't stand it anymore—listening to Barlimer say all that stuff. I just felt guiltier and guiltier with every word, so I scooted away from them a little. I headed over to Jade's party.

As for Uragan's group, they were prowling around the scorpion and checking it out.

"I've never even *seen* a scorpion as big as this before."

"I've heard stories, but I didn't think they were real."

Uragan tried touching it. "I can't believe you killed this thing. Even seeing it right in front of me, it's hard to swallow. Still...this proves it. I understand now why you trust that bear girl so much."

"Well, we can't *not* trust her, not after what we've seen. Even I didn't think Yuna would be this strong when I first saw her."

"She stopped my arm without breaking a sweat too," said Uragan.

Right, he'd tried to push Karina away when we first met.

"Don't look at me like that," said Uragan. "You'll give me a fright. I was tired back then since we'd only just got into town. And then I had the little girl pestering me..."

"Ohhh..." Karina made an apologetic sound as she listened in.

"Being tired is no excuse for pushing kids around."

"That's what I'm apologizing for," he said, then looked to Karina.

"You already apologized," said Karina, "so it doesn't bother me anymore."

"Now then," said Uragan, looking at the part of the scorpion they'd peeled off to reach the panel, "why is the shell missing over here?"

"We started harvesting from it and pulled the lost object from there," I said.

"And the tail?"

"Seems like Yuna cut it off," Mel explained before I could. Nice and succinct.

Now Uragan was touching the scorpion's shell and tapping it lightly. "Very sturdy. Would make a good armor."

"Aw man, I was thinking the same thing!" said Touya.

"And scorpion shell is heat resistant too. A big boss scorpion like this must have even more potent properties than a normal one."

Actually, I'd never encountered a fire-type monster before. Did they usually appear near volcanoes and such? I'd seen snowmin and snow wolves in the mountains, so fire monsters seemed like a real possibility. Maybe I'd try exploring sometime. I'd be fine near volcanoes with my bear gear...if, y'know, I could actually find a volcano.

"Miss, are you going to make any armor...?" Uragan glanced at me, shook his head, and answered his own question. "Ah, but you wouldn't."

I didn't plan to make any, but he shouldn't have assumed either. Also, why'd he say it like that, with that odd look on his face? If he had something to say, I wish he'd just say it to me straight. Then again, maybe he just didn't want to say anything worthy of a good old bear punch.

"Yuna doesn't need any because of her current clothes. She wouldn't look good in armor like any other adventurer," Mel was trying to vouch for me, but that didn't quite sound like praise. To be honest, it almost sounded like she was making fun of me.

Still, if I didn't have my bear gear, maybe I would have been making myself gear from monsters I'd slain, like I did in my game...

"If you're not reporting this to the guild, what're you doing about the monster?" asked Uragan.

"I don't really have plans for it," I said. "I was thinking of just having someone I know harvest from it, then I was going to put it in my item bag."

"You're not going to sell it?"

"It'd attract too much attention. I mean, if I ever really need the money, sure, but..."

Besides, I already had all those profits from my shops in Crimonia and the tunnel tolls. On top of that, there was all that money I had saved up from my old world. I didn't need any cash right now, so I didn't need to sell the scorpion.

"Then would you sell some of it to me?"

"You want some of it?"

"What adventurer wouldn't? It's very rare that anybody finds material like this. Perfect for armor. Gotta seize any opportunity you got, or rue the day you didn't."

"I suppose you're right," said Jade. "It's plenty tough and much lighter than any iron, so now's the time to go for it."

"Jade," I said, "how much would something like this normally go for?"

"I'm not sure. Like Uragan said, you don't come across this stuff often, so there's not really a market rate."

"Then I wouldn't know what to sell it for. Would it be, say, twice as much as a normal scorpion?"

"That's way too cheap. A scorpion like this is way harder to slay than a couple of measly little ones." Jade seemed appalled by my suggestion.

Ugh, but pricing stuff is such a chore.

"Then how about we say it'll be the equivalent of hush money? You can take what you want for free."

"..."

"..."

Everyone, and I mean everyone, was giving me positively *mortified* looks now. What could I say? It really was a chore! What else was I supposed to do?

Going to either the Adventurer Guild or the Merchant Guild would make it a whole thing, and I couldn't just dismiss people who really wanted the materials. I mean, I'd dismiss adventurers I didn't know personally, but...

Still, I fought alongside Uragan's party today. Don't get me wrong—I'd never propose anything like this if they'd skipped out on the sand wyrm slaying or harvesting work. But they were working hard in the heat, which is why I was proposing this to Uragan in the first place.

"Then how about a trade?" Uragan asked.

"A trade?"

"Yeah, you can have this." Uragan produced three cloth bags from his item bag.

What were they? Did they have money in them?

"Three hundred mana gems from the sand wyrms we slew today. I'll trade these for a piece of the shell. And we'll keep mum about you slaying the scorpion too, of course."

Three hundred mana gems, huh? Did I even have a use for them? Then again, if they were trading these and offering silence about the whole scorpion-slaying business, then this wasn't a bad deal.

"I don't really mind. You're sure, though?"

"We can slay as many sand wyrms as we want. It's just a matter of how much time we wanna put in," Uragan said. "But as for scorpion parts, well, we wouldn't be able to get anything like this that easily even if we wanted to. To be blunt, this is a better deal for us. I'm pretty sure you'd get a whole lotta coin no matter where you sold this thing."

"Hey, don't move forward with the deal without letting us have a say," Touya butted in. "Some of those mana gems are ours too."

"You want a piece of the shell as well, don't you?"

"Well, yeah..."

"Then we trade the shell for the mana gems. You'll get your share, of course. We've got more people, so we'll get a little more, but we also were supposed to get a larger share of the gems, so I'm sure you'd be fine with that."

Yeah, I hadn't thought about how the gems were going to be split. Uragan's party had negotiated for more of them, that was true.

Jade's party thought it over.

"Yuna, are you sure you're okay with this?" he asked.

"Yeah. As long as they keep their promise."

Personally, the gems might have been better than money for me. I could just sell them if I needed the cash.

"Then it's a deal."

I took the bag of mana gems. "In that case, I guess you can have the shell you already harvested from the scorpion." I pulled that piece of shell out of my bear storage.

"Wait, but that's huge!"

It was just a piece of the shell, but it was still several times bigger than my bears.

"I don't want to deal with it, so you can divide it up between yourselves. If there's extra, just do what you'd like with it."

"Jade..." Uragan looked at the other party leader. Jade shook his head. Then Uragan sighed.

What was with those looks on their faces?

"All right, then we'll take it!" said Uragan. "You're really fine with this, right? No takebacks!"

"Yeah. Just don't fight over it or anything."

"Ey, Jade, you take this. We'll make armor in the capital. If there's extra left over after that, we halve it. Good with you?"

"Just don't tell anyone I gave it to you," I reminded him. I didn't want to deal with any pesky adventurers or merchants trying to get me to sell some shell.

"I know."

Jade put the shell into his item bag. I wondered how large his bag was. He hadn't missed a beat putting that thing away, so it must've been pretty big.

"Yuna, since you likely don't know this, the pincers and tail are the most valuable parts. Don't go around selling or giving those out for nothing."

"Then do you want the pincers too?"

"As per my last statement, don't go around doing stuff like that. Remember, I did warn you," Jade told me, so I took it to heart.

Still, it wasn't like I needed either of them. Not when I had my bear gear.

344
The Bear Chants the Itty-Bitty Spell

THE DEAL WENT WELL, so we headed back inside. Jade and Uragan's parties talking all the while about what armor they would make with their scorpion shell.

Soon enough, Lasa was calling us for dinner.

"Yuna, please sit over here." Karina latched on to my bear puppet and took me to the seat next to her.

"The food all looks really good." All kinds of dishes lined the table. Everything looked delicious.

"Yes," said Karina. "I'm very hungry, so I'm excited to eat too." She smiled and touched her tummy. It was pretty cute! If I did the same thing, though, it would look like I was holding my gigantic belly.

Everyone took their seats, and Barlimer thanked everyone one more time. "Ladies and gentlemen, I am incredibly grateful that you took on such a trying quest. You have my deepest gratitude for successfully finding the missing object."

"All in a day's work," said Uragan. "Don't worry about it. We were happy to take the quest so long as we were getting paid."

"Yuna really did most of the work," Mel added.

Uragan continued, "So, our job's done then?"

"Yes. I'll give the guild your additional pay, so please remember to collect it."

Everyone had already known about the additional pay, but they were still ecstatic to hear it again.

Since they couldn't know about the crystal panel or the water gem, their jobs were done. Jade's party would leave Dezelt as soon as they could find an escort job to Kars. They were going with Uragan to the capital to make armor from the scorpion.

Huh. I guess they'd have matching armor. That was kind of a funny thought.

Mel invited me to go with them, but I had something else I needed to do here. I had to turn her down.

"Well then, let's meet again at the capital or Crimonia."

If we did run into each other at the capital, it'd probably be at the guild. But...I didn't really want to go to the guild in the capital much. Unlike Crimonia, I still got a lot of curious stares. In Crimonia, sometimes a few people would watch me, but none of them would go out of their way to outright stare.

While I was talking to Mel, Karina began to appear a little sullen. But she smiled when she noticed I was looking at her.

Was something the matter? When I asked, she just said, "It's nothing."

Maybe she was worried about tomorrow.

We were in the middle of the dinner now. Since the food was all fancy and lavish, a lot of the dishes were fragrant from the spices. There wasn't a thing to complain about when it came to their taste. The only issue was that Lasa had made a mistake with how much she made. All the adventurers were eating and eating and eating. Since they were absolutely ravenous, the food was disappearing rapidly. The guys' stomachs were black holes.

She served even more food, but Uragan's party still looked peckish. Mel and Senia were appalled as they watched. Karina and I were too, of course.

There'd been so much food at first! The guys were eating way too much. I wish they'd be more considerate and hold back a little—I mean, we were in the lord of the town's house, for goodness' sake! It wasn't like I was one to talk though, considering I wasn't dressed properly and was never super formal, not even when I talked to the king. Actually, I could've easily been accused of being disrespectful. Not that I would've visited the castle again if he'd said that.

Eventually, the meal ended, and Jade's party headed back to their inn. I was going to stay in one of Barlimer's guest rooms, so I stuck around at the estate.

"Yuna, give my regards to Kumayuru and Kumakyu," Mel told me.

"Let us hug your bears again," Senia said.

They said their goodbyes to me, then all the guys gathered a little farther away.

"All right, let's go out for a drink!"

"But we're splitting the bill."

"You're telling me that Jade, the high and mighty C-rank adventurer, is making us little D-rankers pay?"

"You're no rookies, and I'm not gonna treat a bunch of grizzled guys like you."

It seemed like they were going out for another round, then. I couldn't believe how much they could fit into their stomachs. Where did it all go? I was already so stuffed that my stomach hurt. Weird how just watching other people pig out makes you feel a little more full too. I really needed to avoid eating with gluttons in the future.

Still, that got me wondering...what made someone a rookie adventurer? If they were just someone with less than a year of experience, that made me one. Then again, nobody would've called a C-rank a rookie.

I left everyone and headed back to the room where I was staying. Once I plopped down onto my bed, I summoned my bears in their cub forms. Then I changed into my white bear clothes to sleep.

"Kumakyu, come over here!" I called my bear over so we could cuddle as we slept, just like I promised. Kumakyu looked giddy with excitement when I called them and as they clambered over. My bedclothes matched my bear.

"I'm sorry we didn't spend much time together today. And thank you for protecting Karina."

I made sure Kumakyu knew how grateful and sorry I was. Then I burrowed into the covers with Kumakyu cradled to my chest. Kumayuru didn't even make a fuss about Kumakyu and just curled up next to me.

"Goodnight, Kumayuru." I reached out to pat Kumayuru. Kumayuru crooned in response. I drifted off into sleep with Kumakyu's warmth up against my chest.

When I woke the next morning, I saw Kumakyu sleeping blissfully on my arm. Kumakyu must've stayed in my arms all night...or maybe I just hadn't let go. Well, I couldn't know what happened in my sleep. I was just glad I hadn't kicked Kumakyu away or something, since I would've felt bad.

I changed into my black bear clothes and recalled both my bears.

"Yuna, I am counting on you," Barlimer said after breakfast, when he tasked me with swapping the mana gems. Karina and I headed off to the pyramid in order to finally finish the job.

It was nice out today. Like yesterday, Karina had a hood on over her mantle that blocked the sun. She was riding Kumayuru today—basically, we were switching out.

The desert was quiet. Unlike yesterday, I didn't see any sand wyrms. Guess the large one had gathered them together. Still, why had a giant sand wyrm appeared in the first place? Was it a coincidence, or did it have something to do with the mana gem? I didn't know how monsters thought, so I had no idea.

We arrived at the pyramid safely and then headed right in and made our way to the labyrinth entrances without a break.

When I looked up, I saw those walls again all around us, covered with entrances.

"Which one do we use?" I asked Karina as I stared at all the openings. I peeked into one of them and saw a path heading straight ahead. Another one turned just a few steps into it. You couldn't tell a thing about them just from a glance.

"I'll check," Karina said as she took her panel out of her item bag. She walked from opening to opening, finally stopping at one of them. "This one," she said without hesitation.

"If I look, would I be able to see the map as well?"

"Yes. It reacts to my mana in order to display the map. As long as I'm holding it, you'll be able to see too. But if I let go of it, the map will disappear. Would you like to try it?" She held the panel out to me.

I did want to look at it for myself, but I remembered back to when I was able to enter the barrier to the sacred tree in the elves' village. If I touched the panel and the map stayed, it could bring all kinds of unexpected trouble.

I couldn't explain that to Karina, and I sure wouldn't know what to say if she asked me if I was her long-lost older sister or something. What if she thought Listiel had a love child or something wild like that? No, it'd be better just to turn her down.

"Nah, it's fine. You should keep a hold of it." I really did want to see if my mana would've worked, but I held out.

Glancing up, I could now see that the entrance was just big enough for one full-grown adult to enter.

"It seems like we need to say goodbye to Kumayuru and Kumakyu now," said Karina, looking sad. My bears wouldn't fit while they were their full size.

"It'll be fine. I can cast a spell on them." I looked over at my bears and chanted: "Itty bitty bobbitty boo."

Not that I needed to say that or anything. Nah, I'd just remembered a magical girl anime I watched as a kid. It just sort of came out as a half joke.

My bears shrunk down in response to my chant. They both crooned at us.

"There, now they can come with," I said.

"Y-Yuna, that was amazing. I had no idea they could do that!"

"It's a secret, though. No spreading this around."

She picked up my mini bears and squeezed them in her arms. "Kumayuru, Kumakyu, you are so incredibly adorable! Yuna, could you make *me* smaller too?"

"..."

For a moment, my brain stopped working.

"Can I shrink and ride on Kumayuru and Kumakyu?"

She actually believed in that whole spell thing, even though it was a joke. I didn't want her thinking I could shrink people for real, so I quickly corrected her.

"Sorry, it wasn't a spell. Kumayuru and Kumakyu can shrink, but I can't shrink anything or anybody else. They're special, you see."

"I see..." She looked awfully disappointed.

Had she really wanted to shrink that much? She'd already been riding my bears without having to shrink down, though.

"Also, if you shrank, you wouldn't be able to hold the panel," I said.

"Oh, you're right." She looked at the panel, as if re-membering why we were here.

"Once we finish swapping the gem, you can ride them."

"Okay." She gave me a smile in response.

KUMA
KUMA
KUMA
BEAR

345
The Bear Progresses through the Labyrinth

W E HEADED into the labyrinth. Karina was in front, followed by me, and then my bears. The passage was cramped, and I felt a little claustrophobic in my bear onesie.

"Karina, are you sure you don't want me to walk ahead of you?"

"No, it's okay," she said. "Even attempting to go down the wrong path is dangerous."

If the wrong paths were dangerous, didn't that mean Karina was in danger? She was leading us, after all.

"Make sure you get all of them right," I said.

"Yes. I won't ever get ahead of myself again or go down the wrong one." She held the panel tightly and checked the map several times.

In order to make sure we were really safe, I used my detection skill to check for monsters. Barlimer had said there wouldn't be any monsters as long as we took the right path, but I still wanted to check for myself.

I could only see monsters on the level I was on, so I'd need to check each time we changed levels. I saw some signals pop up here and there, but not many. Hmm…that one was a golem. I guess if you went the wrong way, you had to fight it.

The farther we went, the wider the passage got. I could probably make my bears full size now. "Karina, will the passages shrink again?"

"I'm not sure. The paths are different every day. But I haven't seen it the other times I've been here."

"Then I'm going to unshrink Kumayuru and Kumakyu. You should be safe if you're riding on Kumayuru, even if you go down the wrong path."

"I won't go down the wrong one!" she said, pouting.

Why did seeing a blown-up cheek tempt me so much to pinch it? I kept that urge at bay and turned to Kumayuru and Kumakyu. "Bibbity bobbity big!"

Sure, I didn't need the chant, but I couldn't resist doing it again. My bears returned to their normal size. I had Karina mount Kumayuru, and I rode Kumakyu.

"Kumayuru, make sure you're careful to follow all of Karina's directions," I said.

"Cwoon."

"Can Kumayuru and Kumakyu get bigger too?"

"They can't," I answered. "The only options are their cub forms and this size."

Fun fact: they didn't come in a Goldilocks size. Just adult and cub, and that was all.

"I see." Karina looked just as sad as when she learned I couldn't shrink her. "I was thinking that maybe Kumayuru got really big and fought off the giant scorpion."

That would've made battles so much easier, but imagining the fight just got me thinking of giant Godzilla-style kaiju battles. More importantly, I wouldn't have a chance to fight, and that wouldn't do. It was my job to protect my bears, after all.

Kumayuru stopped at a T-intersection. "To the right, Kumayuru."

"Cwoon." Kumayuru obediently followed Karina's instructions and turned.

"Actually, how did you get back after losing the panel?" I asked.

We already traveled past a few T- and four-way intersections, and it felt like we'd need a map to get back. If we went the wrong way, I wasn't even sure we'd make it back at all.

"Um...we hadn't gotten all that far." She explained that she'd almost gone down the wrong path immediately after getting the panel. That's why they'd been able to make it home at all.

After heading down the wrong path, she'd immediately fallen into a pit. Barlimer grabbed her and saved her life, but he hurt his arm and she'd dropped the panel in the chaos. Her dad got injured *and* she lost the panel passed down from generation to generation, and yet Barlimer hadn't scolded her.

"He said he was happy I was safe, but I think he should have grabbed the panel instead of me."

"Don't say things like that," I told her. "Barlimer cares about you way more than the panel. Don't deny the poor guy his feelings. Yes, you made a mistake, but Barlimer saved you. And you found the panel in the end. None of it was ideal, but you worked hard to fix your mistake. Just make sure you don't do it again."

She smiled brightly. "You're right."

Now we really needed to swap out that gem without anything else happening.

Karina made sure to check the panel at every intersection to ensure that we were going down the right path.

There are people who learn and grow after their mistakes and people who never bother to try. Karina was undoubtedly one of the former.

"Karina, could I take a look at the panel for a sec?" We were riding side by side on my bears now.

"Yes, here you go." She held the panel out so I could see it from the side. It showed our current location as a blue dot in the middle of the screen. Huh...so the map didn't show everything, then. It only showed what was immediately ahead.

The path we'd come from was shown as a trail of yellow. Ah-ha! So *that* was how we were navigating the place. With this, getting back would be a cinch. If only the map wasn't so zoomed in though...it would've been nice to see more.

"Is it possible to see the whole place?"

"No, it only shows what's nearby."

I used my bear mapping skill. Now *that* showed me the entire map. Then again, it'd change each day, so it wasn't going to be useful later.

"Kumayuru, go straight," she said. Karina headed right through a four-way crossing. It reminded me of an amusement park maze, though I had only gone to one once in elementary school.

We went through several more splits after that and

finally arrived at an open area. Ahead of us were some stairs, but I saw a couple of other stairways to our right and left too.

"Which one, Karina?"

"The right," she said, no hesitation in her voice.

I headed over to the right without a word. The stairs spiraled up.

"We climb these?"

"Yes, we go up," she confirmed and headed right on up, still riding Kumayuru.

I really wouldn't have wanted to climb these without my bear gear or my bears. There was no way I'd be able to make it, considering how weak I was.

I thanked Kumakyu as we headed up. A passage led off the stairs partway through, which turned out to be a trap. Karina had checked the map and said no to going down there, and then she'd asked Kumayuru to keep climbing. Partway, she stopped us and had us go through another passage instead.

Without the map, we'd definitely be lost for sure. No wonder nobody entered this maze.

We kept going down the passage until we arrived at another split, but something looked different. The path to the right was brightly lit, and the left was pitch-black.

Human psychology tempted me toward the light instead of the dark.

But then Karina piped up: "To the left. I'll bring out a lamp, so just a moment."

"No need for that." I gathered mana into my bear puppet and created a light. A bear-shaped face appeared in front of us.

"A bear..."

"C'mon, let's get going."

While Karina was awed by the bear light, I headed down the passage. The bear lit the place right up. Karina just stared at the bear. Eventually, I told her to stop since it'd probably hurt her eyes.

"Karina, the panel?"

"Y-yes, sorry." She immediately looked back at the panel. "Um, why is it shaped differently from a normal light?"

"Isn't it cuter as a bear?"

"It is," Karina readily agreed. I could make a normal ball of light too, but I had to stay focused. Otherwise, it'd just turn into a bear face for...whatever reason these things happen to me, I guess. Sighing, I flapped the mouths of my bear puppets open and shut.

We turned another corner and saw another light in front of us. I thought we were entering a room, but instead it turned out to be yet another fork with a light and dark path.

"This time, it's the light," Karina said as she headed that way. The one after that gave us a choice between going up and down, down being light and up being dark.

I really wanted to go toward the light, but Karina had us go up into the darkness. Then we came across a large-ish room. "Is this it?"

"Not yet."

Ah, fine... We had been walking for less than an hour, but it was such a pain going up and down and left and right...

As Karina looked at the panel, I headed toward the next room heedlessly.

"Yuna, stop."

I did as she said. The room was actually a lot bigger than I expected, and I realized it featured a giant hole right in the middle of it. There were three bridges there, each leading to the other side.

"The right one," Karina said.

"What happens if we tried the other bridges? Would they collapse or something?"

"I'm not sure, but I think that's likely. But you could probably make a bridge with your magic."

I guess normally you were supposed to get through the labyrinth by using your wisdom, power, magic, and abilities. But Karina's panel just showed us the right way with its map.

We crossed the bridge and headed forward.

I saw a trap—a golem. Actually, there were probably a ton of traps and maze portions that we hadn't even traveled near. The farther we went, the more I understood why adventurers didn't really want to go through this labyrinth.

That made it all the more impressive that Karina's ancestor and Mumulute had made it through here at all. There hadn't even been a town or lake nearby back then, so it'd probably been even harder. You had to respect the effort.

We kept heading forward without getting lost, all thanks to Karina's map. At long last, we stopped at a door. We'd arrived.

"Yuna, we're here."

I got off Kumakyu and touched the door. Would it open if we pushed on it?

"Please wait," she said. "I'll open it now." Karina dismounted Kumayuru and headed to the side of the door. There was a depression there, and she placed the panel into it. The door slowly opened.

KUMA
KUMA
KUMA
BEAR

346
The Bear Swaps the Gem

THE DOOR OPENED. I guess the panel also acted as a key.

"The door will close a little after I take the panel away," she said, "so please go inside."

Karina picked up the panel and led the way inside. A short while after we entered, the door shut behind us.

I looked around the room. The first thing that caught my attention was a silver cup-shaped object. Little beads of water dripped from of it. The running water had formed something of a fountain.

Karina started walking to the center of the room. There were steps in front of the chalice and a pedestal about a meter tall right ahead of the steps. A gem sat on the pedestal. Karina walked right up the steps and stood in front of the chalice. I wanted to see what would happen, so I headed over. The chalice was a meter wide. I glanced inside and saw the cracked gem sunk at the bottom.

It looked as though the gem was using the last few dregs of its power to produce these droplets of water.

"We just swap this out, then?" We did come all this way to do this, after all.

"Yes."

"Then let's get it over with."

"Okay, I'll stop the water. Just a second." Karina went down the steps and stood in front of the pedestal. She placed a hand on the gem sitting there and channeled her mana into it. The gem glowed a bluish white for a moment, and then the light subsided.

"Now we can take it out."

I turned around and saw that the dribbling water had indeed stopped flowing.

"You can stop the water?"

"It's my first time, but Mother told me how to do it when we came here before. I'm glad it worked." Once again, she went up the steps to the front of the chalice. She rolled up her sleeves and tried to pick up the broken gem at the bottom. I tried to help, but she stopped me.

"Let me do it, please. I want to pick it up and show it how grateful I am for everything it's done. I think this is my duty, as part of the Ishleet family."

I decided to stand back and respect her wishes. She placed her hands into the water-filled chalice. She then carefully picked up each fragment of the broken gem, one at a time, from big to small. This was the gem that had given them water for all of those long years. Graciously, she placed each one in her cloth bag. That gem had created enough water to make an entire lake. It was one thing to think of it as pure fantasy, but to see it—right there, solid and in front of us—was incredible.

While Karina was fast at work, I inspected the room. There was something on the floor, kind of like a summoning circle or a diagram carved into the stone. I guess it amplified the water? The design went up the walls as well, leading to still more intricate patterns on the ceiling. The whole room was enchanted with some sort of amplification spell.

If I'd smashed through without taking a proper route through the maze, I probably would've destroyed the amplification magic. Now more than ever, I was super glad I took this route instead. We wouldn't have been able to replenish the lake with or without the kraken's gem.

Still, this whole summoning circle thing was ridiculous. I thought it'd be interesting to copy it and make another amplification spell somewhere else, but that seemed impossible.

I walked all the way around the room, circling the

central chalice. The water from the chalice was pure and beautiful. Was this the same water that flowed all the way into town? It was pretty far away... I couldn't help but wonder how it worked.

I headed to the back of the room and saw a door on the other side of the chalice. There were two entrances? Did that mean there were two routes to get here? There was a pedestal next to the door and another divot that seemed like the panel could fit inside. I wondered if it'd open if Karina placed the crystal device there.

"That's the exit." She'd noticed me inspecting it from the pedestal above.

"An exit?"

"Yes, in order to get home."

Wait, the entrance and exit were different? Why was that? I looped around the room back to the front of the stairs. Karina had finished picking up the fragments and was coming back down to me.

"My apologies for the wait."

She was sopping wet, so I handed her a towel from my bear storage.

"Thank you." She started to wipe herself down. I wish I had a handy drying spell or something for times like these. Even if *I* could use one, my bear onesie repelled water, so I didn't actually need it.

Then again, it'd be nice to dry my long hair a little faster.

"I really appreciate this, Yuna. I'll wash your towel before I give it back."

"You don't need to. It's not dirty, and it'll dry right away."

I took the towel and put it on top of Kumayuru.

"Cwoon."

That sounded a bit like a complaint. I thought the towel would dry right away, considering Kumayuru was so warm, but maybe that hadn't been such a great idea. Well, I could dry it whenever, so I put it back into my bear storage.

"Do you have the mana gem, Yuna?"

She stared at me with her earnest, serious eyes. She looked nervous.

I pulled the kraken gem from my bear storage and handed it to Karina. She held it carefully in both her hands so she wouldn't drop it.

"It's so much heavier when I think about how the whole town depends on it," Karina said. "What if we place the gem inside and it doesn't work?"

Karina's hands were quivering. I helped her with it, holding her hands in mine.

"Yuna..."

"It'll be fine. You worked so hard all this time. Things will be fine once you swap it."

Karina nodded and slowly made her way up the steps. She stopped at the front of the chalice, let out a little breath, and slowly placed the kraken's gem in. It sank down to the bottom. She stared at it.

"Karina?"

"Sorry," she said and came back down when I called her. "Now we just need to invoke the magic circle."

Karina headed back to the front of the pedestal. She tensed as she placed her hand on the mana gem. She sucked in a breath, bracing her hand. Then she began to channel mana into the gem. The gem on the pedestal glowed bluish white once more. The diagrams on the ground began to glow too. The light spread throughout the room and filled it until it was blinding. Then, steadily, it dimmed.

Karina swallowed her breath. At that moment, water surged out from the chalice—unending, flowing out and out. We'd done it.

I looked up at her now. "Karina..."

As the water came forth from the chalice, tears flowed down the girl's face.

"I'm so glad..." The sight of the flowing water had turned on the waterworks for her too. She didn't try to wipe away the tears at all and instead just stared at the

flow of water. "Yuna... The town... It's saved... Oh thank you, thank you!" she eked out the words between sobs.

I wiped away her tears for her with a handkerchief. "Come on, no crying."

"Yuna..."

I kept wiping her cheeks, but her tears just kept coming. All the tension balled up inside of her had finally snapped. All that stress—from the broken gem, the lake running dry, the lost crystal panel, the influx of monsters, and the fleeing townspeople—had come undone. The burden must have been so heavy.

She shouldn't have had to carry that burden at all, but losing the panel had weighed her down with a gigantic sense of responsibility. But at last, we'd found the panel and installed a new gem. The water supply was back. It was over. Even the monsters were gone. The townspeople probably wouldn't leave now, either. Karina's shoulders would no longer have to carry that weight.

I hugged her gently and let her cry until she was done.

"Thank you so much. Yuna, Kumayuru, Kumakyu, thank you." Finally, Karina stepped away.

"You're okay now?"

"Yes. I'm so sorry for bursting out crying so suddenly." She rubbed her red eyes, and there was a huge smile on her face now. She looked at the water. Finally, she was happy. It was probably a wonderful thing for her to see at last.

For a little while, Karina just watched the water flow.

"It'll be fine. It won't stop," I assured her.

I couldn't actually see into the future, but I wanted Karina to feel better.

"Yes."

"Hey, let's go report to Barlimer, shall we?" We couldn't stick around here forever. Her father was probably worried.

We headed off to the door behind the chalice. So *this* was how we'd get home. Karina touched the gem next to the door. It opened, and I heard the sound of something else moving up ahead—multiple doors were opening, actually, not just one or two.

"Let's go, Yuna," Karina said.

We went down a staircase up ahead. After a while, I heard the doors close behind us, as if they were automatic. Stairs, stairs, stairs, and then a passageway...followed by another flight of stairs and another small corridor.

Finally, we were back where we started at the entrance of the labyrinth.

"We're back," Karina said.

"It's this easy to get home?"

"Yes."

"Weird. Couldn't you just use this path to get there?"

"That's what I thought when I first got here, but it looks like you can't take this path there. Only back."

Once we were out of the corridor, I heard the wall behind us start to move.

"I think it's probably blocked off," she added.

I guess the labyrinth wasn't going to let us use that path, huh? I wondered why.

347
The Bear Returns to Dezelt

AFTER WE FINISHED swapping the gems, we headed back to town.

"Lady Karina!" The gatekeep shouted Karina's name.

"What is it?"

"Did you do something, Lady Karina?"

"Did something happen?" she asked. "I'm not sure. Could you explain?"

"Of course, sorry. A giant spout of water just rushed up from the lake. And then it rained down on the whole town!"

"Wait, really?!" Karina shouted.

"Yes, it's caused quite a stir here."

"Don't worry. The water in the lake should go back to normal now. Father will explain more later."

"I see. We were so worried, watching the water disappear

317

from the lake day by day. I'm glad to hear that things are better." The relief was plain in his voice.

Just like the guard had said, the ground was wet inside the town. The atmosphere there was also completely different. Everyone seemed happy.

A giant crowd surrounded the lake. Everyone was staring into the water.

"Did they come to see the water gushing out?" I wondered aloud.

"They might have," Karina said. "I think we should get to Father quickly."

We headed past the crowd and went to the estate. There we found another crowd. They'd probably come here to ask Barlimer about the waterspout.

"We can't get inside like this," Karina said.

I was wondering what to do when I heard a familiar voice from the house.

"Barlimer will explain later, so please wait a little while, if you would."

"Is that Mel?"

But it wasn't *just* Mel. Jade, Senia, and Touya were there too, trying to calm the gathered townspeople. There wasn't a lot of trouble yet, but it would probably make a huge deal out of things if they spotted Karina.

"Yuna, what should we do?"

If we headed right in, we'd probably get surrounded. "Looks like I've got no other choice," I said.

"Yuna?"

I made my way behind Karina and picked her up, bridal style.

"Yuna, what are you doing?!"

"Hold on tight," I said.

I started running, holding Karina in my arms. Once I built up enough momentum, I leaped.

"AHHHHHHHHH!!!" Karina shrieked.

The townspeople looked up when they heard the commotion.

"What's that?"

"A bird?"

"Yes, a bird."

"No, that's a bear."

"A bear!"

"A flying bear!!!"

I leapt over the shouting townspeople in a single bound and then jumped over the wall into the estate.

A perfect landing! In my head, I imagined a 10.0 score floating next to me. The bear gear could've definitely won me a gold medal or two in the Olympics. Granted, it would've been cheating, but...

A commotion started up outside as the people who hadn't seen me tussled with the people who had. "It was a flying bear!" "Bears don't fly, you fool!" "I know it was a bear!" "I told you there's no way!" On and on they went. Some people probably hadn't gotten a good look at me because of the angle, either. I gotta say though, I was impressed by the people who realized I was a bear just from a split-second glance.

Finally, I put Karina down.

"Yuna, please warn me before you jump! I was so terrified." Karina's legs were quivering even as she stood on solid ground.

"Oh no. Did you pee a little?"

"I did not!" She started to pummel me. Okay, she was fine.

"You're back, Yuna?" asked Jade.

I answered his question with one of my own. "What are you guys doing here?"

"Who cares about *us*? You need to go and get that report to Barlimer. He's waiting for you two."

Oh, right. We really did need to get a move on.

"Yuna, let's go to Father," said Karina, and we headed into the estate. Once we were inside, Lasa was waiting and led us straight to Barlimer.

"Karina! And Yuna too."

Listiel and their son, Norris, were also with him.

"Father, Mother, I've returned," said Karina. "I heard there was a waterspout. Is it true?"

"Yes, but before we talk about that, please give me your report," said Barlimer.

"Okay." Karina told him about swapping the gem successfully, then explained how the water had come out and put things back to normal.

"I see," said Barlimer. "You've been through so much."

"But...this was all my fault for dropping the panel..."

"Thank you as well, Yuna," Barlimer told me. "If you hadn't been there, the town might have been done for." He bowed his head deep and low.

"Father, what about the waterspout?"

I didn't really understand what had happened, but Karina seemed to have an idea of what was going on.

"Karina, you're familiar with the festival that occurs once a year," said Barlimer.

"Mm-hmm. The lake spouts water like a fountain and comes down on the whole town like rain."

"Indeed. That just happened earlier, which has thrown the town into chaos."

"But the festival..."

"You see, there is a reason behind the occurrence."

According to Barlimer, the festival was annual. Water

spurted from the lake like a geyser and fell like rain. That had happened because they'd cleaned the chalice once a year to show how grateful they were. When they cleaned it, that temporarily stopped the magical spell. Then, when the spell was invoked again, the water would spout again like a geyser.

That had eventually turned into its own festival within the town, serving as a way for the Ishleet family to flaunt their abilities. Since we had invoked the spell again during the gem swap and caused another geyser of water, the townspeople had gathered at the lake after seeing it and had come to Barlimer's house to ask about it.

Jade had been one of those people, so Barlimer had asked the party to help with crowd control. Then, he waited for us to come back for our report.

"In that case," I said, "we need to tell the townspeople fast. Jade's party already has their hands full."

"Yes, you're right." Barlimer stood up, preparing to explain what had happened to the townspeople.

Karina's mother Listiel also stood at the same time. "I'll go with you."

"But you're pregnant..."

"It should be fine. And remember, you're hurt," she said. "This is just an announcement, so there's no danger."

"Then I'll go too," Karina offered.

"Me too..."

"Karina, Norris... All right then. We'll go together, as a family."

We all transferred outside the estate, and they explained the lake was back to normal. Barlimer apologized for the anxiety caused by the incident and also told the townspeople not to worry. His message spread quickly, and soon enough the whole town was buzzing, setting up stalls in front of the lake and celebrating like there was a festival going on.

As Karina and I walked around town, we passed the spice shop we visited before.

"Lady Karina," called the shop owner, coming out to greet us. "Is the lake really back to normal?"

"It really is. Everything is okay now," she said. "So... please don't leave."

"Of course we won't. I talked to my family, and we're staying put."

Karina looked ecstatic. In that moment, I could tell she finally felt rewarded for all of her troubles.

That night, I was getting ready for bed after all the mental exhaustion from the day. I wasn't physically tired, but Karina had whisked me along with her all over the place. I stood out a lot wearing my bear clothes, and Jade's party all but interrogated me, so I was genuinely exhausted.

I changed into my white bear clothes and summoned my cub-form bears. They were so fluffy and perfectly comfy, like always. Just hugging them made the fatigue go away.

As I was about to snuggle up under the covers after being re-energized by the healing power of bears, I heard a knock at the door.

"Yuna, are you awake?"

"Karina? I'm up."

Karina walked in holding a pillow.

"What's wrong?"

"Um...may I sleep with you?"

"Sure, that's fine."

I couldn't say no, seeing that pillow in her hands. She happily came over to the bed.

"Yuna, you're...white?"

She looked at this different version of my onesie.

"It's just for sleeping." Although sometimes I wore them when I wasn't sleeping, they were basically like pajamas for when I was tired.

"They look cute too!"

"You've got some cute pajamas as well," I said.

She was wearing an adorable white nightgown. She was way cuter than me, easy.

"Are you going home soon? Then...I'll have to say bye to Kumayuru and Kumakyu, won't I?" She stroked my two bears.

Wait, what about *me*? C'mon, Karina, don't make me cry.

"I'm so sad when I think about not seeing you anymore," she said.

Okay, so she would miss me too, then. "I'll be back."

"Do you really think so?"

"Yeah. I want to buy spices. More importantly, I've gotta visit you again."

If I set up a bear gate, I could make it here in an instant. I just needed a place to put it.

"I mean it," she said. "You have to promise. I'll be waiting, okay?"

"I promise."

Until now, her face had been a picture of gloom, but now Karina's smile bloomed like a flower. "Kumayuru, Kumakyu, let's meet again, okay?"

They both crooned.

"Aww, but I really don't *want* to say goodbye. I'm so sad!" She hugged them both.

"Then I've got something for you."

"Hm?"

I pulled out two bear stuffed animals from my storage. When Karina saw them, her eyes went round as saucers, and she stared in disbelief.

"Kumayuru and Kumakyu stuffed animals," I said. "If you have these, you won't feel as sad, right?"

She took the Kumayuru one into her arms. "For me?"

"Take good care of it, ya hear?"

"Thank you." She hugged the stuffed animals now. Meanwhile, the real Kumayuru and Kumakyu sat off to the side, abandoned. They looked pretty sad that they'd lost out to their stuffed counterparts.

"What should I do, though? I can't hug Kumayuru and Kumakyu while I'm holding the stuffed animals..."

"In that case, why don't you stick with the real ones tonight?" I proposed.

"Yeah, I will!" Karina got off the bed and placed the stuffed animals on a table.

Then she came back and hugged my bears again right before flopping right down on the bed.

"Yuna? Tell me a story."

"A story?"

"Yes, about the town you live in, or where you've gone, or the monsters you've slain. Tell me all kinds of stories, please."

"Hmm... Okay, how about this one?" I started up a tale.

After a while, I began to hear gentle snoring from next to me. She'd fallen asleep while hugging Kumayuru. I called Kumakyu over and gave my lonesome bear a hug.

"Night."

Then I drifted off to heal from the exhaustion of the day.

KUMA
KUMA
KUMA
BEAR

Barlimer Thanks the Bear

IN THE MORNING, I woke up with a slumbering Karina attached to me. Before we went to sleep, she was holding Kumayuru, who was now curled up beside her. I wasn't sure if Kumayuru was happy or sad about being released from her grip, but my bear seemed to be sleeping comfortably. In my arms, Kumakyu was sleeping comfortably too. I got to work waking everyone up from their cozy slumber.

After we finished breakfast, Barlimer told me to come to his office. There was a lot to discuss, he said.

"Yuna, once again, thank you very much," he began. "There are no words to express my gratitude. Thanks to you, I can see Karina smiling. She was terribly hard on herself—no matter what we said to her, she put all the blame on herself. I even caught her crying in her room. As a parent, I couldn't comfort or help my daughter, but *you*...you saved her. I am eternally grateful."

When I first met Karina, it seemed like she was cornered, but she pushed through. Although she was tiny, she worked as hard as she could.

She didn't run when confronted with monsters, and she never complained. Since she was a kid, she could have insisted she was too scared to go. Really, she could have refused to do any of this. But Karina wasn't like that. She knew her role and didn't try to hamper us.

Barlimer seemed pleased when I said all of that.

"Also, Yuna, would you give me your guild card? I would like to record these events."

My client was supposed to be the king, so I guess he meant the quest I went on with Jade and the others?

I handed over my guild card to Barlimer. He took it and placed it upon a crystal panel. Just a moment later, it was over, and the card was right back in my hand—or rather, in my bear puppet's mouth.

"Since you have expressed a preference for not advertising the matter with the scorpion, I have handled this like the kraken incident," Barlimer told me.

"As in," I said, "only important people like guild masters will know about it?"

"Correct. If your accomplishments are ever called into question, I will vouch for you, and I believe King Folhaut would do the same. Please deliver this letter to His Majesty. It details the events that have transpired. I believe he may ask to see the scorpion."

I guess he wrote about the scorpion and stuff in his letter. It wasn't like I could ask Barlimer to lie to the king or something, so I'd just have to live with it.

Still, I knew how the king was. He'd definitely make me show him. He wouldn't spread it around, though—he hadn't spread rumors about the ten thousand monsters I slayed near the capital or the kraken—so that was a relief, at least. That said, he'd tell Ellelaura for sure, and then Ellelaura would absolutely tell Cliff about it. And Cliff would absolutely have something to say.

"I would like to give you something to thank you," Barlimer continued. "Separate from His Majesty's payment."

"That's okay. The king is already paying me." He had prearranged that with me, paying for the kraken's gem from the government coffers. It wouldn't affect the king directly.

"No, that quest was only to bring the mana gem. You also searched for the crystal panel and replaced the mana gem, which were both separate matters. You even slew a massive scorpion. I couldn't let you return home empty-handed."

"Don't worry about it," I told him. "You didn't know there was a scorpion. I can sell the monster parts if I want money, and all I did was go with Karina for the gem swap."

I barely did anything when we were switching out the mana gems. All I did was ride Kumayuru and Kumakyu over with Karina and followed her instructions.

"Yuna, you must be more cognizant of the incredible feats you've accomplished."

I guess I got where he was coming from, but I didn't want to expect anything in return for the things I did. Still, no matter how many times I said he didn't need to thank me, Barlimer wouldn't hear it. He insisted on rewarding me.

Finally, I actually came up with something that I did want. I was going to the Merchant Guild today to buy a house where I could set up a bear gate. After thinking it over earlier, I decided I wanted to set up somewhere in town. At first, I'd considered inside the pyramid or out in the desert, but then people and monsters would start to notice it. Instead, I decided buying a small house in town would be a lot better, since then I could set up a bear gate inside.

"Can you write me a letter of recommendation for the Merchant Guild?" I asked.

"A letter for the guild?"

"I was thinking of buying a house in town," I told him. "But...well, I look like *this*." I gestured to my outfit.

"Indeed, you *do* happen to be rather, ah, ursine."

"Yeah, I get weird looks when I stay at inns, so I was thinking I would buy a house for when I come to visit."

"Um, forgive me, but couldn't you simply...dress differently?"

Right, right. Anybody would ask that. I had an immediate answer for him, though.

"No."

I sure *wanted* to dress like a normal human being, but I didn't have the courage to do that at an inn. Without my bear gear, I was even weaker than a normal girl. Sure, I could dress like a normal human being in a house of my own, but I'd never dare do that while staying anywhere else. Besides, it wasn't like I could set up a bear gate in an inn.

"I'm not sure whether they'll let me buy a house since I'm young and dress weird. They might force me to buy something strange in a bad location or something." I tried coming up with more excuses for buying a house for my bear gate.

Until now, with the exception of Crimonia, I relied on others whenever I dealt in real estate. Gran and Ellelaura helped me in the capital, Atola helped me in Mileela, Retbelle gifted me an entire home in Laluz, and Mumulute gave me permission to make a gate in the elf village. They were the reason I hadn't had any trouble buying houses or building my own all this time.

So, if I had a letter of introduction from Barlimer for this town, I figured buying a house would be no problem.

"You would buy a house just for that, even though you wouldn't live there?"

"It would be small. Besides, I promised Karina that I would visit again."

"Ah, but you may stay here when you visit. My daughter would be delighted."

Yeah, but I wouldn't be able to set up a bear gate here.

"I don't know when I would come to town," I said, "and I don't want to be a bother..."

There had to be another excuse.

"You don't want to be a bother... Hmm. I understand. I'm sorry I was too insistent about having you here. I shall prepare a letter for the guild. If that is to be your reward, I will be happy to write it." With that, Barlimer went right on to start the letter.

"Thank you very much."

"It's the least I can do. I'm just happy to be able to reward you somehow."

Barlimer then stretched out his arm, which still seemed to hurt him. Looked like I had one last thing to do.

"Barlimer, would you allow me to take a look at your injured arm?"

"My arm?" Barlimer rolled up his sleeve and showed it to me. It was red and swollen from when he hurt it while saving Karina from the pit.

"Please keep this between us." I brought my bear puppets near his swollen arm and cast healing magic. I pictured him getting better and the swelling going down. Soon enough, the deep red of his arm turned a healthier color. "There. I think you'll be okay now."

Barlimer rotated his arm. "It doesn't hurt..."

"It'll start hurting again if you push yourself. But it should be fine if you take it easy."

"What *are* you, Yuna?"

"Just a passing adventurer. And remember, don't tell anyone about this." I held my bear puppet up to my mouth.

"I understand. I won't tell a soul. Thank you ever so much."

Every time Barlimer grimaced in pain, Karina would

get sad. She wouldn't have to suffer like that anymore. "Be sure to give Karina a hug later, 'kay?"

"I can't thank you enough." He wasn't lying, either. Barlimer thanked me over and over...

Once we were done talking, I asked Barlimer where the Merchant Guild was and left the room. I was planning to head there immediately, but Karina was standing in the hallway.

"Are you headed somewhere, Yuna?"

"Um, just doing a bit of shopping."

"What are you buying?"

"Just a house," I told her.

"A *house*?!"

"So I can stay there next time I visit," I explained, giving Karina the same excuse I'd given Barlimer. "I get all sorts of attention at the inn since I look like this."

Karina also said that I could stay with her when I came to town, but I told her I didn't want to be a bother.

After that, I went with Karina to the Merchant Guild.

"Here it is," she said after leading me over. It was way closer to the Adventurer Guild than I expected.

"I hope they'll show me a house that's actually...nice," I said.

After all, it's not often a realtor has to deal with a girl in a bear outfit. There was a chance they'd blow me off. If this were my original world, I wouldn't have been able to go to a real estate agent on my own. That was what the letter from Barlimer was for, though. Since I had a letter from the lord of this town, they'd probably take me seriously.

"If there's a problem," said Karina, "I'll have a word with them."

"I'd rather you not."

"Wh-why?!" I could tell she was a little upset, so I explained myself.

"I don't want you to grow up abusing your parents' influence."

Using your power properly was difficult. If she used it to benefit herself, she'd end up hurting the people around her.

"Barlimer is the lord," I continued, "but you can't just act the same way that he does. People won't like that."

I wanted Karina and Norris to grow up without relying on their parents' clout. Sure, they'd probably have that same power someday, but it wasn't good to grow up being able to make everyone follow your orders. If they spent all their younger years bossing people around, they'd stop thinking of other people as people by the time they grew up.

"You're the daughter of the town's lord," I said, "but I don't want you to think you have the same sway as your father. And I don't want you to become someone who just gives orders to others. I want you to be thoughtful and to become a leader who helps the people."

Still, the Karina I saw now seemed like she'd be fine. With the way she was, I was sure she'd keep growing up right.

"I will," said Karina firmly.

349
The Bear Buys a House

KARINA AND I went inside the Merchant Guild. It was just the right time too, since the reception desk was free.

"There's an open spot, Yuna."

Karina grabbed my bear puppet and headed with me to a reception desk. Behind the desk was a woman in her twenties working with her head down, unaware we had approached.

"Excuse me..."

"Oh, yes? Sorry about that... A bear?! And Lady Karina?"

First the receptionist was surprised by us catching her off guard, then surprised by my clothes, and then finally by Karina beside me. A perfect three-hit combo.

The receptionist looked between Karina and me. I could practically see a giant question mark floating above her head. I knew what she wanted to say, but I didn't have any need to explain it to her. Instead, I continued with my mission for coming here.

"I had something to ask about, if I could."

"Um, yes? What is it?" She nodded, still bewildered.

I explained that I was looking for a small vacant house and handed over the letter from Barlimer. The receptionist looked at the letter, then at me, then at the letter, then at Karina. It was like she was on a loop.

"Lady Karina, is this...?"

"I'm sorry. I'm just accompanying Yuna, so I don't know what's in my father's letter," Karina replied, fittingly for the daughter of a nobleman.

"Um...Yuna, is it?"

My name was in the letter, I guess. "That's me. I'm looking for a vacant house. Got any? It's fine if it's small. I wouldn't even mind if it's a little expensive."

It was just for setting up my bear gate, so the size didn't matter much. But the receptionist had a reply I wasn't expecting.

"No, payment won't be necessary."

"Huh?" This time, the question mark was floating above *my* head. I didn't understand, but the receptionist cleared that up right away.

"The letter says that a girl dressed like a bear will buy

a house and that we should help arrange the purchase. Then, it specifies that the Ishleet family will pay for it."

What? Barlimer didn't mention that at all! But remembering his face back then and what he said, it made sense. He tried to get me to stay with him, and then he wrote the letter for me after realizing I was serious about buying a house. Maybe he resorted to this because I wouldn't accept anything else? Maybe that's why he stopped trying to get me to stay at his place.

"Umm...Lady Karina, I wanted to confirm, is this bear... I mean, is this Yuna really an acquaintance of the Ishleet family?"

"Yuna is a very important guest of the Ishleet family, yes."

The guild didn't even trust me with the letter, huh? I guess it made sense, with all the bear stuff.

"I understand," she said, getting right to the point and managing to hold back what looked like an explosion of questions about my appearance. "In that case, can you tell me what you are looking for in a house?"

Other people had also been inspecting me from head to toe for a while. I heard comments from the traders and guild employees like, "It's a bear." "A bear?!" "So cute!"

Karina gave them each a look, though, which got 'em real quiet, real quick. I told her not to abuse her power, but sometimes it's just good to have a nobleman's kid on your side.

I explained to the receptionist that I wanted a small house near a shop where I could buy spices. It'd be useful for when I wanted to pop in for some shopping.

As I was explaining all that, Karina interrupted, "Please make her house close to mine."

"Um, why?"

"I want you to be closer," Karina said firmly.

"S-sure..." I said, bending to the pressure.

The receptionist smiled at that. "In that case, please wait a moment. I'll look for something."

She examined some documents, mumbling things like, "Lady Karina's house is here... The shop is here...which leaves this spot...or what about here... Too big..."

Finally, she came back. "Sorry to keep you waiting."

She spread out a map of the town and pointed out where Karina's house was, along with the street lined with vendors. The same shop we went to earlier was nearby— the one with the owner who'd decided to stick around after all. Seemed like a good situation. After that, she told us about some potential locations. They were all in between Karina's house and the shopping street. I pointed with my bear puppet to one of the houses close to the street.

"Maybe this one?"

At the same time, Karina pointed at a house completely opposite (and closer to her house). "Then this one." She looked up at me. "But why *that* one?"

"Because it's close to the shops?" I countered.

"This one isn't that far away either, so it's not a problem."

"But this one is more convenient for shopping."

We stared each other down. Neither of us budged. Either one of us could have compromised, but we both held out.

"Excuse me," said the receptionist, pointing at a third house. "How about this one?" It was exactly between the ones Karina and I had selected. "This property is relatively new, close to Lady Karina's residence, and close to the shopping district. I believe it will satisfy both criteria."

Karina and I looked at each other again...and gave little nods, forfeiting to her. The receptionist looked relieved. She was a good mediator, which I guess was a requirement for a guild employee.

Now I just needed to look at the actual house to finally make up my mind. If it didn't work out, I'd end up in another battle of wills with Karina.

We arrived with the receptionist in tow at the house I was going to buy. It was right between the shopping street and Karina's house, just like on the map.

I looked it over. "Yup, this is good." It was small, but still two stories tall.

"Are you sure it's not too tiny?" Karina asked.

"It's just for visiting here, so it's plenty."

I didn't plan on having a lot of other visitors over, either. If I did bring someone with me, it would probably just be Fina, and she knew about the bear gate. Even then, we could go back without staying the night, so I didn't need a large house.

"Can I check inside too?" I asked.

"By all means."

The house was pretty new, and the interior was also nice, but there was a layer of dust over everything. I guess a cleaning would be necessary. The first floor had the kitchen and dining room, a bath, a bathroom, and even a small pantry. On the second floor were two more rooms. It seemed like a home that a new couple would live in.

"Yeah, I'll go with this one."

"Th-thank you very much. In that case, we'll return to the guild and handle the paperwork."

We went back together to the Merchant Guild.

"All right, may I have your guild card?"

I pulled it out and handed it to her. This was what my card currently said:

```
Name: Yuna
Age: 15
Class: Bear
Adventurer Rank C
Merchant Rank E
```

"Class...*bear*?"

Jeez, literally everyone seemed to look straight at that one first.

"Also, about payment for the house?" I said. "I would like to cover half."

I had no intention of letting Barlimer pay for it all since I found out he'd arranged for that. But if I paid for the entire amount, I'd be rebuffing his kindness, so I decided to split the difference and the cost.

"Well, that's not..." The receptionist looked a bit troubled when I said that.

"Yuna. This is a gift from my father. Please accept it," Karina insisted.

"I can't just take it all," I told her. "But I want to respect Barlimer's feelings, so I'll do half. I won't compromise any further."

"But..."

"I'll tell Barlimer myself," I assured her.

"All right." And that was that.

I turned to the receptionist again and asked about the price. She looked to Karina for confirmation, got a small nod from the girl, and then told me the cost.

Then I paid half. I just couldn't accept a whole house as a gift.

...What's that? Hadn't I exchanged a picture book and stuffed animal for a whole house once?

Well, I thought better of it after the fact, okay? And so now I was only going to accept half.

After successfully buying the house, Karina and I returned to it to do some cleaning. Although the property had been managed, it was a bit dirty.

We went inside, and I summoned Kumayuru and Kumakyu in their cub forms to help with the cleanup. I wanted all hands on deck, and all paws too. That's what I wanted, anyway, but all they really did was horse around.

Then again, I was going to be saying goodbye to Karina soon, so I wanted to let her spend some time with my bears.

"Karina, I thought you were going to help clean."

"Yes, of course I will. I'm not going to be outdone by Kumayuru and Kumakyu."

I thought Karina would leave when I told her I was cleaning, but she said that she wanted to help. Karina lived with a maid, though, so I was a bit worried she might not know *how* to clean. Then again, even the daughter of an aristocrat knew how to do a little dusting, right?

But it wasn't long before my hopes for her were crushed. I was left almost speechless.

"Karina, Kumayuru is under you!" I cried. She was about to step on Kumayuru! "Watch out!"

At which point she bonked her head on an open door.

"Watch your step!" Karina was so absorbed in watching Kumayuru and Kumakyu cleaning that she ended up slipping on a rag.

"Karina, the bucket!" Next up, she knocked over a pail of water, which flew and splashed down right on Kumakyu nearby.

"Oh, sorry, Kumakyu..."

And that bucket was also what we were using to wash the dirty rags. Kumakyu let out a sad "cwoon" when they realized their white fur had been besmirched. When Karina tried to go over to wipe Kumakyu down with her already-filthy rag, I panicked and quickly stopped her.

"Kumakyu will be okay! Just, uh, focus on the floor."

I recalled Kumakyu and then resummoned them. My bear reappeared, as spotless as ever.

"Kumakyu is clean?" Karina observed.

"No more cleaning with Kumayuru and Kumakyu!" I told her.

Karina deflated. "Aww, b-but..."

If I didn't steel my heart, we'd only end up with more casualties.

It went without saying that I was worn out by the time cleaning was over.

KUMA
KUMA
KUMA
BEAR

350
The Bear Bids Farewell

AFTER CLEANING UP my new place, I headed back to Barlimer to thank him and let him know that I paid for half of the house. He seemed a bit disappointed but also said that he understood.

Then I told him that I'd be going home in two days. I could've gone the day after instead, but I needed to account for the time I saved with the bear gate. Maybe my guild card was date-stamped, but at least the king wouldn't know when I was leaving, so I'd be able to hide that.

The next day, Karina and I headed to check out those birds that were supposed to lay large eggs. Lasa knew I wanted some, so she'd told somebody to let me know when they were ready. She had gotten word that they were a day ago. They would've brought the eggs to the house, but I wanted to see the birds myself, so I went to pick them up.

The birds were in a farming area on the opposite side of the lake from the Barlimer estate. We looked out over the water of the lake as we walked over. There were still a lot of food stalls around the shore.

"Everyone seems to be having a good time," I observed.

"Thanks to you," said Karina.

There were a lot of people anxious about the water, but the town had started to revitalize after Barlimer's announcement. Still, I wondered... If the water supply from the gem ran out again, would it cause a riot...?

No, they'd probably be fine. I was a little worried, but I believed it would work out. I'd done what I could.

I soaked in the town's scenery as we walked and spotted the agricultural zone.

"Yuna, that's it there." Karina pointed ahead. I saw a small hut next to the lake, where large birds were swimming on the water. Were those *the* birds? I'd been picturing ostriches, but these were more like ducks.

Yet the ducks I knew weren't *this* big. These things didn't look like ostriches, but they were about the size of them. I could even imagine a kid riding one. Fantasy world, delivering as always.

"They're so big you could ride them, Karina," I said breathlessly.

"Oh, I have before."

"Really?"

"If you ask the owners, they'll let you," she replied.

Maybe I could bring Fina along next time.

"But you better be able to swim," said Karina. "They only let on kids who can swim, because they'd need to get to the shore if they fell off."

Really? Well, if someone fell and couldn't swim, they'd drown. Which meant Fina wouldn't be able to ride them, but maybe it would be okay if we practiced swimming in the ocean?

Unfortunately, I couldn't ride one myself, what with me being an adult and all. Oh, the woes of adulthood.

"Do you want to try riding one, Yuna?"

Um, ha. No way. Surely I misheard her.

"You could definitely ride one," she said, ruthlessly.

"O-of course," I said, but my heart ached. Maybe I wasn't an adult, but I wasn't a kid, either.

We arrived at the hut where the birds were cared for and found several men working there. They noticed us and were (of course) initially surprised with my appearance.

"A bear? And...Lady Karina?"

People always noticed me first. How could they not when I so bearishly appeared?

"We came because we heard there were some eggs. Are there any?" Karina asked the bewildered man, explaining our reason for coming. The conversation would go smoother with her at the wheel, so I let her handle it.

"Indeed, we do have some eggs," the man said, quite formally. I knew it. Everyone treated her reverently, since she was the lord's daughter.

The man took us inside the hut and guided us to where the eggs were. "These were laid yesterday," he added.

We went inside the room to find two eggs. They were the same size as the ostrich eggs I'd seen on TV. Jeez, this had to equal how many regular eggs? And oh, what would they taste like? I was hyped to find out.

"Is it really okay if I take both of them?" I asked.

"Yes, please take them."

"Thank you."

I paid the man and obtained the pair of ginormous duck eggs.

"You don't need to pay because Father will cover the cost," said Karina, but I wasn't about to let that happen. These would be gifts, and I wasn't going to let someone else pay for gifts I was going to give to another person.

Just like that, I got some good souvenirs for the orphans and Fina. I couldn't wait to see the shock and delight on their faces. Maybe I'd cook a huge sunny-side-up egg? Or make an absolute pudding-zilla? My brain buzzed with good recipes as I thanked the man and left the hut.

Still, the giant ducks had me tempted, even though I said I wouldn't ride them on account of being an adult. They were so close... Must...resist...

Having acquired the eggs and resisted the duck rides, we returned to the estate where Barlimer was working. Sure, he was healed up, but seeing him working so much had me worried. He should've been resting. I gave some sacred tree tea to Lasa and instructed her to only allow him a cup a day.

I saw that the tea worked from giving it to Cliff, and I didn't want Barlimer to burn himself out. A lot of the people I knew loved to work, for some reason. As a former shut-in, the whole thing was pretty confusing.

After that, I went to bed with Karina, like the day before. Of course, I summoned Kumayuru and Kumakyu too. Since I would be returning to the capital tomorrow, I wouldn't be seeing Karina for a while, and even though I had the bear gate, it would seem strange if I came to visit a lot. I couldn't come back very often.

"You're going back tomorrow, aren't you, Yuna?"

"I'll visit again."

"You promised."

"I went through all that trouble to buy a house. Of course I'll come back."

"Please take care of yourselves too, Kumayuru, Kumakyu."

"Cwoon!" Karina hugged both of them close in their cub forms.

"I'll let you sleep with them today," I said.

"Are you sure?"

"So no crying," I added.

"I won't cry!"

The somber look disappeared from her face and was replaced by an angry pout. Much better.

We crawled into bed. It was so large that there was some space between us, so Kumayuru and Kumakyu curled up to the left and right of Karina.

Silence fell on the room.

Then Karina spoke. "Really, Yuna...thank you. If you weren't here, I'd probably still be crying."

I couldn't say a word.

"Before, I was overwhelmed by my mistake. Mother and Father are kind, but when I thought about how it would be my fault that the town would be lost, I couldn't breathe. I couldn't even sleep."

I let her keep talking.

"R-really... Thank you so much."

I could hear sobbing. I hugged her tenderly. Before long, she cried herself out, relaxed, and drifted to sleep.

She had worked so hard. I was so glad that I saved her.

The next morning, I finished my breakfast and said my farewells.

"Come again, Yuna."

"I'll definitely be back," I said, patting Karina's head.

"Thank you so much, Yuna," said Listiel, rubbing her baby bulge. "You saved the town. You saved our next child's future, so thank you."

"I hope you have a safe delivery," I told her.

"This one's my third. I'll be fine."

I reminded myself to bring a gift once the baby was born.

"Awe you leebing, bear?" asked little Norris.

"Yep. Get along with your mother and sister, now," I told him.

"I will!" Norris chirped cheerfully while holding his mother's hand.

He was so close to Listiel that I wondered if he'd be all right when a younger sibling came along. I heard that older kids get less attention when a baby is born. Well, that's just how it goes with siblings, or so they say. It'd be fine.

Finally, Barlimer arrived. "You really helped us. And thanks for the tea as well. I feel so much better, all thanks to you."

He looked much healthier. Even though his injury was healed, he must've still been mentally exhausted. His work had piled up. I was glad the sacred tree tea was helping.

"With a baby on the way, you need to pace yourself with your work," I reminded him.

"True. I can't have myself collapsing. Also, please send my regards to King Folhaut."

I agreed. Finally, I looked at Lasa, who was off to the side.

"Please teach me some new recipes again," said Lasa. "I'll be sure to also learn more as well."

"Sure, I'll bring you something tasty. I want to learn more from you too."

Everyone saw me off as I left. Karina offered to go with me all the way to the town gate, but that would mean I couldn't use my *own* gate, so I politely declined.

"Yuna! Thank you very much!" At the end, Karina sent me off with the largest shout she could manage.

I waved my hand and headed into my new house.

Then I slipped inside, making sure no one was watching, and set up the bear gate in the farthest room. I opened the gate and returned to the capital.

KUMA
KUMA
KUMA
BEAR

EXTRA STORY
Karina's Mistake

I LIVED IN A TOWN surrounded by nothing but sand and desert. At first, no one lived on this land at all, but people began to gather around the lake. Eventually, that led to the formation of the town—a town created by my own ancestors.

My family had a role here, passed along from generation to generation. We were the ones who looked after the lake.

A few times a year, we traveled to the nearby pyramid. In its depths lay a magical contraption that created the lake. By amplifying the strength of a gigantic water mana gem, we could provide plenty of water.

But lately, Father and Mother realized that there wasn't as much water in the lake, and so they went to check on the pyramid. When they returned, they looked somber at what they had found.

It seemed that the water gem had cracked. The gem was still producing water, but the water supply was dwindling.

Father wrote letters to the two neighboring nations and pleaded for a gem to replace the one we needed. However, Father told me that such a large gem would be no easy feat to find. It was difficult enough to get a hold of a large gem, let alone a large *water* gem.

Father collected some small water gems and decided to bring them to the pyramid. There was a possibility that such a plan would not work either.

"Even if they're not able to replace the gem," he said, "it'll be enough to help with the water supply, no matter how little."

We could not know if it would work without trying, so Mother and Father were to visit the pyramid again. But Mother clutched at her stomach, where her new baby was growing. We couldn't let her push herself too hard.

Still, we needed Mother in order to get to the furthest part of the pyramid. We had to travel through the labyrinth within to reach the water gem. The path was winding and treacherous because of the traps, but there was one way to progress through the labyrinth safely. Only by using the map on the crystal panel—an artifact that had been passed down through my family for generations—could we find our way through the labyrinth without getting lost.

But the panel couldn't be used by just anyone. It only worked for those who shared blood with one of the people who created the town—my ancestor.

Mother and I, as well as my younger brother Norris, were the only ones who could use it now. I couldn't let Mother go, not when she was pregnant. And Norris was much younger than me. I was the only one who could go in Mother's place.

"I will go for Mother," I said, which surprised my parents.

But I'd been taken to the pyramid multiple times before. They'd let me hold the map before too, so I knew how to use it.

"I can carry the map for Mother and give directions. We can't force Mother to do anything that would hurt her right now."

The town was only cool enough to live in because of the lake. Outside of town, it was sweltering hot, and that wouldn't be any good for Mother or the baby. Even when she returned from the pyramid before, she had looked exhausted.

Father looked at Mother's stomach and smiled gently. "Then we'll count on you to help, Karina."

That made me so very, very happy. I felt as though Father had acknowledged that I was growing up.

The next day, Father and I set off on a laggaroute to the pyramid. Once we went inside, we made our way to the labyrinth entrance. There were many possible openings to enter the labyrinth, and picking the wrong one would be disastrous.

According to legends and the adventurers who'd attempted the mazes, there were an infinite number of traps there. But I could use the map to find a route without traps, so we didn't need to worry.

"Karina, which entrance do we use?"

I channeled a little bit of mana into the panel, and it showed me the way.

"This one." I chose one of the many entrances and went forward. Father followed behind. Then I went to the right while staring at the panel, then the left, making sure we wouldn't become lost.

"I'm so glad you're here," Father said to me.

He smiled. I was so very happy Father found me so reliable.

"Father, this way," I said.

"Karina, you need to watch where you're going."

I was so taken by being relied upon that I'd twirled

around without realizing I'd reached a crossroads. I went forward...and in that moment, I realized that my right foot had no ground to step on. There was only a pit.

And I fell. But then something caught my right arm in that moment.

"Karina!" Father had grabbed my arm. "Karina, are you all right?"

"Father, the panel! It's slipping!"

The panel cradled in my arm was slowly moving. The precious panel...

"Sorry. I can barely keep a hold of you already." He gave me a pained smile.

"Let me go and take the panel." I tried to move it up in my left arm so Father could take it.

"Don't be ridiculous." Father tried to pull me up, but the panel seemed close to falling.

"Father, please! Save the panel, not me."

"What father would let go of his own daughter's hand?"

He heaved me up, but in that moment, the panel slipped from my hand and tumbled into the darkness of the pit.

"Karina, are you all right?"

"I'm okay. But the panel..."

I looked down into the pit. It was so very deep that I couldn't even see the bottom.

"Leave it for now," Father said.

"But...!"

Father was holding on to his arm. It seemed he was in pain. He must have hurt himself when he grabbed me.

"Father, are you okay?"

"I'm fine. Come now, we can't forget the way we entered. We need to go back."

"Okay..."

Since we didn't have the panel anymore, we couldn't go forward. If we tried, we wouldn't be able to get home at all. But we hadn't gone far yet, so we just retraced our steps.

Father and I walked the path in silence. We hadn't gotten very far and so we reached the entrance again without issue.

"Father...I'm so sorry."

"I'm simply glad you're safe." Father gave me a gentle hug. I still felt terrible.

I wanted him to scold me.

Once we arrived home, Father looked grim as he brooded. If the gem producing our water supply for the lake broke, we could not replenish it or change it for another without the map. With every passing day, the water in the lake disappeared a little more. Even the residents began to stir, and Father became busy dealing with that.

Father submitted a quest to the Adventurer Guild to retrieve the map. At first, several people took the quest and went searching for it, but the pyramid was too vast for them to find it.

I thought it would be best for me to go as well. I knew the general location of the panel, after all. And since my mana was imprinted on the panel, I had a connection with it. I could feel which direction it was in.

I went to the guild and, without my father knowing, changed the quest so that I would be accompanying the adventurers.

It was my responsibility too, after all.

However, monsters began to gather around the pyramid, making it harder to enter. People began to report sightings of a really large monster on top of everything else. Soon enough, the entire pyramid was surrounded by dangerous beasts.

Now there was no one willing to take me there. But I was not dissuaded.

"Please..." Today, I was once again at the guild, begging for someone to join me.

I just needed someone, anyone, to help me...

KUMA
KUMA
KUMA
BEAR

EXTRA STORY
The Girl the Bear Saved: Karina Chronicles

S O MANY THINGS happened in such a short time. The gem that had been creating the lake broke, and the crystal panel we had passed down from generation to generation was lost in the pyramid. Because of that, Father had been hurt and he'd made a quest to the guild to try fixing it somehow...but there were too many monsters around the pyramid for anyone to go near it.

I was a weak little girl, unable to defeat even one monster. All I could do was lower my head and beg. And then Yuna came to rescue me while I was powerless. She solved everything.

The water in the lake steadily grew, and I could see it would soon return to its usual glory. Though we'd been forbidden from playing in the water, children were now enjoying themselves there. When I thought of how Yuna had made sure these kids could smile again, I could really understand just how significant her actions had been.

Even walking around town, I could see smiles return to the once-worried faces of the townsfolk. I doubted anyone would think that a girl dressed as a bear had brought their smiles back. Yuna was a mysterious person, dressed in those bear clothes of hers. She was unfathomably powerful despite her appearance, and she was a kind person who didn't use her abilities to show off.

I remembered when I first met her. It was regrettable how rude I'd been. But she was dressed in that bear costume, and I'd thought she was just being silly about something serious. When I'd first seen her, I assumed that she couldn't be a powerful adventurer.

And yet she hadn't even gotten mad. No, she'd been kind!

I clutched the stuffed bears she had given me. The black one was Kumayuru, and the white one was Kumakyu. They had protected me. Kumakyu had spent a lot of time with me too, which had made me feel so safe.

I hadn't known anything about bears except what I'd learned from books. Books called them savage creatures, which might've been true. Still, Yuna's bears were so incredibly cute. They let me ride them and they even cuddled up to me. They didn't seem savage. Not at all.

As I was thinking about Yuna, there was a knock at the door, and Father entered.

"Are you all right?" he asked.

"Um, what do you mean? Father, I'm not the one who got hurt."

Father had injured his arm trying to save me when I nearly dropped into a pit.

"Lasa said you've looked beside yourself ever since Yuna left," he said.

Oh no. Had I been making Lasa worry? "I suppose I was a little sad, but not enough that you need to be worried."

Also, Yuna had bought a house in town and told me she'd come back. I doubted she would have an easy time of it, but I knew she would fulfill her promise.

"You're right," he said. "We should show Yuna around the town she helped save next time she comes."

Yuna had saved me so many times, but I hadn't been able to do anything for her in return. Next time Yuna came, I would be able to show her around our beautiful town.

"Karina, come over here."

"What is it?"

I headed over to Father. He suddenly grabbed me in a hug and held me up.

"F-Father! But what about your arm?!"

He didn't look in pain at all. In fact, he was smiling. "I'm fully healed!"

"How?! You were in so much pain before."

He'd...he'd hurt himself saving me from the pit. It had all been my fault, and yet—

"I can't tell you the details, but it was Yuna's doing," he said and held me even higher.

"It was Yuna?"

"Indeed it was. My injuries are a thing of the past, we have the panel, the lake is back...Karina, there's nothing for you to worry about anymore. There's nothing to make you fret."

"Father..."

"I'm sorry you had to worry so much until now," said Father gently as he put me down.

"You shouldn't apologize, Father," I told him. "I was so caught up in my head. If I'd done things right in the first place, I never would've dropped the panel or gotten you injured. It's all my fault."

"That may be the case, but you just need to work very

hard and stay careful while you're working in Listiel's place."

"Yes."

So Yuna had even healed Father. Yuna really was always full of surprises.

Today we were going to the pyramid to check the water. It didn't seem like the water would stop yet, but we had just exchanged the gems, so I was still worried. That's why we made sure to check on it regularly. If an issue cropped up, we'd be able to handle it immediately. Father was also thinking of purchasing additional gems, just in case.

Still, Father said that it wouldn't be as easy to get a new gem as it was this time. If Yuna hadn't defeated a kraken, we probably wouldn't have been able to find one at all. That was how valuable a large gem was. Although His Majesty asked her to do it, it still had been Yuna's gem that she had given us.

Even though we were heading to the pyramid, I was going in Mother's place with Father while she was still pregnant.

I rode on a laggaroute with Father. I hadn't noticed until now, but laggaroutes weren't as comfortable as

Yuna's bears. I'd been riding them since I was little, so it wasn't as though I disliked them. Still, I couldn't help but compare them to Kumayuru and Kumakyu's comfortable ride. They were so fluffy and felt so nice.

I hoped I could ride them again someday.

The laggaroute ran to the pyramid. There was not a single monster along the way.

According to Father, the water from the gem ran through the bottom level of the pyramid to the town. That kept the monsters at bay, supposedly. When the gem had stopped producing water, the monsters had gathered.

Father read that from a very old book, so we weren't sure if it was really true. But there hadn't been many monsters before, and they only showed up after the gem broke, so Father was probably right.

When Yuna defeated the sand wyrm, that must've also helped to get rid of the monsters.

Father and I entered the pyramid, eventually arriving at the entrances to the labyrinth.

"Karina, be careful," Father said.

"Yes, I will," I replied. "I won't make the same mistake again."

I firmly held the panel that Yuna had gotten back for me to make sure I wouldn't drop it. Then I checked the turns very carefully.

"This way."

"Ha ha!" While I was looking at the map very, very carefully, Father began to laugh.

"What's funny?"

"I'm simply happy to see my little girl growing up. People make mistakes. The worst thing is to not learn from them. I'm happy to see you understanding your mistakes and making the right decisions."

"Yuna risked her life to get this back. I can't drop it again."

Father seemed happy when I said that too, and he placed his hand on my head.

"Then I'm counting on you to guide me."

"Uh-huh!" I held the panel and led Father in. I wouldn't make the same mistake ever again.

KUMA
KUMA
KUMA
BEAR

Afterword

'M KUMANANO. Thank you for picking up *Kuma Kuma Kuma Bear*'s thirteenth volume. Along with the manga version, this series has already reached seventeen volumes in total!

In this installment, Yuna reached the desert town of Dezelt and met Karina, a girl down in the dumps because of a mistake she made.

Karina accidentally lost an important object because she wasn't being careful and was close to losing hope. Yuna shows up just in time to lend a helping paw to a girl in need.

Yuna also meets up with some familiar faces, including Jade and his party, and an adventurer trying to escape from the feared Bloody Bear.

In the new story just for this book, I wrote about when Yuna comes into the town and leaves, from Karina's perspective.

In the next volume, Volume 14, Yuna, Fina, Noa, and the orphans will all hit the beach! I hope you'll look forward to this next part of Yuna's story.

Finally, I'd like to thank everyone who strived to get this book out. Thank you for drawing such wonderful illustrations, 029. I'm always relying on my editor as well. And also, to the many people who were involved in the publishing of this volume of *Kuma Kuma Kuma Bear*, thank you!

I'm also grateful for the readers who have read along thus far.

I hope we can meet again in the fourteenth volume!

KUMANANO—ON A DAY IN AUGUST, 2019